*For my kids,
those glorious ratbags.*

Copyright ©2025 Alexandra Addams.
Cover and layout design: ©Shanna McNair.
All rights reserved. No part of this publication may be reproduced, distributed, or transmitted in any form by any means, or stored in a database or retrieval system, without the express prior written permission of the publisher.

Published by High Frequency Press.
www.highfrequencypress.com

Postal mail may be sent to:
High Frequency Press
PO Box 472
Brunswick, ME 04011

This book is a work of fiction. Names, characters, places and incidents either are the product of the author's imagination or are used fictitiously, and any resemblance to actual persons, living or dead, businesses, companies, events or locales is entirely coincidental.

NO AI TRAINING: Without in any way limiting the author's [and publisher's] exclusive rights under copyright, any use of this publication to "train" generative artificial intelligence (AI) technologies to generate text is expressly prohibited. The author reserves all rights to license uses of this work for generative AI training and development of machine learning language models.

ISBN: 978-1-962931-17-5
LCCN: 2025901418

THE SELF-MADE SAINT

A NOVEL

ALEXANDRA ADDAMS

HIGH FREQUENCY PRESS

If you want to change the world, go home and love your family.
—Mother Teresa

ONE

Adelaide, South Australia

February 2019

THOUGH JUDITH DRAINGER WAS NEVER SURPRISED BY incompetence, it still made her angry. Take this sodding screen door, for example. She had yanked and twisted the rusty handle several times, yet the tongue stubbornly refused to find its groove in the lock. Now, what was the point of a security screen door if it couldn't keep the world out? Especially when that world was brand-new. New to Judith, at any rate.

She marched outside and to the edge of a porch dusted with yellow pollen. Hands on narrow hips, she faced the street and acknowledged she had far more important problems than a rickety door. Problems such as what to do now that she had moved across the world from London to Australia, a country she'd previously never stepped foot in. What if she hated it here? And why wasn't her daughter, Cassandra, answering the sodding phone?

At the age of fifty-nine, Judith had experienced her fair share of troubles and considered herself to be fairly stout of heart. Still, descending the porch steps, she was very relieved that Rowntree Street, Goodwood, was quite pretty in an exotic, Australian sort of way. "I'll be grateful it's not London chaos," she murmured, pulling her shirt from already damp armpits. "Or Dadaab craziness." She bit her bottom lip and stopped talking to herself.

If only Cassandra were here to make things feel less lonely and strange.

At seven o'clock, the summer evening was still warm, the suburban street draped in wilting sunbeams and shadows before the streetlights came on. She heard the familiar whirr of cicadas and was pleasantly surprised to see jacaranda trees growing on the grassy verges, their purple blossoms and sprawling branches as beautiful as any she'd planted with her camp students in Dadaab, Kenya.

But for goodness' sake, why was it so quiet?

Searching for life on the deserted sidewalks, Judith finally spotted a man coming from the small collection of shops on the corner. He was tall, nicely built, wearing large sunglasses, a jaunty pair of red trousers, and walking a small brown dog. It seemed like fate when he stopped in front of her rusty gate to let his dog sniff at the jacaranda tree. An unwieldy surge of excitement sent Judith hopping along the concrete path of her front garden. Though still airplane-stale, she was determined to impress the natives with her friendliness, so she raised one hand in hello as the other smoothed her cap of brown hair. Yet this gentleman ignored Judith's smile and her wave as he waited for the dog to squat and vacate its bowels among the fallen purple blossoms. When it was done, he simply jiggled the leash and walked away.

Judith was slim but tall and knew the handsome man couldn't possibly have missed her, so she called, "Excuse me, your dog made a mess there!" Yet he rudely hurried on, albeit with the frozen shoulders of a person who knows he's being shouted at.

"Only a twit wears sunglasses at night," Judith scoffed, though no one was around to agree with her. She crossed her arms. On second thought, this pretty street was altogether too foreign, and the evening air far too hot for comfort. She turned to retreat to the relative safety of her house, and it struck her that the old cottage looked like a sad, fat face—two windows for eyes on either side of an ancient screen door for a nose and a silver veranda that curved down over the beige stone front like blunt-cut bangs. All the beautiful flowers in planter boxes from the real estate photos were gone, leaving behind dirty rectangles on the painted concrete steps.

Standing in her sparse front yard, Judith realized that the neighbors might be watching her from behind their curtains, laughing at the strange woman who was silly enough to buy this nasty old place. She lurched up the steps, only to curse and wrestle with the locked screen door, nearly snapping off the handle before she finally wrenched it open. The dark hallway yawned before her, and she stopped short. Then the stupid screen door crashed against her backside, making her squawk in surprise.

"Well, sod you!" she scolded the house, which had so poorly welcomed her. "I'm only here because Cassandra and Emily need me." Yes, by moving to Adelaide, Judith was going to make whatever had gone wrong between her and Cassandra right again. Cassandra had a baby now and needed Judith like never before. Bygones would be bygones. Judith would be the generous mother and Cassandra the grateful daughter. Of course, having a granddaughter would be lovely, too.

Judith jabbed at the hall light switch. A dusty, cone-shaped fixture on the ceiling glowed yellow and illuminated the doors of two smallish bedrooms crammed with unmade beds and too many cardboard boxes. Stomping down the hall, her navy suede loafers made sticky noises on the old floorboards, and she mentally added sanding and polishing them to her to-do list.

In the doorway of the kitchen-dining area, Judith paused, surveying the mess. From this exact spot, she could look across the sea of beige boxes, over the bubble-wrapped armchair in the little living room, and through the open back door into the darkness of her tiny backyard. In the quiet, she heard a distant siren and didn't know if it was an ambulance or the police.

For goodness' sake, even the sirens sounded different here. How unnecessary!

Hot tears stung Judith's eyes, and she pinched the bridge of her nose to stop them falling. Unfortunately, she couldn't do anything about the whispers: *Best get on with it before you go under it, Judith. There's always someone who's got it worse, Judith. Be grateful for small mercies, Judith, and for God's sake, put some lipstick on.*

Judith's mother, the formerly indomitable Mrs. Marigold Henley, had been dead six months already, yet Judith hadn't had a chance to enjoy it because, ever since the funeral, her mother had continued whispering—her personality no less vile for being a ghost now. Mother certainly would've hated this tiny cottage. She would have sniffed and called it humble when she meant awful, then congratulated Judith for not caring about civilized trappings such as wall-to-wall carpet or proper light fixtures.

Such a savage girl, my Judith, Marigold whispered.

Judith didn't always answer her mother, but tonight she needed the comfort of winning an argument. "You would've hated the camp tents I lived in too," she said. "But that was Kenya. That was how we did it. I've always said it's the people who make a house a home. That's why I sent Cassandra to boarding school as early as I could. Unlike you, I saved my girl from our unhappy home, and now I'm here to save her from the one she's made."

Last year, after Marigold had passed and Judith's thirty-two-year marriage to Terry Drainger had finally tottered to its own coffin, she had the really upsetting misfortune of being forcibly retired from her volunteer work with the UNHCR in Kenya. Honestly, after the doctors did that, she could've collapsed, had a breakdown, or taken up knitting or breeding stupid border collies like various friends of hers did now.

Not Judith, though.

Judith had defied the deluge of well-meaning pity and taken on a new mission—she would move to Australia and rescue her precious only child, Cassandra, from a dreadful domestic situation. Here, they would make a new life, free of husbands, all three generations of Drainger women living together. Four, if she included Marigold's lingering spirit.

Fifty-nine is a little old for a new life, Judith.

Judith was proud to say that she had let the divorce settle quickly and only demanded Terry pay the rather exorbitant cost of her special South Australian residence visa, expediting the immigration process so she could get to Adelaide before the year was out.

Terry was so good to you, Judith.

Then—just like that—she was free. Not out of the house on another three-month mission for the UNHCR, she was out for the rest of her life, and just like a mission . . .

"Yes, three months, and I'll make this place a proper home," Judith announced, nodding to the beautiful Queen Anne shelf shoved in a corner of the room. The shelf was the only piece of furniture she'd kept from her mother's house because it was where Marigold had decided to live, post-life, clinging to the walnut shelves. She could still see Mother with her polishing cloth in one hand, can of toxic spray in the other, rubbing at the already shiny wood, lips pinched in eternal disapproval of the world.

This cottage is terribly common, Judith, Marigold whispered.

"Only because it smells like boiled vegetables and cardboard in here," Judith muttered. "We just need some fresh air."

She waded through the boxes to get to the sash window nearest the dining area, the one that looked over a thicket of nettles and onto the green pine palings of her side fence. The window lock was a simple metal bolt in the top corner, and the wooden frame slid up with disturbing ease considering there weren't any bars or a security screen in place.

She leaned out to check the view. With the tall fence in the way, she couldn't see much of anything, which was a relief—she had privacy from the neighbors, at least. A dog barked in a backyard nearby, and the cicadas chittered louder now that night had properly fallen. She held her breath, listening hard. She still couldn't hear any people noises—no shouts, no chatter, nothing normal. Her heart began to race, thudding erratically. Her scalp tightened, her jaw clenched, the blood pounding in her ears made her dizzy.

No! She didn't have time for this nonsense!

She pulled back from the window and squeezed her hands into fists. "That's enough," she admonished the faulty organ thudding in her chest. "There's nothing to panic about. Simply triage. Like Jurgen taught me in the camps. Extreme cases first, immobile wounded, then mobile wounded, and so on."

Talking to me or yourself, Judith? Marigold whispered.

Judith accepted that her personal method of triage was far more intimate than any medical system for grading patients. Hers was the supremely useful ability to take all her feelings and stuff them into separate mental boxes, leaving her comfortably numb and ready to tackle any problem that required a practical solution. It worked for even the really frightening situations, like getting off a long-haul flight and waiting in the chaotic arrivals hall for an hour, exhausted and anxious, before receiving a late text that your daughter really wasn't coming to collect you—*Sorry*, blushing face emoji, four exclamation points—that you were on your own. All alone.

Of course, Judith coped with that particular crisis by packing away her feelings of vulnerability and abandonment in their separate boxes. Numb, she had used a luggage trolley for her four heavy suitcases and worked out how to call an Australian Uber van herself.

Triage made chaos simple. Triage made emotions unnecessary. Judith used her triage for everything now.

Remember when that little camp psychologist suggested your triage was the symptom of a mental disorder? Marigold tittered.

"That doctor was a twit," Judith said and let the matter drop. Pulling the phone from her back pocket, she scrolled through the message exchange with Cassandra from earlier. Cassandra had suggested she might come by the cottage tomorrow with Emily around lunchtime. Or if not, later in the week. Judith's last message asking for clarification still had white ticks. Unread. Forgotten.

Never mind. It really didn't matter that Judith was going to have to get through tonight alone. That was fine. Of course it was. If only she could shake the nasty feeling that she might've made—

Do you think you've made a terrible mistake, Judith? Oh, what a shame.

Judith lifted her chin. "It's always rough on the first night in a new place. I just need someone—"

"Coo-wee!" The shrill cry echoed through the house, followed by the crash of the broken screen door.

Someone had come inside! With instincts chiseled sharp from years of dangerous workplaces, Judith dropped into a crouch behind a packing box and assessed the risk.

"Coo-wee!" the voice cried again. Now Judith was sure the intruder was a woman. She heard quick footsteps slapping their way down the hall to her.

"S'only me." Slap, slap, slap.

The intruder entered the room. "Saw the moving truck and wanted to pop over and introduce meself. Thought I'd do the neighborly thing and bring you a little welcome to Rowntree Street." A tea towel–covered plate was offered to Judith as she rose to her feet again.

Though never one to pass quick judgment, Judith thought the woman made an unfortunate first impression. She was probably in her mid-sixties, short and dumpy, with rounded shoulders. Soft jowls folded around her tiny chin, and wide, owlish eyes blinked behind thick lenses. However, the real travesty was her fleece top with a cartoon kangaroo dressed in an apron and spectacles, "World's Best Grandma" written underneath it. Her beige cotton trousers, ironed with hard creases down the front, were short enough to reveal swollen ankles and bare feet.

"I'm Martha Thompson, and I just live next door, number twenty." The woman, Martha, looked Judith up and down before meeting her gaze. "You've got poor Gladys, God love her, in number sixteen on the other side of you. She won't be visiting, what with all her troubles, but that's a story for another time. Still got lots of boxes, eh? I'd love to help you unpack, but I've got this bad back, you see. It's all I can do to bend down for the oven these days. Still, I made you these biccies—we call 'em Anzacs, like the army corps, you know?"

Gladys, army—what? "I'm Judith Drainger," Judith replied, but Martha was already chuckling.

"Oh, I know who you are, Judith Danger," Martha said, "and even if I didn't, you're the spit of your daughter. Same green eyes, same tiny waist and legs as long as a stork. Only she's a carrot top, and you're brown as a nut. Anyway, I was the one who helped your Cass with the baby while she was taking pictures of the house. She told me you were moving from Africa, or something. It's a big change for you, isn't it? Losing your mum and divorce and all that?"

Judith simply couldn't believe Cassandra had confided in this woman about so much of her private business. "I lived in London and worked in United Nations High Commissioner Refugee camps teaching English in northeastern Kenya for the last ten years." She braced, ready to deflect the awe this usually inspired in a first-time listener, but Martha was perusing the disheveled state of the house, as brazen as you like. Judith cleared her throat, adding, "And my mother had been ill for a long time."

"Still, it's gonna be tough for you getting settled with no man to help." Martha's face crumpled in what Judith took to be a pitying expression. "Cass was so upset when she told me about the divorce—Terry, am I right? Personally, I think it's great you've moved to be closer to her and Andrew and the baby. She said you've never even met your granddaughter! O'course, I got to cuddle Emily a bit when they were here, and she's a beautiful baby, bit on the skinny side, but like you, I guess. Where d'you want me to put these biccies?" Martha didn't wait for a reply and made her way to the kitchen to deposit the plate on the Formica counter.

Judith ground her teeth and fumed.

"Cass gave me a key, and I was the one who let in the delivery guys with your new fridge and microwave," Martha said, with a nod to the stainless steel appliances. She didn't offer the key, and Judith hoped it'd gone back to Cassandra already. "I guess Cass picked you up from the airport?"

"I didn't want to trouble *Cassandra*." It always annoyed Judith to hear her daughter's beautiful name shortened to something that sounded like a cough.

"That's a shame." Martha blinked and pursed her thin lips. "You're her mum. It's not right to let you get about on your own in a new place."

Judith decided it was time to take back control from this nosy neighbor. "Look, it's been so lovely to meet you, Martha," she lied, using her superior height to herd the woman back down the hallway. "As soon as I'm settled, I'll have you over for tea. Until then—"

"No worries, Judith." Martha didn't seem at all perturbed to be escorted out of the house. "Your screen door's broken, if you hadn't noticed?"

Judith opened the offending door to hurry Martha along.

"The people here before you had a teenager, and he was forever banging and slamming the thing at all hours of the day and night," Martha continued, her feet planted on the threshold. "O'course, I could have my husband, Paul, have a look at it for you. He's not good for much, but he's all right at fixing things."

"That's really not necessary."

"It's no trouble," Martha said as she finally stepped out of the house and slipped those pudgy feet into a pair of green rubber clogs. "The noise really bothers me, so I'll send Paul over, eh?"

Judith watched Martha's square figure trundle down her concrete path and make the short trip right next door. Her heart pounded, and she felt a desperate need to reinforce that this interaction was over. "Please don't send Paul tonight," she called out. "Goodbye, Martha."

"No point saying goodbye," Martha called back. "I'll only see you later."

Judith accidentally let the screen door slam in her own face. Sodding thing! Now she knew her neighbors were bothered too, she resented it even more.

For goodness' sake, she'd only been in the house for one sodding afternoon!

Stomping back to the kitchen, Judith spied Martha's "biccies." She lifted the starched tea towel. They were flat brown discs, knobby and not particularly attractive. She took one between her index finger and thumb and, raising it to her lips, nibbled the edge. The combination of butter, sugar, and oats danced across her tongue. Her stomach growled, and she shoved the entire thing in her mouth. It was heavenly.

The wicked sound of crunching filled the silent room.

Judith wiped the crumbs off her lips with shaking fingers. She took the plate to the sink. There was a plastic rubbish bin underneath it, and the biscuits thudded against the sides with a hollow sound. She grabbed the nearest poison at hand and doused them in dishwashing liquid.

"There, no more," she said as her heart rate slowed again.

Wasn't she awful! Marigold whispered.

Judith folded Martha's tea towel in a neat square and placed it in the center of the plate. She thought of Martha taking the time to make the ugly biscuits, bending her sore back over to get them from the oven, all for a pitiful new neighbor with no mother, no husband, and no daughter to pick her up from the airport.

"I never asked for help," Judith muttered, "and there's nothing I hate more than a martyr."

TWO

THE NEXT MORNING, EARLY ENOUGH THAT THE SUN hadn't hit the tops of the cathedral-tall eucalyptus trees in the lane behind her house, Judith stood on her back step with a cup of Australian Breakfast tea, colored terra cotta by a dash of skimmed milk. Jet lag had meant she'd been up half the night listening to the house creak and groan around her. She was exhausted but had still forced herself out of bed because no one could argue with the sunrise. The beautiful morning was already hot, the air redolent with the astringent scent of dry gum leaves. A chorus of delightful warbles and piping bird calls, including the laughing cry of a kookaburra, reminded her that though she was very far from home, it might not be all bad here.

"Billy! Billy!" The shrieks came from that Martha Thompson next door. "Get yourself to school." A pause, then, "No, I am not kidding. School, Billy!"

Idly, Judith wondered why Martha had a young child living with her. She sipped her strong tea and let loose a yawn. The backyard was a simple rectangle bordered by a shoulder-high pine fence. There was a small shed, which she had opened to find an oily lawn mower smell and nothing else. A hexagonal clothesline—a Hills Hoist, she'd been told—sat near the shed, a plastic peg basket trailing down its one leg. All very boring. It seemed to Judith that the single redeeming feature of her rough yard was a lone lemon tree, heavy with green fruits waiting to turn yellow. Beautiful and clearly productive, the fruit tree looked like a wealthy refugee, so out of place yet stuck by circumstance.

Judith knew nothing about gardening and wondered if Cassandra did. Maybe she could ask her daughter to help with all the decorating too? She had never had to make a proper home from scratch before. In the camps, you had a tent with a stretcher bed and a locked trunk to store your things. Simple.

Never ask someone to do something you can do yourself, Judith, Marigold whispered.

The shouting from next door had moved to Martha's front garden. "Billy! You put one foot in that hoon's car, then so help me, God, I'll—" There was a loud squeal of tires and a car engine roaring away.

Right, this Billy was a teenager. That wasn't going to bother Judith as long as Martha kept the shouting down. Taking another sip of tea, she noticed a confetti of old cigarette butts in the dirt by the corner of her back step. Streaks of black soot decorated the concrete where they'd been stubbed, and she thought the orange filters looked strangely delicious.

Cigarettes—her solitary vice. She had only quit when she got pregnant with Cassandra thirty years ago. Cigar-puffing Terry hadn't approved of women who smoked. Neither had Marigold. She'd said smoking made a lady look common—a cardinal sin.

Judith couldn't smoke with a baby in the house, anyway. She smiled at the thought, and a thrill of anticipation trembled the mug in her hands. Today she would finally get to meet her granddaughter. The hospital photos taken straight after the birth never did a newborn baby any justice, and Emily had been no exception, looking all bruised and puffy. Surely by now, she would be just as beautiful as Cassandra herself had been at four months.

Judith tossed the dregs of her tea onto the dusty lawn and made her way to the kitchen. She rinsed her tea mug under the spluttering tap. The window above the sink looked directly at the side of a steel-gray fence and about six inches of the top of Martha Thompson's window. She noted Martha's curtains were white with orange spots on them and then realized that her own kitchen window was completely naked. Curtains were added to the growing chores list, and her shoulders slumped under the weight of all that had to be done.

"Stop that moping," she scolded herself before Marigold could. "Best get on with it before you go under it."

She checked her wrist before remembering her phone and Fitbit had both died overnight. So, time being of the essence and wholly digital, she became determined to find her missing chargers. There'd been no sign of them in any of the suitcases, but she might have packed herself some spares in the boxes that had left London with the moving company three months before she had.

Barefoot, she padded into the second bedroom across the hallway and began opening the alarming number of boxes that had *office misc.* written on the side. She unpacked recklessly, putting things on the floor in wonky piles, and tried not to think about the reunion to come. It was perfectly ridiculous to be nervous to see her own daughter, even if it had been two years since Cassandra had moved to Australia to be with *that Andrew*.

That Andrew was Andrew Caster, an Australian dentist ten years older than Cassandra, with curly blond hair and not particularly nice teeth. Cassandra and the dentist had only been going out for a few months when Cassandra had declared herself in love and ready to move to the other side of the world when Andrew's UK work visa expired.

She was always losing her head over a boy, the silly girl! Marigold hissed.

Oh, and the goodbye party had been just awful. All the hours stuck with a drunken Andrew as he extolled the virtues of the Australian paradise that was his home city of Adelaide: a big country town where families could live in peace and harmony, away from the violence and dirt of London. Oblivious to Judith's horror, he claimed Cassandra would be so happy in Adelaide she'd never want to come home again. And he called her "Jude" all night, despite being asked not to several times.

After the initial flurry of calls home, Cassandra hadn't said much more about her life here. While Judith was the first to admit that it had always been hard maintaining communication with her sensitive daughter, during their many Skype calls, she had watched Cassandra grow even more distant and, she thought, sadder. Then, when the surprise pregnancy came, the calls had stopped altogether.

Worse still was that Cassandra had never said anything negative about Andrew. In fact, it was the opposite—she gushed about him and their oh-so-wonderful relationship. That was a big red flag for Judith, because no man was that perfect. With a mother's instinct, she knew something was very wrong in Cassandra's world, and she was determined to fix it for her. No, *with her*, because it would still be Cassandra's choice if she wanted to bring Emily to live together with Judith as one extended happy family. Of course, they would have to share custody with that Andrew. Judith hoped he'd be civilized about it.

While Judith really wanted it to be just that simple, she couldn't shake the feeling she was missing something important.

And are you quite sure Cassandra wants you here, Judith?

She removed a stack of tea towels that had been shoved in a rather valuable Kenyan pottery vase. "I can't believe she thought describing a summer drought and the blowflies would stop me from coming," she murmured.

Remember, she even suggested you were in shock from my passing and not fit to make proper decisions.

Judith frowned and paused in her rummaging. "She must've been terribly worried for me when you died."

Perhaps it's you that has her worried? The doctors said orthorexia was causing your nervous heart condition.

Judith scoffed, as she had scoffed since it'd been written on the medical form banning her from any more missions to Dadaab. "Orthorexia! I don't have an eating disorder. Since when is concern for good nutrition a syndrome? It was that chubby young doctor who had a problem with me working in Africa, that's all."

Maybe she would have kept shouting at Marigold if the dust from the packing paper hadn't made her sneeze. Searching her pockets for a tissue, she heard people talking on the street. Then the loud squeak of her front gate. The conversation continued to the front door, and she could make out Cassandra's piping voice now. Peeking through the bedroom window, she saw the edge of her daughter's figure.

Judith's heart lurched, horrified to realize that she was still in her pajamas. Oh, she looked an absolute state!

She'll think you've let yourself go, Marigold hissed.

"No, I—"

Cassandra was already knocking. Climbing to her feet, Judith flapped her hands under her armpits, as if that might dry the sweat patches. Breathless, she arranged her expression—smile stretched wide and eyebrows high—then threw open the textured-glass front door. Cassandra was facing away from her, holding one of those infant car seats with the sun hood pulled up. Judith saw a bunny blanket and a baby's foot kicking. Her heart pounded like a kettledrum. This was it. This was the moment that would make everything right again. The funeral, the divorce, forced retirement—all that would pale in comparison to reuniting with her daughter and meeting this precious baby.

"Nice to see you again, Martha!" Cassandra called and then turned, squinting through the screen door netting. "Oh! Hello, Mum."

"Morning, Judith!"

Judith's gaze skittered to Martha shouting from her front yard. Today her neighbor was wearing a green T-shirt decorated with glitter that sparkled in the sunshine, her upper arms jiggling as she waved.

"Mum?"

Tears suddenly blurred her vision. Judith wanted to fling open the screen door, but Cassandra was too close to it. She stood frozen, holding the handle, rendered speechless by the gravity of this moment.

"I was just chatting to your neighbor, Martha," Cassandra said. "She's got a heart of gold, hasn't she?"

Judith, open the door for your girl! Marigold hissed.

"You're in the way," Judith said, sounding gruff as she choked on a wave of emotion. "Of the door, I mean. Sorry."

"Sorry," Cassandra echoed and took a step back. Judith opened the screen door, but the metal edge knocked the top of the car seat when Cassandra tried to come in. The baby wailed.

"Stupid door. Sorry." Judith turned on her heel and had led Cassandra down the short hallway to the kitchen-dining area when it finally struck her that she'd forgotten to hug her daughter. Sod it! She was already making a terrible mess of things. Like always. Cassandra would be cross now.

"Sorry we're a bit early." Cassandra's lovely, expensive boarding school accent had changed. Her vowels were flatter, more nasal. "I did text."

"Well, you'll have to excuse me not being ready—I know I look a state." Judith swiped at her sweaty pajamas again. "But you'd never really said when you were coming."

Cassandra raised a fine red eyebrow. "I didn't?"

Judith winced. She reached to give Cassandra a shoulder pat that didn't quite make contact. "It's my fault. I've only gone and lost my chargers, and my phone died. Silly sod that I am!"

Cassandra lowered her eyebrow. "Hmm."

A quiet fell between them so dense that it made Judith's head feel buzzy. She had a powerful urge to tell Cassandra that she still smelled the same, like vanilla and flowers, and how happy that made her. She also wanted to say that Cassandra looked pale and exhausted and how worried that made her. She also wanted to ask for a hug now.

"Would you like to meet your granddaughter?" Cassandra asked, sounding vague, like she was thinking of other things too.

"Absolutely!" Judith cried and threw herself over the car seat, but Cassandra was already moving away to put it on the dining table. Correcting course, Judith prepared herself to be delighted at this first precious encounter. Yet when Cassandra stepped away, she revealed one of the ugliest babies Judith had ever seen. The little thing had a head that looked far too large for her skinny body. Pale blue eyes goggled out of a face tinged yellow with jaundice, and her tiny nostrils flared. The fragrance of sour milk hung in a cloud over the car seat.

Shocked, Judith blanked on the baby's name. "Why, she's just . . . lovely, darling!" she said. "Shall I, can I, do you want me to pick her up?" As if to answer that uncertain request, the poor baby promptly released a stream of orange-flecked vomit down her chin and whimpered in discomfort.

"Oh, dear, what's happened now?" Judith shouted, far too gaily. "The silly sausage!"

Cassandra pulled out a packet of wet wipes from her giant handbag as Judith hovered behind, apologizing on behalf of the baby for being *such* a messy girl. "She's quite small for four months," Judith added, keen to impress Cassandra with her grandmotherly knowledge.

"My beautiful girl is five months old now." Cassandra scooped the baby out of the car seat and onto her hip, the movement causing more vomit to spill from the baby's mouth.

Judith wanted to ignore the fact that Cassandra was dumping all the soiled wet wipes on the dining table. If she said anything, it might upset Cassandra even more. It was so hard to know what would set the girl off. She was very sensitive even to helpful criticism.

Instead of fussing, Judith retreated to the kitchen to make tea and desperately try to remember the baby's name. Amelia? Emma? For goodness' sake, what was it? When she couldn't procrastinate any longer, she returned to the dining table and placed a mug of tea in front of Cassandra, next to the mounting pile of used wet wipes. The baby reached from her mother's lap, and Cassandra moved the hot tea back across the table to Judith like an unwanted gift. Judith lined the mug up next to hers.

Cassandra dabbed at the baby's wet onesie with another wipe, and Judith tried to think of something sympathetic to say. The baby whimpered in the silence.

"I'm sorry there's no biscuits to have with our tea," Judith blurted. "I suppose you still want to lose all the pregnancy weight anyway." She caught a frown from the googly-eyed baby.

"Andrew says he loves my new curves." Cassandra rolled her eyes, but her little smile said she believed him. "He doesn't want me getting skinny again."

Judith had already sized Cassandra up and could tell that she was at least a stone heavier than she'd been at the goodbye party. Though now probably wasn't the time for sensible advice to lose the weight before another month passed. Cassandra would certainly misunderstand that Judith was only trying to help if she was under that Andrew's influence. Or worse, maybe she was taking after her dreadfully obese father, Terry.

"Lovely." Judith took a sip of her tea.

"It's thirty-seven degrees outside," Cassandra said. "You should get air-conditioning in here, or it'll be unbearable before too long."

"The heat doesn't bother me, darling," Judith said. "Dadaab got much hotter than this."

Cassandra flung another dirty wet wipe on the pile. "Of course," she said. "Nothing could ever be harder than life in the camps."

Judith didn't know how to answer that when Cassandra already seemed so irritated. She sipped her tea, and the sound of her swallowing was loud in their silence.

"It's nice to see Grandmother's shelf again," Cassandra said, nodding at the Queen Anne dresser half-covered by a dust sheet and tucked in the corner. "It was her pride and joy, wasn't it?"

"A gift from Baroness Stockwell herself," Judith and Cassandra chorused. Cassandra giggled, and Judith added, as she always had to, "Her mother was just a kitchen maid, you know?"

Cassandra's smile faded. "I thought you said you weren't keeping any of Grandmother's things."

Judith didn't want to lie, yet neither did she want Cassandra to think she was completely barmy. "It just . . . spoke to me," she said.

Cassandra tucked the baby against her chest. "I wanted to go back and visit her," she said, her voice cracking. "It was so hard being trapped over here, pregnant, knowing she only had you to help her."

Judith waited for Cassandra to get to the point, but her daughter seemed a little lost, her gaze drifting around the room. Judith decided to return their conversation to a more relevant topic, the one that was probably concerning Cassandra most. "Of course, the house needs a lot of work before I even get settled," she said. "The photos on the internet made it look so much nicer than it is. Never fear, I'll get it all sorted!"

Cassandra's eyes narrowed, and Judith knew she'd said the wrong thing before her daughter started. "Honestly, Mum, I could only do my best when you told me to drop everything and find you a cheap little house in a city you've never even visited before!"

Judith flinched from the shrill force of Cassandra's words. Her first instinct was to fight back, yet seeing her exhausted daughter sitting there with that skinny little baby, she only said, "Darling, don't blame yourself, please. I'll just have to work a bit harder than I imagined." She looked around the box-filled room. "After all, what else have I got to do?"

Cassandra's eyes glassed over. "Well, I would've thought—"

Judith didn't find out what Cassandra would have thought because the baby released another cascade of vomit, and they were both distracted by the minor emergency of finding more wet wipes and undressing her.

"Is she not well?" Judith asked, careful to use her mildest tone.

Cassandra struggled to drag the stained onesie over the baby's large head. "She's fine, Mum," she said. "We're starting solids this month, and with her jaundice and colic, it's hard for her to keep food down."

The half-naked baby directed its bulging eyes at Judith as if begging her to give Cassandra some sensible advice.

"If she's not thriving, then perhaps it's a problem of lactose intolerance," Judith suggested, studying the baby's bony ribcage and bloated tummy. "It's quite common, you know."

"There's nothing wrong with her!" Cassandra spoke in that shrill tone again. "I weigh her every week and took her to a pediatrician already. He said to give her more milk until I find something she likes to eat."

Judith thought the pediatrician sounded like an idiot. "It's not as dramatic as all that, Cassandra," she said. "I do know something about infant nutrition, and I can help, you know."

"I'm not being dramatic!" Cassandra said as she surged to her feet. She looked between Judith and her whimpering baby and seemed to struggle with a decision. "Would you just cuddle her for a minute, Mum? I have to run to the loo. I'm despair—desperate."

Judith flung her hands out, clapping twice to show Cassandra she was ready to take the baby into her lap. "The little bathroom first on your right down the hall," she said, pleased she'd remembered the bar of soap and hand towel that morning. As soon as Cassandra was out of sight, the baby whimpered, heartbroken. Judith thought it was time for a chat. She sat her granddaughter on the edge of the dining table, legs dangling. The baby's head wobbled, and a blue vein throbbed under the pale skin of her forehead. Judith thought it was sad that Andrew's ordinary genes seemed to have trumped Cassandra's lovely ones. "Right, Emma? What are you doing to my daughter?" she whispered. "And what is she doing to you, Amelia?"

Clearly as sensitive as Cassandra, the baby's face scrunched, and she let out a hideous wail. "No, no, stop that," Judith scolded and stood to press the damp, vomit-scented baby to her chest, only succeeding in making her cry louder.

Cassandra entered the room at a run. With red-rimmed eyes, she regarded Judith holding her screaming daughter, and something in her middle seemed to crumple.

Judith felt an acute sense of failure in her first act as grandmother. "I don't think she likes me," she joked, handing the baby off.

"She didn't sleep well last night and needs a nap." Cassandra's tone was flat. "I'm sorry. Even when I do all the right things, she's still out of sorts."

Judith nodded, relieved that Cassandra was finally admitting she needed her mother's help. When Cassandra pulled a Ziploc from her handbag, extracting a pink rubber pacifier, Judith started immediately. "Darling, any cheap soother will cost you thousands of pounds in orthodontic bills later."

"Now who's being dramatic?" Cassandra asked the baby as she tucked her into the car seat again. Whisking up the pile of used wipes, she took them to the rubbish bin in the kitchen. Judith saw her looking down for a long moment—and knew it was at the mess of soggy Anzacs.

She braced herself for a lecture. None came, though Cassandra's lips were pressed in a hard line when she collected the car seat from the table and slung her handbag over her shoulder. Judith followed her to the front door, feeling tongue-tied despite all she wanted to say.

Cassandra stopped on the threshold. "I'm really sorry, Mum, this wasn't quite the reunion that I'd hoped for. I honestly thought that we could talk more about—"

Judith saw the pain in Cassandra's eyes and leaped to forgiveness, giving it generously so that her girl wouldn't blame herself for their interrupted lunch. "Never mind, darling. That's life with babies, isn't it?"

Cassandra's cheeks flushed red under the freckles she'd never tried to hide. "I wasn't blaming this on Emily."

"Emily!" Judith gasped the name in relief. "No, of course not. It's not Emily's fault at all. She's *lovely*."

Cassandra stared at her for a long moment, and Judith couldn't quite place her new expression. "Okay, we need to go," she said. "Goodbye, Mum." She marched to the silver Subaru parked in front of the cottage. The stupid screen door slammed in Judith's face before she could get by, and she pushed it open with a curse. Cassandra was already putting the baby in the back seat.

"No point in saying goodbye, darling. I'll just see you later!" Judith shouted. "You and *Emily*!"

THREE

IT TOOK A TEMAZEPAM-INDUCED GOOD NIGHT'S SLEEP to help Judith shake off the jet lag, though not her worries about Cassandra and Emily. She was sure that yesterday some important thing had not been said, some vital action had not been taken, and she had failed to convey how delighted she was to be in Cassandra's life again. It was also clear that Emily wasn't thriving and Judith had done nothing except irritate Cassandra with her suggestions.

Yet—moping about mistakes solved nothing, and Judith was a firm believer that if you couldn't fix one problem, then you should fix another.

Standing in the kitchen, stirring her second cup of tea, she decided her priority was connecting the house to the internet, then reaching out to Cassandra to see if she knew any good homewares shops for furniture, then she should unpack all these boxes, then call the delivery company to pick them up, then—

Look at my Judith, trying to make a home. Marigold cackled. *Wonders will never cease.*

Then she should make another list of chores that could be done when she finally had a fully charged phone.

Walking to the second box-filled bedroom, Judith imagined what it would be like to have Cassandra and Emily in here, filling the house with their noise and laughter.

Then you can feed poor Emily properly. Such an unfortunate-looking child.

"Food. I'll need to get in food, won't I?" Judith said, ignoring her mother. Though the new car hadn't been delivered yet, the shops were only half a mile from her house, which was perfectly walkable on a lovely sunny day. Wonderful! Judith grabbed her handbag and marched out the front door in such a hurry she didn't even think to put lipstick on.

Naturally, she had researched the nearby options and, at the end of a short stroll, was delighted to find that the collection of shops matched their online photos. She visited the bakery attached to a busy café, Beans and Brew, the IGA mini-mart, Costello and Sons Fine Butchery, and the Goodwood Greengrocer. There was also a lovely wine shop, Goodwood Quality Cellars, with a gregarious young man behind the counter who reminded Judith of one of Cassandra's old boyfriends from university. This was the only reason she might have chatted to him overlong and been convinced to buy a bottle of gin made somewhere called Kangaroo Island. By the time she headed home with bulging shopping bags, her cotton shirt was stuck to her back with sweat, and she was cursing herself for not being more presentable. What must that young wine shop man have thought of her?

Walking down Rowntree Street, Judith was desperate to get home, when just ahead of her she spotted a familiar-looking man wearing bright red trousers and getting pulled along by a little dog. Her heart beat a double tap, and she hurried despite her heavy shopping, already planning her diatribe for the inconsiderate dog owner. So excited to catch her quarry, she didn't notice that Martha Thompson was standing with a group of women at her front gate before it was too late to cross the road.

"Hello, here she is!" Martha called out in a tone that suggested Judith might have missed an engagement. "Come and meet the girls, Judith."

Judith could hardly avoid the four women—they took up the entire sidewalk. Beyond them, the figure in red trousers disappeared off down the street. Her heart was still pounding for the planned confrontation, and she found it disorienting to be surrounded by a cloud of sweet perfume and cheerful introductions. More than that, her hands were swollen mitts of pain. If she had to put her bags down, then she wouldn't be able to pick them up again, which would necessitate the need to ask strangers for help and make a nuisance of herself.

"Hello, everyone," she said and tried to sidle past a very plump lady in a fuchsia-pink shirtdress. "I'll just get inside. I've got cold things here."

"Put it down before you fall down, love," Martha said and stepped out of the gate to intercept her.

"Oh, yes, put it down," other voices murmured.

"No, really, it's fine!" Judith had to stagger away when Martha reached for her bags. "Really, Martha, don't!"

Martha blinked owlishly for a moment, and the corners of her mouth turned down. "Have it your way, Judith. I'm only trying to help."

The chatter around them died. The feeling of everyone's eyes on her made Judith clumsy as she hurried away, tripping on the cracked concrete path in her front yard and lurching up onto the porch. "Sorry!" Judith shouted. "Just need to get inside. Sorry."

"What's that accent?" she heard somebody ask as she tried to find her keys.

"British," Martha answered, and as if that explained everything, there was a chorus of knowing *oh*s.

Judith felt flushed as she negotiated the key with a sore hand and pushed her way into the house. She'd been warned about how Australians saw Brits. Andrew had been very clear that they were viewed as pompous and stuck-up. "Course, it all depends on the accent too," he'd extrapolated. "Your sort of plummy one doesn't go down too well, Jude."

Judith put her groceries away in the empty cupboards, the loaf of bread and minute steak in the freezer, and the salad vegetables next to the lonely carton of skimmed milk in the fridge. She immediately plugged in her new chargers and began charging her phone and Fitbit with a profound sense of relief. Soon she would be able to count everything in her life again, from the seconds on the clock to her own steps. With everything neatly arranged, she ran her swollen hands under cold water, cursing at the pain. She caught sight of the elegant gin bottle. Perhaps one glass could be considered medicinal?

Why not get drunk? You've already made a terrible impression on the neighbors, Marigold sniped.

Even through the closed kitchen window, Judith could hear Martha's friends. Someone was shouting "A spider the size of a kitten!" while the others laughed uproariously. Judith dried her hands on Martha's tea towel and left it hanging on the oven door.

Right, enough nonsense. She would go out and properly introduce herself, disproving their ignorant notions of British snobbery. She had got to the front door when her heart began pounding like she was nervous. Which was silly. Still, Judith thought maybe she should just plan to get the mail. And if the women still wanted to say hello, then of course she would be open to a chat.

Squinting in the sunshine, she made her way down the path and headed for the steel mailbox next to her front gate. Its very position seemed designed to make someone interact with the world instead of simply having one's mail slipped through the front door. Another odd Australian thing to get used to.

She studied the three letters that had arrived for the previous owners, Mary and Tom Phillips, then looked over to the women. Using the envelopes to shade her eyes, her other hand rose to wave hello. No one waved back. Immediately angry with herself—and with Martha too, quite frankly—Judith turned on her heel and stomped toward the front door. Unfortunately, this time when her toe caught on the cracked concrete, the world tipped forward, and she could suddenly see underneath the front porch. Her face pressing into the dry grass, she tried to roll over and immediately heard a squawking sound. She was horrified to realize it was her own cry as pain exploded in her ankle.

What've you done now, you clumsy thing? Marigold whispered.

"Judith! Judith!" Voices shouted close by. Judith smelled a powdery perfume, and beige cotton–clad thighs loomed in her vision.

"Is she knocked out?" someone asked.

"Don't think so, Marg, her eyes are open," another said. "Martha, she all right, you think?"

"Better take her to the hospital," yet another voice added to the hysteria. "I'd take her, but I've got that appointment with the podiatrist to get to."

"I'll take her—she's my neighbor," Martha said.

"You've got a heart of gold, Martha, really you do!" the voice with the podiatrist appointment said.

"Please, don't fuss." Judith was trying to get off the ground when she felt a waterfall of wetness over her left eye.

"Oh, that's a lot of blood!" someone screeched.

"Not to worry, head wounds bleed a lot," Martha said. "All right, chook, let's get you on your feet and to the hospital."

"Oh, Martha, mind your back!" someone else protested.

"Never mind my back. Poor Judith's in real trouble," Martha replied, resolute in her martyrdom.

When Judith tried to protest again, her voice was only a whimper. Sod it! She really did need help, and Martha was the only one offering it.

FOUR

JUDITH HELD A DISHCLOTH FILLED WITH ICE CUBES TO her head during the drive to the hospital in Martha's car. She clutched the empty ice cream tub that Martha had thoughtfully placed on her lap in case she needed to vomit. Watching the eucalyptus trees flash past the window, she tried to focus on Martha's inane chatter.

"Me, I've lived on Rowntree Street all my married life," Martha was saying. "Which is a fair old whack of time, forty-odd years and change. Before that, my family lived a couple streets over, further toward Mitcham. That's where I went to school, Mitcham Girls High. You're not from here, so you won't know it, but it's a great school. O'course, my parents are dead now—s'truth, Judith!" Martha flung out a hand across Judith's chest. Only then did Judith realize she'd listed forward, forehead touching the dashboard.

"Stay awake, love!" Martha shouted. "Tell me about you, eh!"

Judith pressed her back against the car seat. The pain dug its claws into her brain and made it hard to concentrate. "Yes," she managed to whisper. "My parents are dead too."

"Do you have hobbies, Judith? Anything you like to do for fun?" Martha asked, then shouted, "Judith! Hobbies!"

"I never had any," Judith whispered, "fun."

When they took her life in Dadaab away, all she had left were duties, chores, and difficult things that must be done without complaining. Mustn't complain. Care for your mother who hates you. Support your husband who despises you. Worship your daughter who ignores you. Help others before yourself. Join a charity. Join two. Soup kitchens always need hands. No one has to like you when you're giving them hot food. No one even looks at you. They've got their own problems, their own people who can't stand them.

But it all added up, didn't it? Somewhere the points for goodness, for helping others, accrued. You were still a good person even if no one liked you. Right?

Judith felt a softness against her cheek. Snatching the tissue from Martha, she dried her tears.

"It's no good getting old, is it?" Martha said. "Judith!"

Judith roused and risked nodding her sore head.

"No good at all," Martha continued. "Women our age. We keep falling apart at the seams. Here's the hospital now. Look, lots of parking spots too. It's our lucky day!"

Finally the drive was over. Even through a haze of pain, Judith found much to admire at the Royal Adelaide Hospital; it was very modern and shiny, with walls of clean windows and glass doors. Unlike a London public hospital, there were beautiful flower beds in the front, and the parking was reasonably priced. She was quite dazzled by the bright lights in the elevator as Martha manhandled her to the second-floor emergency department. After a short stint with a nurse who looked younger than Cassandra, they were taken to a screened cubicle on a busy ward. Judith was heaved onto a bed and left, now only gently bleeding, to wait for the attending physician.

"It's all right, love," Martha said, scraping a plastic chair across the floor to sit closer to the bed. "You can have a good old cry if you need to."

Judith hated crying in public as much as she hated being looked after. There was nothing that made her feel more like a fraud than having the attention of white-coated doctors in a hospital as busy as this one. "It's just a bit of a bump, and my ankle only swelled a little," she croaked. "There's no need to fuss."

Get off that bed, Judith, Marigold whispered. *There's always someone who's got it worse.*

"For God's sake, I'm trying, Mother," she muttered. Marigold had no business being this far from her Queen Anne shelf anyway.

"What'd you say, love?" Martha was frowning in a worried way, so Judith stopped talking altogether.

The next few hours were blurry and busy for Judith. She had her vitals taken, then was eased into a wheelchair and pushed through a maze of white corridors to get an X-ray for her ankle. She was wheeled back to her curtain-shrouded cubicle, annoyed to find Martha rummaging through her handbag for Judith's personal identification and insurance cards. She also had a good look at an old photo of Terry that Judith had forgotten to toss. It was a recent one of him, taken on a Saturday morning, looking particularly bloated and hungover in his bright yellow golf shirt, scowling at the camera—at her, really. She liked looking at it to remind herself of what she'd left behind. Now she was embarrassed at what Martha must think of him.

When the analgesics were administered by a young intern called Shane, Judith was so relieved she could have kissed his pimply cheek. She quickly changed her mind after Shane decreed that she was to have her ankle wrapped in a flexible cast for four to six weeks and arranged an MRI to check for swelling on the brain. He even admitted her for an overnight stay to observe the head injury. Again, very much unlike a London public—they seemed determined to keep her in a bed under unnecessary care.

Shane left the cubicle curtain open when he was fixing her cast, and Judith could see Martha making yet another phone call in the hall. She heard "Oh, Cass!" and then "That's a shame" and watched Martha's face fall as she checked her wristwatch. Apparently, Cassandra wouldn't be coming, and Martha wouldn't be leaving.

Chin up and mind you don't make any more fuss, my girl, Marigold hissed, and Judith trembled with the force of her mother's mortification.

It was early evening when Judith returned from her MRI scan and finally said goodbye to a hovering Martha. She breathed a sigh of relief at having one less person making her feel ridiculous.

"Your friend's lovely. Heart of gold, I bet?" said the night shift nurse, Bianca—of Italian descent, though her accent was broad Australian. She had moved Judith to an empty ward and helped her into a blue cotton robe before wishing her good night. Judith took the oxycodone tablet from the tiny paper cup on her untouched dinner tray. She welcomed the impending oblivion and tried to get comfortable for sleep.

A hospital is never dark, but Judith also had a little light shining on the wall above her head that she couldn't find the switch for. Bianca had placed her by the window so that in the morning she would have a view of the hospital garden. Now all she could see was her own reflection in the dark glass. She thought her expression looked like Cassandra's had yesterday. Pinched and angry. Clearly her daughter was still too upset to visit her own mother in the hospital.

Judith turned away from the window and slid down the narrow bed. The pillow crinkled under her cheek, and the cotton pillowcase smelled a bit like vinegar. Determined not to feel abandoned or anything ridiculous like that, she squeezed her eyes shut. The narcotics made her head swim.

She still didn't feel quite asleep even when she dreamed of being back in London, sitting at the dining table with Marigold and Terry, Cassandra only tiny in her wooden high chair, wailing. Marigold was taking food off the baby's plate and giving it to Terry, who was eating with his greasy hands. They were both laughing, and Judith just couldn't stop crying.

She woke with wet eyelashes and a sore throat. Fortunately, she spent the rest of the night getting interrupted by nurses to check her vitals every three to four hours. Though it all felt like a lot of work for these busy professionals, she was grateful she didn't have a chance to dream again.

Early the next morning, after getting Shane's all-clear, Judith tried to arrange an Uber to go home. A lovely nurse helped her limp on crutches to the waiting area, where Judith was outraged to see Martha already sitting near the table with the magazines. She was wearing a white fleece top with two cartoon koalas hugging each other and those hideous green clogs.

"You took your time, Judith!" Martha shouted and waved with her whole arm. She made a show of heaving herself out of the plastic chair—hands on knees, letting out a long groan of effort—then shuffled across the nylon carpet to Judith wobbling on her crutches.

Hands on hips, Martha gave Judith's rumpled clothes such a hard look Judith wanted to snipe that even a bloodstained T-shirt was better than anything with puffy-paint koalas on it. Thankfully, she controlled herself.

"Next time, I'll bring you fresh clothes," Martha said. "Let's get you home, eh? I've got lots to do today."

Judith was so preoccupied with her own humiliation at having to limp out of the hospital behind Martha that they had driven halfway back to Goodwood before she realized Martha was annoyed too. Stopped at a red light on a busy intersection, she sniffed wetly before fishing a tissue from her sleeve and blowing her nose. Judith knew it would be churlish of her not to apologize to Martha for the inconvenience of the pickup. Even if she hadn't asked for help. "It was very kind of you to come and get me this morning, Martha," she said, testing the waters.

"You know, I've got a terrible cold now." Martha snuffled her mucus as Exhibit A. "Must've been sitting in that waiting room yesterday. The air-conditioning was freezing, and I got a chill. O'course, hospitals are always filled with the worst germs too. Every trip's a danger."

"I'm sorry to hear that." Judith turned to the window and took a deep breath of the air freshener that didn't smell like any ocean breeze she could recall. "You know, it really wasn't necessary for you to stay the day. The doctors saw me quite fast, and they were happy when the MRI returned clear. My ankle is just a regular old sprain."

As if she didn't just hear Judith telling her she'd been surrounded by people, Martha said, "Like I'd leave you on your own! I couldn't get hold of your Cass for love nor money, and you needed someone. I did catch your girl this morning, but she said it'd be too hard to come in with the baby and everything. She'll pop by later, though."

Judith was quite sure she'd heard Martha talking on the phone to Cassandra yesterday. Was she lying to protect Judith's feelings? But, why? She decided to change the subject just in case. "You know, Martha, Cassandra actually prefers her full name to Cass."

"Well, she's not backward in coming forward, your girl." Martha sniffed. "I'm sure she would've told me. Nicknames are an Aussie tradition. Believe me, Cass would've been in trouble at school with that ginger hair and freckle face."

Judith couldn't stand to hear Martha ridiculing her daughter's rare complexion. Cassandra had cried over it enough as a teenager. "Unless you two are friends, then I wouldn't—"

Martha nodded. "Yeah, Cass and I got close when she first started looking at the cottage. She's the one who asked me to see to your fridge delivery. It's how I knew when to drop the bit of shopping over before you got in. You know, the milk, tea bags, dish soap, few loo rolls. I'm sure you didn't think a fairy had put them there." Martha tossed an annoyed glance Judith's way.

"Thank you, but I'd . . . " She'd thought Cassandra had done all that for her. Judith was as embarrassed to be the victim of this kindness as she was by Cassandra asking a perfect stranger for help in a family matter. What was wrong with the girl?

Martha slammed on the brakes when a black Holden Commodore cut into her lane. "Look at this young hoon weaving about like he's in the Formula One," Martha muttered. "Maybe use your turn signal next time, champ! S'truth, I don't know who teaches these kids to drive nowadays, Judith."

Judith didn't know either, so she said nothing.

At the cottage, Martha insisted on coming inside to get Judith settled. Promising to shower later, Judith dressed in the only pajama pants that could fit over her ankle cast and a clean T-shirt, then collapsed into the armchair in the living room, her leg elevated by a packing box. She checked her phone again. There were no messages. Surely Cassandra couldn't be too far away. It would be such a relief to see her after the flurry of pain and strangers and new experiences.

"You want some lunch, Judith?" Martha called from the kitchen.

"No, thank you!" Judith shouted back and winced when pain stabbed behind her eye. The doctor had said her bruised head would be sore for a couple of days and told her not to be brave with the pain in her ankle. He'd prescribed her some heavy-duty oxycodone, a twenty-pack, and strong paracetamol to get her through the worst of the recovery. He'd winked at her twice during this short chat, mentioned he was divorced too, and squeezed her toes through the blanket with what Judith thought was inappropriate familiarity considering he was a health professional.

Martha came over with a cup of tea and put it down on another packing box. "Good thing you didn't want to eat. There's not much in the house," she said, her soft chin jutting. "I'll have to remember you don't like Anzac biccies."

Judith blanked. "Oh, the biscuits—" She scrambled for an excuse. "Martha, I accidentally dropped the whole plate and had to throw them out. I'd only had a couple too. They were delicious!"

Martha pressed her lips into a straight line and blinked in her owlish way.

"You've been very kind," Judith added, trying to sound sincere while also praying that Martha would leave. "Thank you for the lift today. It was unnecessary but much appreciated."

Martha pulled a tissue from her sleeve and blew her nose before putting it back, all wet and scrunched. She sniffed again. "I'm sure you would've done the same for me, Judith."

Both women contemplated this for a quiet stretch, then Martha slapped her forehead. "S'truth, I almost forgot your pain pills."

She bustled off, then returned to deliver a glass of water with two boxes, white with different-colored stripes. She waggled one at Judith. "These paracetamol pills are to take with food," she said. "You're sure you don't want me to bring over a ham sandwich or something?"

The idea of bread and ham greasy with mayonnaise made Judith's stomach turn. "Cassandra will get me something," she said.

"Just make sure she does, Judith. These other tablets are oxycodone, and they'll make you real sleepy." Martha continued talking at full volume as she left the room and made her way to the front door. "Why a doctor would give you something that strong is beyond me. S'more like something you'd have after proper surgery, isn't it? You be careful, love. See you later."

Judith heard the front door close and heaved a deep sigh. She reached for her mug of tea and was happy to find it made strong with just a dash of milk. Heaven. She took another deep breath, and her nose wrinkled. The back door was closed, making it hot and stuffy with the chaos of open boxes and strewn packing paper. The mess made her feel like she should get back to unpacking. The pain told her to keep her behind right in the chair.

Judith wondered how to distract herself until Cassandra arrived. Her television was still sitting on the floor, black cords in a messy tumble, separate from the black boxes that they needed to be connected to. The books were still packed in cartons. Maybe she should shower.

When she tried to get up, the leg muscles pulled ferociously at her sprained ankle, making her yelp. It seemed like bed was the only decent option, and for that she'd need her crutches. Sod it! They were at the front door, where she'd told Martha to put them. Maybe Cassandra could—

Cassandra's not coming, is she? Marigold whispered. *You made her angry, and your girl can hold a nasty grudge.*

"That stupid Martha told her to stay away," Judith muttered and felt tears boiling behind her eyes, as hot as her sudden fury. Fumbling with the little white boxes of pills, she didn't bother to read the instructions, just popped two from a blister pack and swallowed them down. Eyes closed, she told herself to breathe normally. She should be angry at the accident her clumsiness had caused, not Martha. Her poor neighbor was just a woman who needed to become involved in other people's business to feel useful. Judith should've apologized to Cassandra—

The medication started slipping like gray waves through Judith's head, washing away the guilt and thudding pain, enveloping her in comfort. Past experience reminded her that the oxycodone would soon combine with the ibuprofen she'd taken at the hospital that morning and could trap her in the armchair. Rocking to her feet, she winced and limped through the house, one hand dragging along the wall, then along the kitchen counter, then along the hallway wall. When she reached her bedroom, she fell into bed, pulling her clumsy leg in under the duvet. She let out a groan that could've been a sob and gave in to the comfort of oblivion.

FIVE

JUDITH FELL INTO A FOGGY HAZE, THAT SHE WAS TOO tired to fight off. Whenever she woke, there was only pain and an echoing quiet in the house. No one told her if it was day or night, and no one told her to get up and eat something. No one needed her for anything. It was just like after her mother had died. The only difference being it was now her name on the neat little box of pills. She kept taking her oxycodone and fell asleep over and over again.

A sunbeam falling across Judith's face finally woke her up. She blinked carefully, assessing herself, and was relieved to find that her head didn't hurt anymore. Dragging herself to sit against the headboard, she looked about the room that didn't yet feel like her bedroom. The previous owners had left their ugly, faded curtains, which tinged the light a dismal gray. Her packing boxes were lined up along the walls like unwanted visitors, making the air dusty with their cardboard smell.

Rolling to the side of the bed, she reached for her phone, which was resting on one of the boxes serving as a nightstand. Left on silent, it was filled with messages and missed calls from Cassandra. She checked the date and groaned. She'd slept away almost three days. But of course, she'd known that. Hadn't she? Sod it. Did it really matter?

Scrolling through, she noted that the last text suggested Cassandra might come by for a visit tomorrow. That meant today.

Her heart thudded in a chest that felt suddenly hollow. It had taken three days to visit her own mother after an accident, really? Wasn't that just a little callous of Cassandra? "Unless she's still punishing me," she muttered. "Trying to teach me a lesson."

That girl of yours is spoiled rotten. I always said it, Marigold whispered.

"I don't know why she hates me so much." Judith picked up the box of pills.

What? I never said she hates you.

"You didn't have to," Judith whispered. She watched her fingers pop the oxycodone tablets from the blister pack. The last two. She knew it was wrong when she swallowed them down with a mouthful of stale water. Just one more time wouldn't hurt. She dropped back on her pillows, eyes already closed.

A loud knock at the front door startled her alert. Judith assessed the situation. What was happening today? There was the sound of a baby crying and two adult voices talking. One of them was Cassandra's high, piping pitch. Judith realized she'd made a dreadful mistake taking the tablets and struggled out of bed.

Gritting her teeth, she limped to the front door. Her crutches were still where Martha had put them in the corner. She propped them under her arms and pulled the door open, squinting when the heat of the day hit her in the face like a slap. Cassandra was already standing with the broken screen door held out.

"Mum!" Cassandra pressed a hand to her mouth. "Martha said it was just a sprained ankle."

Judith almost didn't recognize the man standing behind Cassandra. The dentist, Andrew, now sported a groomed beard, and a heavy belly pressed against the buttons of his denim shirt. His cheeks were red and his hair spiky, as if he'd just rubbed forehead sweat through it.

"How are you, Judith?" The baby wailed miserably from the car seat in his hands. "Emily says hello too," he added with a laugh.

"Hello, Andrew." Judith shuffled back to let everyone in. "Is Emily all right?"

"Mum, how about I help you get in the shower? You probably want to freshen up a bit."

Judith didn't miss the judgment shading Cassandra's tone. "I've only just got up, darling. I don't suppose anyone looks well so early in the morning."

"Actually, it's going on three in the afternoon," Andrew helpfully informed her. "You've slept the day away." He walked off down the hall, swinging the car seat as though that might quiet Emily's screaming.

Cassandra frowned, and a bossy, take-no-nonsense expression spread over her freckled face. "Shower time!" she sang, as if to a young child.

In the tiny bathroom, Cassandra helped Judith undress, which was very irritating to say the least. After all, Judith had managed to change her T-shirt yesterday. Or maybe that had been earlier today? Although she did agree it was damp with sweat and smelled terrible. Sitting in her knickers on the closed toilet lid, Judith trembled in the cool air as Cassandra undid the Velcro tabs and pulled off her ankle cast. Her stomach gurgled in the silence, the intestinal music embarrassing them both. Judith wondered if she might be in a bad way when Cassandra had to physically lift her up and put her under the showerhead. Then she discovered she had to lean on the tiled wall with both hands just to hold herself upright, which frankly was a great flapping red flag that she was weaker than she should be. Oh, dear. Cassandra would be cross with her again.

"Mum, when was the last time you ate something?" Cassandra asked. "Be honest with me, please."

Judith leaned back under the hot spray and let it run over her ears. Honestly, she couldn't remember. Did she eat on the day she'd hurt her ankle—or had that been just a cup of tea? "I had an egg and toast for dinner yesterday," she lied and made a fuss of wiping water out of her eyes. It was her duty to dismiss this moment of vulnerability as the aberration it was.

"Toast doesn't trouble your gluten allergies anymore?" Cassandra asked. For no good reason, Judith felt a stab of sudden shame and turned into the corner of the shower cubicle to hide her sunken breasts and jutting hip bones from view.

Now you've made you girl worry about you, Judith, Marigold hissed. *Doesn't she have enough on her plate?*

"How's Emily doing?" Judith asked, trying to restore the mother–daughter balance between them. "Have you got her eating anything yet?"

It sounded like Cassandra said, "At least she tries to eat," but Judith stuck her head under the shower spray again, so she didn't quite catch it.

Judith couldn't make eye contact as she allowed Cassandra to help her out of the shower and wrap her in a towel that smelled musty from being in a card-board box.

After dressing in a fresh T-shirt and pajama pants, flexible cast back on her sore ankle, Judith was exhausted and tried to get back into bed. However, Cassandra stood in her way. "Mum, please come out and have something to eat," she said, but it sounded more like a command.

"I'm really all right," Judith said. "Just need a bit of a rest." She couldn't quite remember how long it would take for the oxycodone to work, but it had to be hitting her soon.

"C'mon! Emily wants to see you." Cassandra actually clapped to harry her along. "Chop, chop, Mum."

And who could resist that? Not Judith.

She had only just sat down at the dining table when Andrew launched a conversation at her, reporting that he'd done his best with the television and stereo equipment in the living room, though he couldn't find her cable box and the television couldn't be centered on the cabinet because of the short cords. Fortunately, he didn't seem to need Judith to respond to any of this. He was sitting at the dining table, bouncing Emily on his knee, tapping away on Judith's laptop without so much as a by-your-leave. Emily had vomited again without him noticing, and a small pool had formed on the floor. When Judith directed Cassandra to the mess, she was too tired to insist that a bottle of disinfectant spray would be more effective than her apple-scented wet wipes.

"Andrew, sorry, what are you doing with my laptop?" Judith asked.

"I guessed your password was Cassandra's birthday." He grinned and spun the screen to face her. A window filled with colors and words flashed chaotically. "It's an online supermarket, Mum."

Judith recoiled in horror.

Did he just call you Mum? Marigold gasped.

"It'll be handy while you're laid up." Andrew showed her that he'd already filled in her address and other private details, including her credit card number. He must have ransacked her purse to find the card. "Martha left some soup in the fridge, but you've only got a fancy bottle of gin in the cupboard!" He laughed so loudly that even Cassandra frowned at him. "I'll let you finish up the order yourself, yeah." He snapped the laptop shut, still chuckling.

Judith's heart rattled in her chest. For goodness' sake, what was going on? Martha had been in her house depositing soup without permission. Now Andrew had crossed every polite boundary of social interaction by interfering with her handbag, and he expected her to be pleased about it! She simply couldn't stand having to be grateful for things she hadn't asked anyone to do for her. It was only to erase the frown from Cassandra's face that she squeezed out a thin "thank you" to Andrew.

She needn't have bothered, as the dentist had started tucking into a large plate of something greasy with pasta and cherry tomatoes that Cassandra put in front of him, hot from the microwave.

Cassandra put a plate with a much smaller serving of the pasta dish dish in front of Judith. "Please eat something, Mum. I made this with tomatoes from my own garden."

"Cassandra, sorry, I don't think this pasta is gluten-free," Judith said. They both knew it was an excuse—that there would always be an excuse. "But I'd love a cup of tea, if you're making one?" she continued quickly.

Cassandra raised an eyebrow, exchanged a glance with Andrew, and returned to the kitchen. "I'm sorry it took me so long to visit, Mum. It's just Emily's going through a stage, and I can't disturb her routine too much. It'd be great if you and Martha became friends. It'll be a weight off my mind if I know she can help out."

Ask her why she never got to the hospital to see you, Judith. Ask her why she called Martha instead of you.

Judith pursed her lips and stayed silent.

"Yeah, she's got a heart of gold, that Martha," Andrew said through a mouthful of food. "She was so nice when we were trying to get the house sorted for you. She watched Emily and had us over for a cup of tea afterward. She makes a cracker Anzac biccie, doesn't she, love?" This he directed at Cassandra. "And she's got heaps of experience with babies. Cass was nattering with her for ages about how to get around all of Emily's problems."

"Emily doesn't have problems," Cassandra said as she brought two mugs of tea to the table. "She's just a bit sensitive, and she's teething, which even your mum agrees—"

"Well, I think that Martha's a natural grandma type, and I'm sure she can show you the ropes, Mum." Andrew pushed his plate away. "My mum's always over at ours too, if you need anything. She gets along with everyone."

Judith saw the slight movement when Cassandra shook her head at Andrew. He rolled his eyes in response. "Our house is like Central Station most days as it is." He gestured to Judith. "The more the merrier, eh?"

"I keep things calm for Emily," Cassandra squeaked and did that tiny head shake again.

Judith wondered what they were really saying to each other.

Cassandra cleared her throat. "Mum, when I moved here, I thought it was amazing how welcoming Andrew's friends and family were," she said. "For the first time in my life, I felt completely . . . at home. Of course, sometimes all the questions and curiosity can come across as a bit nosy, but when you give people a chance, you'll find that they're just being friendly and you can—"

Home? Home is with you. What's she talking about, Judith?

"Sorry, if by friendly you mean walking into a person's home uninvited, like Martha does, then yes, I do find that a bit too friendly," Judith snapped.

"Actually, what Cass means is that people round here will do anything for their neighbors," Andrew said, his chin wobbling with sudden emotion. "They'll take you to the hospital when you fall over and make you decent meals when you can't cook for yourself. They'll give you the shirt off their back if they have to. If you call that being nosy, then I don't know what to tell you." He turned to Cassandra, daring her to dispute his statement. Cassandra looked from her partner to her mother, and Judith saw the resignation stamped on her beautiful, freckled face.

That boorish twit of a man was trying to make her choose between them. Judith was incensed. Cassandra needed to be shown how to handle that kind of manipulation. If Terry had taught Judith one thing, it was how to keep her poker face in a fight.

"Mum, I know you're a bit fragile right now," Cassandra said, her reedy voice yanking Judith's heartstrings. "But I've got so much on my plate with Emily and the house, I can't possibly look after you, too."

Tell her to stop being so dramatic—

"For goodness' sake, I'm quite all right on my own!" Judith shouted, louder than she'd meant to. "I was always alone at home with your father working such long hours, and then on my missions with lots of different teams. I'm a tough old girl, don't you worry!"

"Everyone needs people, Mum, and I did warn you that it would be hard to leave your old friends behind," Cassandra protested, almost as if she were trying to convince her mother to act like a burden. Judith knew all about maternal burdens. She'd had to nurse Marigold for those last six months. Ungrateful, bitter Marigold, who'd made Judith's life a hell right up until the doctors had taken her back into the hospice. She promised herself that she would never do that to Cassandra. Never ever.

"I do miss my friends, and we chat almost daily," Judith lied. "My colleagues are always writing too." Suddenly she listed to the side, catching the table to stay upright. Sod it, maybe she should have eaten something after all.

Cassandra yelped. "Mum, you just went gray!"

Judith stared at Cassandra's hands clinging to the dining chair, her daughter's nails bitten to the quick like always. It suddenly became very important that she couldn't remember the last time she had hugged Cassandra. Or tickled her or made her laugh . . .

"What meds are you taking, Mum?" Andrew asked, his booming voice pulling Judith's focus back into the room. "Are you feeling dizzy or nauseous at all? Cass, she didn't eat a thing just now."

Judith wanted to roll her eyes, exasperated by being talked about like a child. Unfortunately, she was feeling too numb to answer for herself.

Cassandra rushed to Andrew with the boxes from Judith's bedside. "Is this what you took this afternoon, Mum? Oxycodone?"

Judith wanted to lie, knowing the truth would only worry Cassandra. Still, the habits of a lifetime were hard to break, and she couldn't lie to a doctor—even if he was only a dentist. "I know they're very strong. I'm not s-silly."

Andrew examined the box. He looked up, and this time Judith couldn't avoid his gaze. "You shouldn't take these if you're having this kind of reaction. Do you understand?"

She used every atom of strength to lift her chin. "There's none left now, so don't . . . choo . . . worry."

"Cass, she's about to drop!" Andrew leaped from his chair. He and Cassandra each took a side, and Judith only hoped she was dreaming the indignity of being put to bed by her daughter and *that Andrew*. Still, even in a dream, it felt lovely to have the covers pulled up to her chin and tucked around, very much like someone cared about her.

Oh, Judith, pull yourself together, Marigold whispered in one ear, but in the other she could hear Andrew ask Cassandra, "Why wouldn't she just take the paracetamol pills?"

"Because you need to take them with food, and she won't eat." Cassandra's voice caught, like she might cry. "Daddy said her panic attacks were getting worse too—maybe that's why she took the oxycodone."

"You've got to stand up to her if you want to help her with this orthorexia and anxiety, Cass," Andrew said.

"I told you she'd be like this," Cassandra said. "She's just so—"

She was so what? Judith really wanted to know, but the chemical fog had crept in, and she drifted off to sleep before she could hear Cassandra's answer.

SIX

WITHOUT THE DELICIOUS OXYCODONE, JUDITH SOON righted her days and nights again. It really hadn't been a problem. She enjoyed medication but always knew when to stop at the end of the prescription. She'd never shame herself by asking for a refill. She wasn't an addict, for goodness' sake! Which is exactly what she told Martha, who had taken to dropping by every day this week with soup and crackers. That was fine, too. She had deleted Andrew's online supermarket order.

Wednesday lunchtime found her sitting in an armchair angled to view the backyard and drinking a cup of cooling tea. The day was already too hot for comfort, and she imagined she could see the grass shriveling in the fierce sunshine. There was the annoying sound of a leaf blower at Martha's house turning on and off at irregular intervals, but she still thought the fresh air was worth the racket. The lemon tree remained vigilantly green despite the heat, and she admired it even more.

Today she had her laptop open to a housewares website and was selecting furniture to decorate the living room. She wanted things that were not only on sale but could be delivered immediately, so that meant she was forever hobbling on her crutches to remeasure the room with her smartphone app to be sure everything would fit. This made the whole process very tiring, despite her initial excitement.

It was more important than ever to stick to her plan and get the house in order for Cassandra and the baby. The encounter with that Andrew reminded her why he wasn't right for her daughter. The man was just another Terry, a dominating fool trying to drive a wedge between mother and daughter. Cassandra needed protecting from this one, too.

It had been three days since her daughter's last visit, and Judith didn't want to admit how keen she was for Cassandra to see her showered and dressed. She had even left her soup bowl on the dining table, the scraps evidence of a meal eaten. There'd been a texted conversation yesterday in which they had planned for Cassandra to come around today, ostensibly to help with the unpacking and have lunch. Judith had tried everything to change her mind when Cassandra called to cancel.

"If you haven't slept all night, then come and nap here. I'll watch the baby for you," she had offered, as a proper grandmother should.

Cassandra's voice wobbled with tears. "Emily will only sleep in her own bed, and she'll only sleep when she's eaten something, and that's what I'm trying to do now. She takes forever to have a proper meal, so I really won't be able to visit today. Anyway, it's not like you could carry her around with your poor ankle."

"Look, have you tried—"

"Everything! I've tried everything," Cassandra snapped. Emily wailed in the background, and Cassandra sighed into the phone, saying, "Oh, Emily, not again." Judith could imagine the sour scent of vomit and winced in sympathy. "Mum, I have to go," Cassandra said. "We'll plan a visit for another day. So sorry."

Judith held the phone after Cassandra hung up, Emily's pained cry still echoing in her ears. After her years of experience in the camps, she knew exactly how malnutrition presented in an infant, and Emily really wasn't well. Who was this stupid pediatrician telling Cassandra to keep forcing milk down the baby's throat without looking for an allergy or issue in the gut? Why didn't Cassandra recognize there was a real problem with Emily? Surely she knew what a healthy baby looked like.

Judith had moved to South Australia to help Cassandra find her way again because when she'd met that Andrew, she'd definitely lost it. In the past, Judith had always ignored Cassandra's boyfriends, finding them to be generally smarmy, spoiled twits. Andrew was a proper man at least, which was also the problem. He had the life experience and the financial means to lure Cassandra across the world and away from her family, even her beloved father. That couldn't be what Cassandra wanted. Not really. She'd never even mentioned needing such a big adventure to Judith. If she had, Judith would've been the first in line to take her to Kenya. Now Cassandra was living the life Judith had warned her against—made vulnerable by not working, financially dependent on a man, and far from home with a little baby to care for.

Judith could only curse her bad luck that this sodding accident had transformed her into an invalid. It was ridiculous to blame the cottage, yet if that garden path hadn't been so cracked, she would never have tripped.

"Stupid house," she muttered. "But I'll not let you ruin my plans." She returned to her housewares websites, determined to turn these unfriendly walls into a home that Cassandra and Emily deserved.

Engrossed in her work, she didn't hear the front door until Martha shouted, "Coo-wee, Judith, s'only me!" Martha always began her conversations from the hallway, even before she could see Judith. "S'truth, it's hot today. I almost cooked on the way over. I tell you, this heat is no good for me with my poor back. Thirty-eight Celsius, they said on the radio. That's too hot!" Martha came to stand in the living room doorway, fists planted on round hips. She was wearing a pink T-shirt dotted with the printed faces of tabby kittens. "How're you today, Judith? Feeling better?"

"I'm very well, thank you, Martha," Judith replied, closing her laptop and managing to smile.

Martha never believed her. "You still look a bit peaky to me, poor love."

"Really, I'm fine." Judith struggled forward in her chair, reaching for the crutches. "I was getting ready for a visit from my daughter when—"

"Oh, yeah, poor Cass, eh?" Martha rushed to grab Judith's arm. "She just called to say you sounded a bit shaky on the phone and could I pop over? O'course, I've got enough to do, but she was teary herself, and she's got the baby not sleeping again, Judith."

Judith burned under Martha's reproachful glare. Was this woman really trying to chide her for worrying Cassandra? "Well, I think—"

"Anyway," Martha interrupted, "don't mind me saying, but you look like a bag of bones these days, Judith. I know Cass thinks you need to put some meat on yourself as well. She's got enough to do just feeding that little baby of hers without worrying about you too, now, doesn't she?"

Judith's jaw dropped. She'd always thought herself immune to feminine guilt trips. Years of her mother's razor-sharp attacks had left her with a very thick skin. She'd never encountered such a blunt force as Martha and her patronizing disapproval of Judith's eating habits on top of everything else. Furious with Martha and furious with Cassandra too for calling her, she could barely squeeze the words between clenched teeth. "Let me show you out, Martha."

Martha walked behind Judith to the front door. "Look at you on those crutches. You're doing a good job!" she said. "If you've not eaten, why don't you come over to me? I've put out a nice spread."

Judith stopped at the door. She looked down at her portly neighbor but found it hard to be haughty in the face of a lunch invitation. She had smelled the baking cakes in her own kitchen that morning. "Well, I really couldn't put you to any trouble," she declined. "Maybe another day?"

"Go on, you'll be doing me a favor," Martha said. "I've made far too much, as usual."

Judith felt her anger toward Martha soften even as she tried to think of another excuse. If only Cassandra hadn't already betrayed her by announcing that she was lonely and hungry with nothing to do. "It's kind of you to insist—"

"Yeah, I'm insisting, so hurry up." Martha already had Judith's house key in her hand. "It's not like you're the type who needs to get tizzied up for a bit of lunch."

Judith looked down at herself. Dressed in a T-shirt and jeans, she wasn't in any way ready for a formal lunch engagement. Anyway, what did Martha mean she wasn't the type to get tizzied up? She didn't think of herself as beautiful, but she'd always dressed to make the best of what she had.

And today not even a bit of lipstick, Marigold tutted.

With only the choice between false modesty or prideful protest, Judith instead swung out the door. She took her time negotiating the two porch steps, then the cracked garden path, finding herself scanning the path, finding herself scanning the concrete for the spot she had tripped over a week ago. Ahead of her, Martha opened the rusty front gate.

Judith found Rowntree Street to be exactly as empty and oddly yellow as it had looked through her screen door that morning. The smell of hot pavement and pollen enveloped her, making her nose itch and her scalp prickle. She immediately had to stop and sneeze.

"Bless you!" Martha said and offered a tissue that Judith couldn't take with her hands full of crutches. "Wattle pollen's a nightmare this time of year."

Judith was just about to mention that she didn't have pollen allergies when a couple of birds chattered loudly in a nearby tree. The small colourful parrots never appeared in her own yard, though their melodic screeching was a familiar sound on the street. For rather common birds, they always garnered a lot of attention from passersby, and Martha was no different. "Rainbow lorikeets!" she remarked. "Aren't they pretty? Don't get them in London, I bet."

"No, not there." Judith hadn't been much for birdwatching in London, though in Dadaab she'd enjoyed following the vibrant kingfishers and chatty gray parrots who lived in the trees around the camps. Those parrots could even mimic human voices, and Jurgen had one that he'd trained. Whenever Judith asked, he'd brought his pet gray to the schoolhouse to delight the children.

Now, why was she thinking about Jurgen? Judith felt her heart thump erratically. Maybe because he would be so pleased she was trying to make a friend, no matter how annoying they might be. Jurgen had always paved the way for Judith with new people or sorted out misunderstandings between her and other volunteers in the camp. Everyone had adored Dr. Jurgen Haag. He had written to her after Marigold's funeral, a simple little note. She'd immediately emailed him in return. He hadn't responded. She understood. But not really. They'd shared so many adventures working together on several rotations. It was Sod's Law that just as she became single, she wasn't allowed back to Kenya to see if anything might grow.

"It's been a while since you were outside, isn't it?" Martha interrupted Judith's thoughts. "I've not even heard you in your yard this week."

Judith squinted and didn't deign to reply. No wonder Cassandra was worried about her with this spy next door putting ideas in her head. She tried to hobble-swing faster to Martha's gate and then up her redbrick path, ready to get this lunch over and done with so she could go home and reach out to Jurgen properly.

"Here we are!" Martha sang as she skirted past Judith and pulled the security door open.

Once inside, Judith was assailed by the glory of air-conditioning and a babble of female voices. Oh, no, not a party! Her stomach dropped, and her heart rattled. Now she was being forced to meet new people while she was injured and completely underdressed. To make matters worse, Martha made Judith take her shoe off at the door, putting her single navy slip-on in the row with the pairs of ballet flats and patent leather loafers.

Martha herded Judith, barefoot, down the hall and straight into the kitchen and dining area. Her house had a similar layout to Judith's, only much bigger and more modern. Martha had a lovely large kitchen with pale green tiles and gray granite countertops. In the dining area, there was a long oval table with ten ladder-backed chairs, though not all of them matched. The walls had sand-striped wallpaper and were covered in framed photos of various sizes. Judith caught sight of the floor-to-ceiling window and its orange-spotted curtains, visible from her own kitchen window.

"Here she is—our invalid!" was how Martha introduced Judith to the four women sitting around one end of the table.

The women jumped up and began cooing at Judith, offering her a seat and a glass of water at the sight of her flushed face. She scrambled for her social graces as her gaze fell on the feast. Astounded by the amount of food across the white crocheted tablecloth, she counted a long platter of finger sandwiches, another of mini quiches, a plate of smooth-topped scones with bowls of jam and cream beside them, an enormous iced cake on a glass stand, a jam roll snowy with icing sugar, and a selection of cut fruit with a chocolate sauce for dipping. Not a bowl of salad or piece of grilled chicken to be seen. This wasn't lunch, it was high tea. Judith hated high tea.

"You're looking well, Judith." The woman who addressed her was remarkably fat, yet despite this, she was very pretty, with wide blue eyes and blond curls set in a Marilyn Monroe style. She wore a black-and-white striped shirt, its buttons open to the top of her pillowy bust, and a thick

Tiffany choker with a locket detailing the store's New York address. She looked to be the youngest of the group of women by at least thirty years.

"Thank you," Judith croaked, finally remembering her manners. "I'm sorry—you are?"

The woman laughed gaily. "Of course, you won't remember us! We only met on the day you took your tumble. I'm Chantal."

"It's lovely to meet you," Judith said.

"And this is Marg," Martha said, returning to her place at the head of the table with a pot of freshly brewed tea. She indicated a lady with bobbed white hair and a navy polka-dot dress. "Marg used to be in real estate—now she's retired and writes articles for the local paper."

"Hello, Judith, nice to meet you properly!" Marg shouted. She had the rigid smile of a shy person determined to be friendly, which made Judith wonder why she spoke so loudly.

"This is Bev." Martha pointed to the lady next to Marg. "Bev used to work in finance, but now she's president of our local gardeners' society." Probably around Judith's age, Bev had a very chic haircut and a gray blouse that looked just as expensive. Her wristful of bracelets tinkled when she waved at Judith from across the table. Judith waved back, then tucked her hands in her lap, feeling silly.

"Judith, lovely to see you again," Bev said.

"And you, Bev." Judith swallowed the "erly." She guessed it would be rude to take the full name when she'd been offered the short version.

"This is Cate." Martha nodded at her last guest, a petite woman with short auburn hair and tiny eyes. "Cate's divorced like you, Judith, and quite recently too."

Cate pursed her lips so tightly they went white. "Better off without him," she said. It wasn't clear if she was referring to Judith or herself.

Flustered, Judith's crutches slipped from her sweaty grasp and clattered to the floor, making her feel an even bigger fool in front of these well-dressed Australians. "I am so sorry to interrupt your lunch. I had no idea when Martha invited me that I'd be an interloper."

"No worries at all." Chantal had a smile that made her eyes almost disappear into her round cheeks.

"When Cass called Martha, we told her to invite you over." Cate's voice was as dry as her sunburned nose. It was apparent she had no talent with comforting people when she added, "You poor old thing."

"You all know my daughter, Cassandra?" Judith felt a flash of fear. Had they all met the dentist and Emily too?

"No, but we heard about her from Martha!" Marg shouted. "Such a sweet girl!"

"Marg." Martha touched her own ear. "Bit loud, love."

Judith cringed with embarrassment for Marg as the woman fiddled with the tiny device behind her ear. "Thanks, darl," Marg said. "They've been playing up today."

"So, you're from England, Judith," Chantal said. "Whereabouts?"

"I used to live in London—Belgravia," Judith said and automatically braced herself to wave away all the *ooh*s and *aah*s that her address usually incurred.

Chantal just smiled blankly. "I've never been to London," she said. "Love to go one day, though."

"I love London!" Bev exclaimed. "God! Adelaide must seem like a country town in comparison." She rolled her eyes at the very idea, and Judith decided she might like to be Bev's friend.

"My grandma was from Cork," Cate said with a proud tilt of her chin.

"That's Ireland, not England," Judith said.

"Same country, though," Cate replied, frowning.

"Don't tell an Irishman that!" Judith said, ending their debate with a forced smile.

"If you say so." Offended, Cate frowned more deeply.

In the silence, Judith heard a clock ticking in the kitchen and the gurgle of a dishwasher.

"You must be so happy to be close to your daughter," Bev began again, with an encouraging smile. "I bet you can't get enough of the new baby."

Judith thought of Emily and the vomit dribbling down her chin. "Of course," she agreed. "Emily. She's *lovely*."

Silence again as the women exchanged glances. There was the sound of a lawn mower whirring outside. God, this was excruciating! Judith plumbed the depths of her mind for an excuse to leave.

"Cake, anyone?" Chantal asked, her voice pitched high and jolly in a clear effort to cover the awkwardness.

"That looks beautiful, Chantal!" Martha rubbed her dry palms together in excitement. "Your icing technique is really coming along."

Chantal had pulled the double layer cake over to slice it. It was covered in smooth, pale pink icing, with lavender cream roses in a circle on the top and a scattering of sugared violets. She cut large, even pieces for everyone at the table, describing the ingredients as she handed out the slices of wickedness.

Stop! Judith wanted to warn the lovely young woman, you'll only get bigger and take us with you.

Greedy girls are lonely girls, Marigold had always cautioned whenever Judith had reached for anything sweet. Too late, every woman at the table had picked up her fork and was sampling the chocolate mud cake with ganache filling, showering Chantal with compliments. Not wanting to offend, Judith cut a tiny bite of cake and raised it to her lips. Her mouth began watering immediately. She put her fork down.

Martha was looking at Judith's plate with disapproval. "Judith, you have to keep your strength up if you want to get better. Cass'll only worry for you."

Judith thought she might throw her fork at Martha's head if she had to hear her call Cassandra *Cass* again. She searched the room for a way to change the conversation and gestured to the wall of photo frames behind the dining table. "Martha, I didn't know you had such a large family."

Martha smiled as she made a big deal of slowly rising from her chair and presenting the wall. "That I do, Judith, that I do," she said. "Let me introduce you to my kids." The women around the table began conversing in low tones and piling their plates with food. Clearly they knew what was coming, and it wasn't going to be quick.

"These beautiful kids are my biological children." Martha pointed out two boys and a girl, all young teens, posed in an awkward studio portrait. "That's my oldest, Andrea. She's a dental technician. There's Jakey and Peter—they both work the mines in Queensland. Peter's looking for something down here soon. O'course, this photo was taken a fair few years ago, so they're older now. Now! As you can see here, I've got . . . " Martha tapped her finger on a picture of two babies lying side by side, wearing identical yellow onesies and bemused expressions.

Judith hazarded a guess. "Twins?"

"Twins!" Martha nodded, smug. "My Andy had twins, first try, right off the bat. O'course, it's a lot of hard work for her, and now they've moved to Brisbane she doesn't have me around anymore, but twins are really special."

And because Cassandra only had one baby, it was less special? Judith felt as bemused as the babies in the picture.

"Now comes my—"

"Her heart children," Cate piped up, as if she'd seen this show before and couldn't wait for the next bit.

Martha assumed a somber expression. "That's what I call them, Judith—my heart kids. These are the kids I've fostered over the years, or kids that came into my life who just needed a bit of love and a hot meal.

Our house was always open, and I never turned a hungry kid away." She paused to let the gravity of her generosity fall over everyone at the table.

Judith was impressed to see that Martha had taken in dozens of children over the years, though she couldn't bring herself to congratulate her for it. Her firm belief was that if you wanted to help people, wonderful, but you shouldn't ever expect thanks.

Charity is its own reward, Marigold would have sniffed, at this point in the conversation.

"She's got a heart of gold, our Martha," Marg said. "Always looking out for others, never thinking of herself. She's generous to a fault!"

"It's who I am," Martha said, horrifying Judith by accepting the compliment with no protest.

"And we love you for it, Martha," Bev said as she helped herself to another scone. "Mind you, that Billy boy has been causing a bit of grief, hasn't he, love? Not sure how you put up with him."

Martha sighed the sigh of the long-suffering and rolled her eyes. "Billy's trouble, all right, Bev."

Chantal leaned in, touching Judith's elbow to get her attention. "I'm one of Martha's heart kids too, Judith," she said. "I was a ratbag teenager, running with a bad crowd. We were up to all sorts—stealing cars and getting into trouble with the police. Martha saved my life." She started flapping a hand in front of her face. "Oh, Martha! I always get so emotional when I talk about you."

Martha circled the end of the table to hug Chantal. "Aw, love," she said, "You were always a good kid, and now you're a wonderful mum yourself."

In the next moment, Chantal had recovered from her tears and was reaching for her smartphone. "Do you want to see a pic of my little Eddie, Judith?" she asked. "He's only six months old and is the cutest baby in the world!"

Judith was shown a photo of a fat, laughing baby wearing denim shorts and a button-up shirt. Now, that was a healthy baby, she thought and felt a pinch of longing for a picture of a fat, happy Emily.

"What did you do, Judith?" The question floated over the table from Bev. "Before you moved here?"

Judith bristled at the past tense but nevertheless had to answer. "I was a volunteer for the United Nations, working in the UNHCR camps, mostly in Dadaab, northern Kenya. I did some day-to-day administration and taught English in the camp schools that I helped set up. I also worked in the medical tents when we were understaffed." She smiled, preparing to make the usual joke. "Which was only every Monday through Sunday."

"That must have been extraordinary work," Bev said. "I bet you had to be tough as old boots. Kenya's mostly desert, isn't it?"

"It was harder for the refugees having to live their whole lives there," Judith said, firmly steering the admiration from herself to the lost Somalis and South Sudanese who'd been forced to make a home in camps she'd only worked in.

"But it must have been so dangerous!" Chantal held her fork halfway to her mouth. "Weren't you scared?"

This was a normal reaction from other women, and Judith had her stock answers. "My job was incredibly rewarding, and I worked with wonderful teams. I learned so much living among the different communities of mostly Somali refugees who escaped the conflict and poverty in their own country. What a lot of people don't realize is that Kenya is extraordinarily beautiful. To me there's nothing in the world as magical as a sunset over the plains of Dadaab. Of course, the older camps in the Lagdera District are actually more like towns than camps. They've got proper markets, with an organized police force, schools, and hospitals. It goes without saying that one had to be careful moving through the camp at night, but it was no more dangerous than midnight in the backstreets here," Judith said, breathless as her monologue came to a halt.

"Not here." Cate seemed personally affronted by the suggestion that Goodwood had backstreets and that they might be dangerous.

Judith didn't bother with a reply. Talking about Dadaab had made her heart race and tears sting her eyes.

"Now I suppose it's grandma duty for you every day?" Bev continued her gentle interrogation. "Or are you planning on working again?"

Could she work here? It honestly hadn't yet occurred to her.

She was saved from having to respond when Martha rejoined the table and thumped another fresh teapot down near the jam roll. "I always believe that charity begins at home," she said, nodding in agreement with herself. "Help thy neighbor and all that. No need to go looking for trouble overseas when we've plenty of our own in need. Take my current foster kid, Billy. He's a sixteen-year-old ratbag from a broken home, but the two things have got nothing to do with the other, if you get my meaning?"

Now, that didn't make any sense at all. Judith's head was spinning. The smell of cake coupled with Martha's self-satisfaction was too much to take. She had to get some air. Struggling to stand, she grabbed her crutches. "Excuse me, ladies, I really have to—"

"Guest loo's down the hall, Judith," Martha said. "First door on the right. Sing out if there's no toot paper."

Mortified, Judith stamped the rubber heels of her crutches on the floorboards and swung herself around, almost crashing into a man as he walked through the living room doorway. Despite his size, he dodged her easily and ducked around the kitchen counter. Judith hadn't finished stammering an apology when her jaw dropped open. Tall and broad-shouldered, with messy, sun-bleached hair and a deeply tanned face, the man might've been the other side of sixty, but he looked every bit the picture of Australian masculinity that Judith had been promised by the movies. He was wearing long shorts with a button-up shirt in thick green cotton. He smelled of sunscreen and cut grass. Cobalt-blue eyes scanned the room, taking in the food on the table and the women surrounding it.

"Here he is." Martha's expression was stony. "Hungry, are you?"

The man bobbed his beautiful head, shy and uncertain. "Didn't want to interrupt. Was just gonna grab a quick cuppa, love." His accent was so broad and his voice so low that Judith didn't catch a word of what he said.

"Judith, this is my husband, Paul," Martha said in a tone that suggested she wished he wasn't. "Paul, Judith just moved into number eighteen. I told her you'd fix that front door of hers. Have you done it?"

Paul shook his head and flashed Judith a look of such pure hunger she felt it like a punch to her empty stomach. "I took your bins out this morning when I did Gladys's," he said by way of unnecessary apology. "I'll fix the door when you want, eh?"

"Lovely, brilliant, thank you so much, Paul." Judith pushed the words between her widely smiling lips.

Paul ignored this and shuffled to the fridge.

Martha rose from the dining table with a huff. "Oi, get out of my kitchen before you hurt yourself." Paul backed out of her way and moved to the living room door again.

Judith followed Paul, needing to know she hadn't imagined the electricity between them, the attraction which had burned in his eyes. "Lovely to meet you, Paul," she called, trying to make him turn again. "And thank you for taking my bins out!"

Paul left without a backward glance.

"Never mind Paul, Judith, he's got no manners and never did," Martha grumbled. "He only comes in when he wants his tea." She began filling a plate with sandwiches and cakes.

Judith thought Paul was after more than tea and was giddy with the thrill of it. He was even more handsome than Dr. Jurgen Haag, and he had taken her bins out!

"You've got a heart of gold, Martha," Bev said. "After everything you put up with from that man."

"You're a saint, Martha." Marg nodded in agreement.

"I wouldn't put up with any of his crap," Cate added.

Martha glared at the divorced woman. "I do everything for Paul, like I promised I would forty-odd years ago, Cate, and I never break my promises. Marriage or otherwise. Not that it's done me any good, but there you are." She shuffled out to deliver the tea and cake to her much-maligned husband.

Judith sank down into her chair again, an unfamiliar buzzing in her chest. "My goodness, don't you think Paul looks exactly like Paul Newman?"

"Who?" Chantal was clearly too young to know.

"The pasta sauce guy?" Cate asked, doubtful.

"Paul has exactly the same blue eyes. They're just . . . electric."

"Well," Bev said heavily, as one with the duty to reveal some serious gossip. "It's those electric eyes which've gotten him into more trouble than you'd think possible."

"Poor Martha." Marg shook her head.

"Poor Martha," Chantal agreed.

"She's had to put up with all sorts from him over the years," Bev said.

"Things that would make your hair curl," Marg added, her frown inviting Judith to share in the communal disapproval of their friend's husband.

"He worked in *Africa*," Cate whispered. "For *years*." She folded her hands and sat back as if this should be explanation enough.

Judith felt her heart lurch with delight. They had so much in common already. "I wonder which country he was in?"

"It was a diamond mine. That's all I know," Bev said just as Martha walked back into the room and the conversation returned to more inane topics, like the tourist sites Judith should visit after her ankle healed.

She now found herself enjoying the luncheon at Martha's table, even eating a whole finger sandwich while waiting for Paul to make another appearance. Of all the women, she thought Bev was the most fun, though she couldn't quite bring herself to ask if they should exchange phone numbers. She was certain that Bev was a busy woman and probably didn't have time for new friends, let alone invalids like Judith, for goodness' sake.

When it came time to leave, Martha made up a plate of cakes and scones. She sent Cate to accompany Judith home with it.

"I promised Cass I'd feed you, and I will," Martha called from her front step as Judith hobbled away, embarrassed to be scolded like a child in front of this new group of women, one of whom might be a friend soon.

Poor Martha? Poor Paul, more like! Judith frowned down at the uneven path. She couldn't imagine having to live with that holier-than-thou busybody. No wonder he had worked away too. She remembered how happy she'd been to leave Terry twice a year for her three-month missions. Africa certainly had been a wonderful place to get away from the London life that had been organized by her mother and dominated by Terry. And of course, the work was terribly rewarding, no question.

"It's a doer-upper, isn't it?" Cate said as she watched Judith struggle with her house keys. "The Phillips family—Tom and Mary, who lived here before you—moved to a much nicer place in Burnside. That's a few suburbs away." She waved her hand at the patchy lawn in Judith's front yard. "I don't envy the work you'll do making your yard as good as

Martha's. Even Gladys, from number sixteen, has a lovely one. But that's down to Paul—he does it for her. She's an old biddy, Gladys, and a gossip too, so don't listen to a thing she says. It was her that spread it about Mary Phillips having that affair with Paul. I think it's really why they moved away, but you didn't hear that from me. So. You all right now?"

"Yes, thank you, Cate, it was lovely to meet you." Judith took the cake plate and shut the door before Cate could even reply.

Standing in her dark hall, she waited for the squeak of the gate as proof the irritating woman had really left. Hobbling with a single crutch under one arm, she tried to carry the plate in the other hand. She'd just made it to the kitchen when her grip weakened and it fell with a crash. She assessed the pile of cake and shards of china with something like satisfaction. Her stomach growled angrily at the waste. She was happy to ignore it. There was no way she would give in to that particular temptation when Paul Thompson was right next door. Here was a handsome man followed by gossip and romantic scandal. Judith had never dallied outside her own marriage. It might just be a bit of innocent fun to find out if Paul did.

Tell me, Marigold whispered. *Was it awful?*

"Lunch was nice, actually," Judith said, feeling lighter than she had in forever.

Don't you dare return the invitation until this nasty little house is fit for company.

Marigold's words brought Judith back to earth with a thud. Her mother was right. She had priorities. It was time to get back to work. She clomped into her bedroom to finally make a start on unpacking those horrid boxes.

SEVEN

JUDITH KNEW IT WAS WRONG TO CALL CASSANDRA TOO often. Luckily, throwing herself into house chores was a useful distraction. Though unpacking boxes while using crutches wasn't easy, what really made the work hard was that she didn't care for any of the things she pulled from the crumpled paper. She had packed these boxes months ago when she'd been emotionally fatigued after cleaning out Marigold's house with its hundreds of Wedgwood dishes, porcelain figurines, and linen table napkins saved for the company who never came.

Determined to be civilized about the divorce, Judith had only asked Terry for two days to clear her things from their Belgravia terrace. On the first morning, she'd found the dusty gift box of lingerie under Terry's side of the bed that was never meant for her. That time her triage worked too well. Zombie-like, Judith had drifted around their family home thinking *mine, mine, mine*, grabbing everything she'd ever bought or received as a gift. Yet now these crystal vases and hand-painted fruit bowls didn't feel like hers at all. In fact, it was unsettling to be reminded of that awful time and her awful marriage. The expensive things went back in their boxes, and she retaped the lids, wondering if charity shops did pickups in Adelaide.

It wasn't all doom and gloom, though. The lovely discount furniture Judith had purchased online had started to turn up in large trucks. Her favorite piece was the couch, a deep three-seater in chocolate-brown leather that was as comfortable as it looked. It was a floor model, the leather heavily scratched on one arm, and Judith loved that it was already worn in. She put a wonky little brass side table next to it, and that spot became her new favorite place to sit with a cup of tea. The wooden bookshelves had arrived in a darker stain than she'd anticipated, but they were easy to assemble while sitting on the floor with her new electric drill. Finally she had a place to unpack her huge collection of books and the empty silver picture frames. The frames were only empty because Terry was a vindictive toad who had insisted on keeping all their original family albums and photos, going so far as to tear them from their frames. Judith had been forced to download a scanner app on her phone and copy every photo left.

It was a happy day at 18 Rowntree Street when Judith's new color printer was delivered by the mail carrier. Settled on the couch with her ankle elevated, she spent hours on her laptop searching through Cassandra's baby pictures—such a beautiful, happy girl—to find matching ages for the few digital photos she had of Emily. Though when she put them side by side, the contrast was a little too stark. Emily's bright red face and yellow wrinkles clearly showed she had been born without a decent layer of fat under her skin and had suffered terribly from the jaundice Cassandra mentioned. Judith remembered her own happiness at having a healthy baby girl. Poor Cassandra didn't even get to share that joy if Emily was sickly from the start. What a shame.

What a shame you were too selfish to give Cassandra a sibling. Marigold repeated the words she'd whined dozens of times when alive.

The very idea of a second baby still gave Judith a shudder. What if she'd had that little rugby player son that Terry had begged her for? Could you imagine? Yet another reason to celebrate the sensibly controlled diet that had caused her periods to stop for months at a time.

Of course, Judith had loved every day of her year at home with baby Cassandra. She had been such a happy little thing when her routine was structured, every day exactly the same. Into bed she'd go, and hours later, she'd be up again. Exactly the same time every day. In one end the food would go and, minutes later, come out the other end. Exactly the same time every day. Same. Same. Same.

Only once Judith had mentioned putting Cassandra in a papoose and taking her off to Nairobi to see friends, and Terry had lost his mind. He had categorically forbidden Cassandra to go on any trips outside their regular French beach resorts. He said he'd claim kidnapping, knowing Judith couldn't have even a shadow of a criminal record if she wanted to return to her volunteer work.

Honestly, Terry and his stupid parenting rules had driven Judith to distraction. Though not a couple prone to unnecessary conversation, they had made time to argue over everything about their daughter. Yet of all their disputes, the worst had been the year-long screaming fight when Judith demanded to change the fiercely academic school Terry had chosen for Cassandra. The poor girl had languished at the bottom of the class for most of her primary years before Judith succeeded in sending her to a much more supportive school with a fine arts focus. The only difficulty was that it was a boarding-only school.

Even though Judith had been told that her daughter was crying herself to sleep in the dormitory every night, she felt a deep satisfaction that Cassandra had not only escaped the awful school but also her parents' miserable home life. No matter how much it hurt, she knew she'd done the right thing for Cassandra. She was sure of it. There was nothing else she could have done. Was there?

And what thanks have you had from that ungrateful girl? Marigold whispered. *She's done nothing with her fine education. She didn't even marry that Andrew before she had his baby.*

"Oh, stop it, Mother." Judith had never waited for thanks. "Cassandra is an interior designer, or a set designer, or something. I just need to help get this baby off her hands, and she'll be free to work again."

Then you'll tie those apron strings back on, will you, Judith? Marigold's whisper turned to a cackle. *You'll be a grandmother to Emily like I was to Cassandra?*

"I—what?" Judith was shocked at the thought. "I'm sure we'll get a nanny for Emily. I'm not taking over Cassandra's life like you did to me. I'll still get to work too."

Cassandra is not you, Judith.

Cassandra hadn't called or visited that week, which was just fine. Completely fine. Judith reached for her phone and touched the screen to make it light up again. No message yet. Completely fine. Judith didn't want to be a nuisance sending too many messages. There was nothing that irritated her more than someone who couldn't take a hint. Still, the lingering problem remained. Cassandra did need her, and honestly, how could you help a daughter if you didn't interfere at least a little bit?

Everyone does better if they mind their own business, Marigold whispered.

Of course Marigold would say that. She'd spent her life friendless and alone. Judith's father had died before she was born. Marigold never mentioned him, and Judith was not encouraged to ask any questions.

"For goodness' sake, I just miss people," Judith murmured, and her stomach growled loudly as if in agreement.

The camps had been constant chaos. Thousands of people awake and active at all hours—"the makeshift city that never sleeps" had been Jurgen's joke. Always someone needing an immunization or a bowl of rice. Inner-city London was no different. Around every corner was someone needing a couple of pounds or a hot meal on a cold night. Always something happening. So many chances to be a nameless saint. Not that Judith thought of herself as a saint.

Outside her cottage, a passing car revved its engine, rattling the living room windows, before it raced off down Rowntree Street. A dog barked somewhere distant. Birds warbled in the yard. Inside the house, her kitchen tap dripped in the sink. Her stomach gurgled again. Her hunger was undeniable, but it annoyed her to always be thinking of food.

Cassandra hasn't even invited you over to her home yet, Marigold whispered.

"Cassandra is probably even more disorganized than I am," Judith said, tapping the screen of her phone to find no messages there again. "She's a young woman with a baby and doesn't want the stress of visitors." It was Saturday, though, which meant tomorrow was Sunday—a family day.

I was the one who always did the Sunday dinners when Cassandra lived in London. Marigold needled a sensitive spot. *Maybe she doesn't want to have to endure one of your attempts at a roast again?*

"Would you be quiet!" Judith's stomach cramped, and she felt a little lightheaded. "I did a fine enough job of Sunday dinner when you left me alone." She stomped to the kitchen, turned the kettle on, and dropped a tea bag in a fresh mug.

Well, careful you don't start slipping like those women next door. Keep trim for Terry.

Lurching to the fridge, Judith took out the carton of skimmed milk and chose to ignore the fruit yogurt she'd bought in a moment of weakness. "I never kept myself trim for Terry," she protested. "It was the children in the camps who made it hard to eat. It wouldn't have been fair of me to flaunt a full stomach when theirs were always empty."

Well, no man can love a woman who eats more than him.

Judith snorted. "I think I have a few other priorities before finding someone to love me." But now she was thinking about Paul again, and there was a lot to think about. She was smiling when she finished making her tea.

Planning on going back to the couch, Judith hobbled carefully to the other side of her kitchen counter without her crutches, watching the hot tea trembling in the cup. "Might be too soon, I think," she cautioned herself.

There was a loud *knock-knock*, then the sound of the screen door squeaking open. Judith was shocked to see a tall figure coming inside her house, uninvited. Wait a minute, was that—?

"Coo-wee, Judith, s'just me and Paul!" Martha shouted from behind her husband.

Judith lit up with an almost violent intensity as Paul caught her gaze with those cobalt-blue eyes. Her hand holding the tea mug rose to wave hello and doused her front in hot liquid. Squawking, she hopped backward, and her flexible cast skidded, sending her crashing to the floor in a heap.

How humiliating, Judith!

She tried to get back on her feet by grabbing the edge of the kitchen counter and wedging her good leg under her.

"I've brought Paul to fix this screen door for you." Martha said, then took in Judith struggling on the floor. "Jeez Louise, what've you done to yourself? Paul, get in here! Judith needs help."

Paul was already standing next to Judith. She found herself briefly fascinated by the long, corded muscles of his calves covered in curly blond hair. Thick woolen socks scrunched down over the top of his brown leather work boots, still decorated with bits of the grass he'd just been cutting.

Martha must have noticed Judith staring at Paul's feet because she shouted, "Boots, Paul!" Judith felt flushed and realized what a mess she was in.

"You want me to help or take my boots off?" To Judith's surprise, Paul sounded open to either option as he waited for his wife's command. If Judith had ever barked at Terry like that, she would have received a mouthful of sarcasm and then heard the incident brought up for months afterward as he regaled dinner parties with a performance of "Judith, the Harridan Wife."

"Help her up, o'course." Martha rolled her eyes at her beautiful husband's stupidity. "I would meself, Judith, but my back's playing up again."

"No, really, I'm all right," Judith protested as Paul lifted her into his arms, enveloping her in the scent of fresh laundry and male musk. She gave an odd, squeaky laugh as he heaved her against his side. "I'm sorry, I must be so heavy for you."

"It's fine."

Paul's compliment and his nearness flustered Judith so much she forgot to stand on her own two feet, his hands holding her hips. She told herself to stay calm as he led her to a dining chair, but when his upper arm brushed her left breast, she couldn't contain the wild corners of her mouth.

"All right, off you go and fix that door." Martha fanned her husband out of the room with flapping hands. "Sorry, Judith, you'd think he was raised in a tent."

"There's nothing wrong with tents," Judith said, gazing down the hall to watch Paul. He'd left his tool kit next to Martha's rubber clogs and was crouched over it, knees splayed in a way that made his drill cotton shorts ride up his thighs.

"You're looking a bit flushed, Judith."

"Tea, Martha?"

Martha was busy mopping up the spilled tea on the floor with a couple of kitchen towels. "I'll make it, chook," she said. "You stay sitting."

While waiting for the kettle to boil, Judith was irritated to see Martha poking in the few open boxes that were scattered around the dining area. "I haven't seen Cass this week. You did tell her you're still laid up, right?"

"*Cassandra* is very busy," Judith said. "I'd be helping her with the baby if it wasn't for this blasted ankle cast!" She flicked a glance down the hall to Paul, now with a drill in one hand and a metal hinge in the other.

"I think Cass's all right for help," Martha said. "She's got Andrew's mum over most days, then a cleaner comes in a couple times a week, and there's a young girl who does some babysitting for her."

Judith's jaw dropped. When they had visited, Andrew had mentioned his mother coming over just in passing. How did she not know Cassandra had this much help?

Martha had moved on to perusing the photos on the Queen Anne shelf. "You haven't got any photos of Emily up yet?" she commented. "Lots of other people's kids, though."

Still reeling from the news that Cassandra had no practical use for her company, Judith looked for solace down the hall. Unfortunately, Paul had moved out of sight.

Martha picked up a picture of Judith with the head girl and two prefects standing in front of their school, next to a huge jacaranda tree. "This is you, is it? Must have been a while ago. You look so young."

Judith bristled. "Actually, that was taken while I was on mission in Nairobi two years ago. I was working with the Girls Empowerment Program, learning new strategies to take to the camp schools in Dadaab."

"Nai-robby? Now that would've been dangerous for a white woman," Martha said, seeming confident that Judith couldn't contradict her.

"You learn to look after yourself," Judith replied, already annoyed. Why did no one ask about the work? Why did they always harp on about how hard it must've been on her delicate white lady sensibilities?

Martha pointed at the three girls in the picture. "Who're the kids?"

"Those were students from the school where I taught English." She rose from the table and held out a hand for the frame. "They were my teaching assistants. In fact, I just heard that the taller girl, Nathalia, has started university this year."

"What happened to the other two?" Martha asked.

"Constance and Zenya? I really wish I knew." Judith felt her heart pinch as she gazed into the girls' happy faces. "It's so hard keeping track. There's so much movement between the schools and the camps and families being reassigned or sent back to the awful conditions that they were trying to escape in the first place."

Judith sat down in her chair, feeling the weight of loss. "Of course, I never knew where exactly the UNHCR would assign me in the camp. Three months fly past when you're working like that, and then it'd be another three months for me in London waiting for a new visa before I could get back again. Of course, not all my kids would be there when I got back." She felt the familiar burn of injustice for all that she had in her own life without having had to earn it—a wonderful education, a safe home, a future free of violence—and all those children had been deprived of through no fault of their own. Yet when she looked for understanding, she only saw an expression of disapproval on Martha's face.

"I guess if you're changing around all the time, it would be too hard for the kids to find you," Martha said. "Believe me, I had enough trouble getting my kids to school some days. Well, you know how it is."

Judith gaped. Was Martha really comparing the school drop-off to the chaos of running a school in a refugee camp?

"Don't get me wrong, it was wonderful work you did, Judith," Martha said, dusting the shelf edge with her shirtsleeve. "I just choose to help those around me in need, like my family—and my neighbors," she added with a pointed look. "Cass mentioned it was really hard on her with you leaving to go to Kenya all the time when she was little."

Oh, Cassandra had mentioned that, had she? Overwhelmed by a sudden jealous fury, Judith decided it was time to cut through Martha's pompous attitude and get to the issue at hand: Martha thought by staying home, her charity work was more valuable, which therefore proved she was a better mother than Judith. "Are you saying the African refugees didn't deserve my help because I'm white and privileged?" she asked.

Martha had the gall to look surprised, her heavy brows rising above the frames of her glasses. "I only meant to say it doesn't hurt to look to your own, Judith. You don't always need to go to the other side of the world to help them over there when there's plenty that needs your help here."

"By 'them,' you mean African people, don't you?" Judith was incensed. She felt something akin to happiness as she leaped straight into her favorite diatribe for anyone who dared ask her why she gave her time and energy to the refugee crisis in Kenya. "Martha, you have no idea what the people of Somalia and South Sudan have suffered because of political strife, famine, and overpopulation. If you had any interest beyond your own backyard, your heart would bleed for the millions dying of preventable causes while the West sits back and 'looks to its own.' You, Martha, who have lived in a safe, wealthy country all your life, how could you think to judge those who've suffered through wars and starvation and extreme poverty—"

"We've got poverty here in our safe, wealthy country too," Martha argued, raising her voice above Judith's. "It might not be glamorous looking after ratbag kids or teenagers with drug problems, but it's useful work, and it helps people in my town."

"Well, that's just small-minded and . . . racist," Judith hissed. "I think it's time you left, Martha."

"If that's how it is, Judith." Martha raised her double chin high. "I know when I'm not wanted."

"As do I," Judith said, so triumphant to have the last word that she didn't realize how ridiculous she might sound saying it.

Martha left.

Judith sat, hands flexing on the tabletop, boiling in her self-righteous fury. It was impossible to ignore the sound of Paul's power drill fixing her security door, and she wondered what Martha said to him when she stormed past. She began mentally preparing herself to defend her anger at the suburban housewife who'd dared challenge—

Her phone pinged loudly.

Hands still shaking with adrenaline, Judith snatched it up and saw a message from Cassandra inviting her to lunch tomorrow. She felt a cascade of relief. Finally! A chance to tell Cassandra what sort of woman this Martha really was. Maybe then Cassandra would finally stop confiding in her about their private family business. How could Cassandra think Judith would ever be friends with an ignorant fool like Martha Thompson?

EIGHT

AT MIDDAY ON SUNDAY, JUDITH TOOK AN UBER FOR THE five-minute drive to Cassandra's house. Cassandra hadn't offered a lift. Which was of no account. Judith wouldn't want to bother her with such a trifling thing anyway. She spotted a lovely florist on the way and stopped the driver to pick up a hostess gift to go with her bottle of wine. She chose an elegant bunch of white, long-stemmed lilies framed by large palm leaves. Yes, two gifts were probably overkill, but Cassandra loved pretty things in the house, and she'd appreciate the flowers.

As Judith resettled into the back seat of the air-conditioned Uber, she imagined how nervous Cassandra must be today. Sunday lunch with the family was very stressful for any young woman, and she didn't want Cassandra feeling any undue pressure to perform miracles. She had her own reasons for being nerve-racked too. She had decided it was time to sit Cassandra down and discuss the real reason for her move to Adelaide. It was the right thing to do but was probably going to be very emotionally complicated, and because she'd been told often enough, Judith knew she wasn't good at emotionally complicated situations. Afterward, Cassandra would certainly need some time to understand that what Judith was offering her was a chance to fix a bad situation, to rebuild, to stand on her own two feet like Judith should have done all those years ago.

It's not as if the silly girl is married to that Andrew. Marigold whispered so loudly that Judith checked the rearview mirror to see if the driver had heard it too. Thankfully, his eyes stayed on the road, and only the sound of sports on the radio filled the silence.

Judith dabbed the sweat from her forehead with a tissue.

Silly. Girl. The way Marigold spat the words, they could hit a body like bullets, piercing the heart.

Silly. Girl.

The only words as bad were "Sunday lunch."

Judith and Terry were newly married, having just moved into their first terrace house in Kensington, when Judith volunteered to host Sunday lunch for the extended family. Marigold had broken the first cardinal rule by arriving early, sending Judith into a flurry to get ready ahead of time. She had then remade Judith's lumpy gravy, scoffing at her all the while.

Silly girl.

When dinner was served, Marigold claimed it was too tough for her teeth.

Silly girl.

Terry's mother, Elizabeth, had pushed her own plate away with a relieved titter, both women enjoying Judith's humiliation. Terry had laughed at her too and eaten a double helping of the beef, claiming he enjoyed indigestion.

Silly girl.

Judith had kept her upper lip stiff and done her crying in the laundry room. When she served the sticky toffee pudding for dessert, no one noticed her red eyes. Especially not Marigold, who had been too busy flirting with her trophy son-in-law, the newly crowned barrister.

Judith felt breathless under the weight of memories. She tried to dismiss her misfortunes, reassuring herself that plenty of people had it worse in this world. A bossy mother was no tragedy. Ridiculous to get so upset over nothing. She was being silly. Silly girl.

The Uber had pulled up in front of a bluestone bungalow with a peaked tile roof. There was a hip-high white picket fence and rosebushes lining the pebbled path to the porch. Judith had to double-check the number before she could believe that this gorgeous house really belonged to her daughter.

She fussed with her belongings as she left the cool of the car and braved the hot sunshine. She thanked the driver, though he hadn't helped her with anything, and slammed the door. He drove off before she could jump back in.

Silly girl.

On her crutches, Judith could barely manage with the wine and flowers but eventually struggled up the garden path. The front door had been painted an azure blue so glossy she could see her reflection in it. A deep breath, and she was ready. The doorbell needed to be pressed twice, just to be sure it chimed. Hearing heavy footsteps inside the house, she raised the corners of her mouth high. There wouldn't be any crying in laundry rooms today.

Andrew opened the door, greeting Judith with a wailing Emily on his hip. "Mum, you're early!" Judith's heart sank. He kissed the air near her cheek and stepped back. "Darl, your mum's here!" he shouted, though they'd already entered the airy open-plan living, kitchen, and dining area. Australians clearly didn't like houses with too many walls.

"Mum!" Cassandra peeked over the kitchen island she was cleaning. She had a white streak of baby vomit on the shoulder of her blue T-shirt, and her hair was in a messy bun.

"I can't be early," Judith said, flustered by how pained Andrew and Cassandra seemed to be. "You said twelve noon on the message."

"You're in Australia now," Andrew said with a quick laugh. "Twelve normally means closer to one. Anyway, I was going to come pick you up when we were ready for you."

"Well." Judith tried to shake off the anger she felt at being faulted for something she couldn't possibly have known. "Then I'm sorry."

"No problem, family's welcome anytime." Andrew finally reached to take the string bag with the bottle of wine from Judith's aching hand.

"I did tell Andrew you would prefer to make your own way here," Cassandra said.

Not sure how to answer that, Judith held out the bunch of flowers. "I have a gift for the lovely hostess."

Cassandra only swiveled to Andrew, her expression stricken. "Oh, no, Andrew's allergic to that type of lily," she said and kept spraying the kitchen counter with pink cleaner, the cloth squeaking on the pale stone.

"We can put them on the outside table, love," Andrew said. "Mum wasn't to know. No harm done."

Disappointed by the rejection of her rather expensive gift, Judith noted how nervous Cassandra seemed and presumed it was because of Andrew. Him and his ridiculous allergies!

Andrew joined Cassandra in the kitchen, and they rudely started a whispered conversation, so Judith took the chance to look around the home. Though the façade of the house had been kept very traditional, the interior was renovated and thoroughly modern. There were lots of great big windows everywhere, and the few walls had been painted white and left bare of artwork, the floorboards stained a pale gray. The furniture was in coordinating shades of beige and light blue.

Judith was very impressed by Cassandra's simple yet bold decorating style. Everything looked placed just so. She thought the large white candle scenting the air with frangipani perfume and the gentle hum of an air conditioner in the background made for a pleasant and restful atmosphere. Yet she couldn't see any preparation for a formal lunch. The broad dining table hadn't been set. There was no tablecloth or silverware to be seen, only a pile of paperwork and a laptop at one end.

"Can I help with anything?" Judith asked as she made her way to join Cassandra and Andrew in the kitchen.

"Actually, I'd love you to hold Emily." Andrew guided Judith to the dining table and held out a beige fabric chair, encouraging her to sit down. "I've got baby sick in my hair, and I need a shower."

"Really, Andrew?" Cassandra sounded a little hysterical. "Mum just got here, and you're dashing off to the shower?"

"Won't be long, love," he promised and gave the whimpering baby to Judith. Moving back into the kitchen, he embraced Cassandra and whispered something that made her smile. She pushed him away as he smacked her bottom and left the room laughing.

Frowning at Andrew's disrespectful display of sexual domination—she was right there, for goodness' sake!—Judith tried to sit Emily on her lap. Contrary, the baby refused to bend at the waist and instead stood on the edge of Judith's knees, little toes gripping painfully through her linen trousers. It could have been her imagination, but she thought Emily looked thinner than she had a week ago. Wearing a pink dress with embroidered ducks on it, her skinny legs were sticky, and she smelled like baby wipes and sour milk. The poor little thing was not thriving.

"Hello, Emily," Judith said. Emily cocked a tiny ginger eyebrow at her grandmother's falsely cheerful tone, looking as if she was considering crying again. Her stomach gurgled. Judith's stomach gave an answering growl that surprised Emily enough to raise her other eyebrow.

"Did you sleep well?" Judith called to Cassandra.

"No, she slept horribly," Cassandra called back.

"And why aren't you sleeping?" Lowering her voice, Judith directed the question to Emily. "Is it because you're hungry and nauseous all the time?" The baby answered with a wet burp, and a little string of vomit dribbled down her chin. Her pout deepened. Judith braced for a scream when Emily suddenly spotted Judith's necklace of blue crystal beads. For the very first time, there was a lift at the corner of her granddaughter's lips. "Help yourself," Judith told her. Happily, Emily allowed herself to be folded, sitting on Judith's lap as she shoved the blue beads between her gums.

Cassandra came over to the table with a dish of green mush for the baby and a mug of tea for Judith. She put both out of reach of Emily. Judith was so proud to show what a helpful grandmother she was that she turned Emily on her lap to face Cassandra.

"Mum, what's she got in her mouth?" Cassandra lurched out of her seat in a sudden panic and came around the table.

"It's just my necklace, darling," Judith replied. "I don't mind her chewing it as long as she's happy."

Cassandra wrenched the beads out of Emily's mouth, making her wail. "When was the last time you washed that thing?"

Judith was confused by the question. "Honestly, Cassandra—"

"Emily gets sick all the time." Cassandra held the weeping baby high on her shoulder, as if protecting her from Judith. "We sterilize everything she puts in her mouth so she doesn't pick up any bugs to make her worse." She strapped Emily into a plush high chair with beige cushions that matched the dining chairs. Staring down at the screaming baby, Cassandra's expression suffused with despair. "Wonderful. Now she's too upset to eat, even though she's probably starving from throwing up all morning." The baby rubbed her eyes with tiny fists and slumped down in the cushioned chair, her cries petering out to whimpers.

Judith looked from mother to daughter, daughter to mother. Both were upset. Both were exhausted. If Cassandra really thought that Emily's constant vomiting was due to gastroenteritis, there was a big problem, and Judith knew that she had to step in. Yet how? Cassandra looked like she wasn't going to hide in the laundry room to cry her eyes out, and the baby certainly couldn't tell anyone what was wrong. Judith tried to be gentle. "Darling, do you always put milk in Emily's food?"

Cassandra rubbed her own eyes, mirroring Emily. "Of course. Breastfeeding was a nightmare. I had to wean her onto formula at four weeks, and she's still not happy."

"Are you quite sure it isn't the lactose?" she said. "You know I have a lot of personal experience with intolerances."

"Or maybe Emily hates my food too," Cassandra muttered as she got to her feet and headed back into the kitchen. She might as well have put her hands over her ears like when she was little.

Judith knew this was too important to stop trying. "Darling, listen. I don't think that you're doing anything wrong—it's just Emily wouldn't be so cranky all the time if she was healthy, don't you think?"

"Things have changed since your day, Mum," Cassandra said in a tone that meant *for the better*. "Her pediatrician said she just needs to get her sleeping sorted, then she'll get her meals right. It's a chicken-and-the-egg thing."

Chicken and the egg? Judith wanted to give that doctor a piece of her mind. Clearly the baby was underweight and her digestion was miserable. However, Cassandra didn't return to the table, and Judith didn't think her advice would be any more appreciated if she kept shouting it across the room.

It was only a few minutes before Andrew returned from his shower wearing a clean striped T-shirt that hardly covered his large stomach, his blond hair still wet. He scooped Emily out of her high chair and blew a raspberry on her neck. "I'm starving, Cass," he announced. "Are we eating now?"

Judith cursed the twisted ankle that kept her from leaping into the kitchen. Stupid man, to think Cassandra could just pull together a Sunday lunch as easily as that. It took hours of work. "I can make the gravy."

The words slipped out, and Judith cursed herself again. "Or set the table, whatever you like, darling," she added.

"I didn't have time to cook." Cassandra disappeared into the fridge, only to pull out a stack of plastic takeaway containers and a foil-lined paper bag. She got bowls and plates from a cupboard.

Aghast, Judith watched as a cold roast chicken was slipped from its foil-lined bag onto a platter. All the salads in their plastic boxes were unceremoniously placed at the end of the table where she sat. There was a fork or spoon sticking out of each one. Andrew sat down with Emily on his lap opposite Judith, and Cassandra took the head of the table, still handing out cutlery to her mother and husband.

"Napkins, darl?" Andrew suggested. Cassandra got up and brought a roll of paper towels to the table, avoiding Judith's gaze.

"Nothing's fancy, Mum," Andrew said, holding his plate out for Cassandra to fill for him. "We've got the best chicken 'n' chip shop in Adelaide just on our doorstep. Cass told me Sunday lunch was a big deal to your family back in the day, so we're happy to have you over to ours."

Judith eyed the picnic lunch spread out before her. "Thank you both for inviting me, Andrew. I'm happy to be here—and see your beautiful home for the first time too," she replied. Very politely, considering.

Of course Cassandra picked up on her tone. "Sorry," she muttered. "I've been so busy."

"We should've had you over much sooner," Andrew agreed, his gaze on Cassandra as she continued piling food on his plate. "Emily's a lucky kid to have two grannies in her life now."

Judith's stomach clenched when she recognized Cassandra's irritation—the pink cheeks, narrow eyes, and pinched lips. She almost felt pity for Andrew. Yet he just gave Cassandra a big, goofy grin, seemingly oblivious to her anger.

"Mum's been busy too, Andrew," Cassandra said, still glaring at him. "She's been trying to decorate that *horrible* cottage I chose for her."

"So you did get my texts!" Judith was relieved. "I wondered if my new Australian number wasn't going through sometimes."

"She got them," Andrew said, now frowning at Cassandra. "Cass loves decorating—it's a wonder she's not helping you more with all that."

"Mum's fine on her own," Cassandra said.

Andrew turned to Judith. "My parents are excited to meet you, Mum," he said. "We'll have to set up a barbecue with everyone. Right, Cass?"

Judith hoped Andrew would stop with his jibes. For goodness' sake, she didn't need any help irritating Cassandra. She did well enough at that on her own.

"I could do with some help on the decorating," Judith said to pull Cassandra's attention. "I've no idea what colors to paint the walls. What's better: butter lemon or pale pink?"

"Can I serve you some lunch, Mum?" Cassandra asked.

Judith really didn't want Cassandra to feel worse about this terrible Sunday lunch. The chicken had been cut into chunks and was sitting in a puddle of its own glistening juices. The salads were shiny with dressing, and there was even a "salad" of pasta and potatoes covered in greasy pesto. A traditional roast was something that Judith could usually negotiate. Where were the boiled vegetables? The dry baked potatoes? The lean meat?

"I'll serve myself, darling," she replied. "You eat before Emily needs you again." She managed to wrestle some skinless meat from the chicken and picked out a few pieces of celery and olives from a Greek-style salad.

She hoped her meal wasn't being judged when she looked up and saw Cassandra communicating with Andrew using only jiggles of her eyebrows. Andrew gave Cassandra that goofy grin again and shook his head. He noticed Judith watching them. "Cass, you forgot the wine, love," he said.

Cassandra flew to her feet and retrieved a cold bottle of white wine and three glasses. When she set it on the table, he made a joke about having to open the bottle with his teeth, sending her back to the kitchen to retrieve the bottle opener. "We're both pretty tired, aren't we, Cass?" he said. "Emily isn't sleeping much at all, and Cass is up with her three or four times a night, which of course keeps me up too. Most nights, I sleep in our little office so I can be okay for work, but the weekends are tough."

"Cassandra was a very good sleeper," Judith offered by way of keeping the conversation going, even though she would have preferred to stab Andrew with a fork for the way he bossed her daughter around.

"That's because I had a night nanny," Cassandra snapped.

"Who told you that?" Judith asked, surprised. "You slept next to me your whole first year, darling."

"Then maybe you could show us how it's done," Andrew said. "We'd love a good night's kip."

"I'd love to!" Judith said. Yet not a moment later, Cassandra clearly kicked Andrew under the table. How confusing. She decided to change the subject before Cassandra was furious with either of them again. "Oh, you'll never guess, but I had a run-in with that dreadful neighbor of mine—Martha."

"Oh, not Martha!" Cassandra seemed more stricken than the situation warranted, and Judith felt a stab of jealousy.

"Well, let me tell you about Martha." Judith enjoyed telling a story. She was always careful not to embellish the facts and gave her own opinions to let her listeners know how to react properly at every turn. Yet despite how clear her tale was, Andrew and Cassandra just couldn't seem to keep up.

Andrew scratched at his head, making his hair stick up in tufts that Cassandra reached over to smooth for him. "She didn't actually say anything racist, did she?" he asked. "Not that she doesn't like black people or anything, just that she wanted to help people in her own town."

"She said 'them over there.'" Did Judith really have to draw them a picture?

"Martha is a sweetheart, Mum," Andrew assured Judith. "It's hard to imagine she hates anybody." He reached out and took the last chicken leg—with his hands and not the tongs, she noted with disgust.

"Martha has a heart of gold," Cassandra said. "I know she loves her family and all her foster kids equally. She's done so much for so many. I'm sure she never meant anything offensive to African people by her comments."

Judith raised her eyebrows at Cassandra as she sided with a dentist against her own mother.

"I'm sure it was just a big misunderstanding," Cassandra was using Andrew's decisive tone too. "If you made an effort, you'd see that you and Martha have so much in common. Remember, she looked after you so well when you had your accident. We should be grateful to her for that alone."

"Yeah, a quick apology, and it'll be water under the bridge." Andrew spoke through a mouthful of chicken.

Judith sat back in her chair and stared at her untouched glass of wine, watching condensation trickle down the sides. During the conversation, Emily had almost fallen asleep against Andrew's chest. Cassandra took her to bed, leaving Andrew and Judith to sit in an uncomfortable silence. He slurped at his second glass of wine. "Cass really is happy that you moved to Adelaide, you know," he said, as if Judith might've thought differently. "We know it was tough for you to visit when Emily was born, what with your mum passing away and that, so it means the world that you're here now."

A-ha! Judith heard it again. The accusation that she hadn't been there for Cassandra in the past. Andrew was just like Terry, so judgmental and arrogant she could hardly stand it. Cassandra was far too permissive, not strong like Judith had been. Thank God she had her mother's help to get free of him.

When Cassandra reentered the room, both Judith and Andrew were sitting in silence. "How about you get the dessert, darl?" he suggested before Cassandra could sit down again. "You're going to love this, Mum," he said as another plastic box appeared from the fridge. "It's the chicken shop specialty—gluten-free tiramisu."

Surely Cassandra wouldn't dare? Judith watched as her daughter split the entire dessert into three bowls. Cassandra's cheeks were flushed, which meant she knew exactly what she was doing when she put a heaped bowl in front of her mother.

"Try it, Mum," Andrew insisted. "It's lactose-free too, so eat as much as you want."

Judith scraped a spoonful of the dessert and shoved it in before she could tell Andrew to shut up. The sweet mascarpone and espresso flavors coated her tongue in pure, decadent joy. The chocolate powder mixed with the soft ladyfingers and easily slid down to her grateful stomach.

"Good, right?" Andrew was as proud as if he'd made the dessert himself.

It took all of Judith's willpower to put the spoon down and not take another glorious bite. "It's very nice," she conceded, fussing with the square of paper towel to wipe chocolate powder from her lips. Out of the corner of her eye, she saw Cassandra finish her own bowl and then carefully scrape the sides to get every last bite. Again she wondered why Cassandra and Andrew were both so heavy and yet the baby was too light. Emily was seen regularly by doctors, and Cassandra had so much help in her life. Maybe Judith was wrong about there being a problem?

After lunch Andrew convinced Cassandra to give Judith a tour of the ground floor of the house. The upper level held the primary bedroom, a little office, and Emily's bedroom, where the baby slept too lightly to have people walk past her door.

The house really was lovely. Cassandra had wonderful taste, but it was very much an adult space. Judith knew all the beige fabric was going to be filthy as soon as Emily started walking. There were so many potted plants to upend on the carpet. So many books and knickknacks to toss on the floor. Judith wondered where all the toys were until she saw a basket by the side of the couch, hidden from view. A few bits of colored plastic poked from the top.

"The toys get disinfected every day," Cassandra seemed rather desperate to tell her. "I keep everything super clean for Emily—of course only using organic products. I've got a sterilize option on my dishwasher, so it's easy to do."

Judith spied a low shelf, set with a small collection of frames. It seemed like a safe topic. "What lovely pictures," she said. "Are these Andrew's parents?"

Andrew came into the living area and put his arm around Cassandra. She sank against him like she needed the support. "That's my mum, Emily, and my dad, Robert, at their anniversary party," he said. "It was forty years for them last month."

Judith couldn't hear him anymore over the blood pounding in her ears. She was grateful for her crutches as she reeled from the news, surprised at how deeply it hurt. "Is Emily an old family name?" she asked, interrupting Andrew blathering on about his parents' happy marriage. "Is that why you chose it?"

The dentist shrugged. "No, but Mum was pleased as punch when we gave it to her first grandchild. It was sweet of my Cass to suggest it." He gave Cassandra a kiss on the forehead.

"I loved the name," Cassandra murmured. "It was always on my list."

"Right under Marigold, I'm sure," Judith said. She swung herself out the glass patio doors and onto the wide covered deck, continuing the tour and enduring Andrew's talk on the landscaping plans, to be completed as soon as they could afford it. The yard was very pretty, with flower beds along three sides and a patio with tan paving stones. The large rattan sofa, coffee table, and two matching armchairs had apparently been a generous housewarming gift from Andrew's parents. Judith remembered the fruit basket she had sent and stopped wondering why she'd never received a thank-you note for it.

"How about I leave you ladies to chat out here?" Andrew suggested, his attitude so blasé Judith immediately knew it to be fake. "I'll go make the tea and bring it out to you."

"That's okay," Cassandra protested, "you can stay."

"I've got some work to do anyway, love." He squeezed her shoulder. "You two talk."

Judith sat down in a chair facing the yard as Cassandra watched Andrew leave. Only when the patio door closed behind him did she pull out the other armchair and fold herself into it, silver-painted toenails curling over the edge of the cushion as she hugged her knees to her chest.

"I've never known a dentist to work on weekends," Judith joked to break the silence.

"Andrew runs his own practice, so there's a lot to do besides just see patients."

Reminding herself to be careful, Judith moved to a more neutral topic. "You have such a beautiful home, darling," she said. "Did you do all the decorating yourself?"

Cassandra nodded. "It's taking ages, and the budget's small. It's not all antiques and wall-to-wall carpet, but I think lots of white feels stylish and comfortable."

"Oh, yes!" She was relieved to agree with Cassandra on something. "It was your father who liked all the antiques and things. I love your plain decor."

"Plain," Cassandra said. "I guess you would call it that."

Sod it. Judith could instantly tell from Cassandra's frosty expression she'd used the wrong word. "Plain is beautiful to me," she said, determined not to lose the whole conversation now.

Andrew came out with two mugs of milky tea and a sugar bowl with no spoon. He gave Cassandra another squeeze on her shoulder and left. Cassandra took a deep breath, and her cheeks flushed, making her look younger than her years. "Speaking of Daddy, I thought you might want to talk about the divorce. I mean, I would like to talk about it. We've never really had the chance, have we?"

Judith felt her heart rattle in her chest. "Of course, it's only natural that you'd have questions, though you should know the lawyers are handling the wills and the trust your father set up."

"I'm not talking about money." Cassandra sounded insulted, which was confusing, as she'd been complaining about just that very thing with her renovations. "I wanted to ask you about something far more important."

Judith couldn't seem to pull enough air into her lungs. She nodded for her daughter to continue.

"Did you—I mean, why did you divorce Daddy?" Cassandra's words ran together in a rush. "What happened? Was there, maybe, somebody else? That Dr. Jurgen guy you were always talking about?"

Judith laughed, shrill and mirthless. "Cassandra! That's certainly a lot of questions." She held up her hand when Cassandra opened her mouth again. "I'll try my best to answer." She looked out over the flower beds, brave enough to talk, not quite brave enough to look into Cassandra's accusing stare. "I suppose the simplest explanation is that your father and I were just living very different lives, and neither of us wanted to change that, so it felt much kinder to part ways than force each other to fit. We hadn't enjoyed being a couple very much, especially in the last few years with the pressure of his work and my sick mother—"

"Please don't blame Grandmother," Cassandra interrupted, chopping her hand on the table between them like it marked a line. "She always loved Daddy, and I was so angry when he told me that she could've stayed at home until the end. It was you who wanted her back in hospice. I was pregnant, so it wasn't like I could come and look after her myself. I was just lucky that he gave me regular updates."

Judith's whole body shook with a toxic mix of anger and adrenaline. "How would Terry have known anything about my mother's care? He never visited her!"

"He knew I was worried about her," Cassandra said. "Just like she worried about him when I left for Australia."

"Cassandra, your grandmother worshipped your father. Sometimes I thought she was too happy to step in while I was away on missions. It wouldn't have surprised me if one day I found her in my bed!"

Cassandra narrowed her eyes. "Mum, *really*. It just annoyed you that Grandmother was an old-fashioned homemaker. That it was her, who made our house a home. My happiest memories are of those weekends home from school when it'd just be me, Grandmother, and Daddy. We'd have scrambled eggs for tea in the kitchen and read comics together."

Judith crossed her arms over her chest, trying to contain all the hurt at having missed that picture of domestic happiness. "Sounds delightful."

"Was there anyone else?" Cassandra asked again. "Someone who wanted you to leave Daddy?"

"No, Cassandra." Judith was finding it difficult to choose her words with her heart pounding so erratically. "There was no lover asking me to leave my husband. The husband, I will add, who couldn't ever give me a compliment or even stand to look at me naked. No one had to make me leave Terry—I just needed the chance." Was she hoping to shock Cassandra with her reply? She wasn't sure, but it was an odd thing to tell her daughter and not one she'd been planning to say.

"And when Grandmother died, that was your chance to leave Daddy behind?" Cassandra asked, her words just as sharp. "To take the money and run?"

With a nauseating jolt, Judith realized the truth—Cassandra thought she was the enemy here, that Terry and Marigold had been victims of her disloyalty and faithlessness. Well, this would be fixed right now! She gripped the arms of her chair with both hands. Cassandra thought her father the wounded hero, and Judith would bet she never asked him about his other women. All the years of late-night meetings at the private club, the calls with "unknown 1" or "unknown 2" on his phone. And then there were Marigold's lectures, delivered with a cup of tea and a mouthful of poison, detailing every one of Cassandra's faults. How unattractive Cassandra was and how she needed her nose fixed. How silly Cassandra was and how she should be pushed into marriage instead of university.

"You have no idea, young lady, how I protected you from those two—"

"Mum, please, I don't want to fight!" Cassandra shouted, then lowered her voice, casting a guilty glance at the patio door. "I just need to understand. When I'm alone at night walking the floor with Emily, it's all I can think about. You and Daddy seemed in love to me. I never heard you fight when I was home. So what chance have I got? How am I going to keep my family together if you and Daddy couldn't make it work after thirty years?"

Judith knew the moment was now—it was time to rescue Cassandra from this terrible situation she'd trapped herself in. She leaned forward across the space between them and touched the back of her daughter's hand. "It's your choice, Cassandra," she said. "If you want to be with Andrew, that's okay. If you don't? Then you and Emily will always have a home with me. I can help you get back to work and be in control of your own life again. I'm here for you two, not him."

It took Cassandra a moment to understand, then her eyes widened in horror. "No, Mum, that's not what I meant at all!" she said. "I love Andrew, and I would never take Emily away from him. We discussed it, and I want to be home with her. She comes first for both of us."

Judith pulled back, pressing hands together in front of her chest as if to protect her vulnerable heart. "Well, of course, if that's what you really want, then I'll support you, but—"

"But if I want to be like you, then you'll be happier?" Cassandra demanded, her eyes bugging wide like Emily's did. "If I dump my baby in boarding school aged ten so I can leave to help everyone else in the world? Even if my daughter needs me, even if she begs me to come home because something truly awful happened to her?"

Judith sat back in her chair, shocked. She regarded Cassandra's pale face, framed by wisps of strawberry-blond hair. For God's sake, the child was still clinging to that day, as if Judith wouldn't want to change it too. "Cassandra, that was the only time—"

"It was the *worst* time," Cassandra hissed, jabbing a finger at her. Judith flinched though it wasn't close to touching. "You never asked about any of it because it only happened to me and not one of your refugee girls."

"No, I didn't ask because I couldn't fix it!" Judith replied, hating herself for escalating a conversation she should be ending.

"I didn't need you to fix it. I just needed you!" Cassandra covered her mouth with a hand, trying to stifle the shriek. When she spoke again, her voice was choked with tears. "You chose to stay in Dadaab because the girls over there had been hurt worse than me. Their pain was always more than mine, even when the injury was the same."

"Cassandra, that's just not true," Judith began, ready to defend herself yet again. "After the massacre, the flights were canceled because of the military coup, and I couldn't get a seat until the following week. Of course I wanted to be home with you after what happened."

Cassandra stood up, pressing bloodless fingertips on the tabletop. "It was a dark night, and I was walking home when I got jumped from behind. Those two men kicked and punched me. They broke my arm when they took my handbag. I thought I was going to die, and for a long time afterward, I wished I had. That's what happened to me, Mum."

"Darling, I know all this." Judith felt helpless to divine what it was that Cassandra needed her to say. "You were also eighteen, very drunk, and with that stupid boy Dante, who left you to get home alone, despite your promises that you were done with him and you would always take a taxi at night. I read the whole police report so you wouldn't have to talk about it again." With an entire bottle of dry gin by her side, she didn't add.

"I really wanted to, Mum, but Grandmother said it would upset you too much." Cassandra sniffed. "Now I think maybe I should've. If Emily was ever attacked, I would want her to tell me what happened, not be worried that I was going to blame her for it!"

You're losing her, Judith. Marigold's presence was so solid at Judith's shoulder she could smell her mother's lily of the valley perfume.

Judith flailed in the mire of emotional issues that Cassandra had dumped between them. Cassandra was stuck in the past, and Judith was only thinking of the future. "I'm so sorry. I never blamed you, and it's been ten years—"

"Why are you here, Mum?" Cassandra asked, tears falling from her wide eyes. "Is this a midlife crisis? I imagine you've got big plans once you've done your allotted time with me and Emily. What's the escape plan when this all gets too hard?"

Judith gaped at her daughter, and the words slipped out before she could stop them. "Cassandra, you are my escape plan!"

"No, Mum. Not me." Cassandra dropped the words like rocks between them. "You don't get to make me your mission."

"Hey, darl?" Andrew appeared in the doorway holding the baby. He stared from Judith to Cassandra, concerned. "Emily needs you."

Cassandra rushed to her crying baby. "I'm going to take Emily upstairs and try to get her to sleep again. Andrew, could you please see Mum out?"

"Sure." Andrew touched Cassandra's arm as she passed, but she just shook her head at him.

Judith was trembling as she retrieved her crutches and rose to her feet.

Oh, dear, even if she wanted to leave him, it wouldn't be to go with you, would it? Marigold whispered.

Judith made her way through the house to the front door and then slowly negotiated the step down to the path with Andrew by her side, sensibly not offering her any help. She fumbled with her phone, thankful there were cars all over the little blue Uber map.

"You have a lovely home, Andrew." She forced the words out, feeling sick to her stomach. "Thank you so much for lunch."

"It was a real treat, Mum." Andrew opened the gate to let Judith and her misery hobble through. "Look, I couldn't hear what you and Cass were talking about just now, but you should know she's exhausted. It makes her pretty bloody cranky, and I mean cranky all the bloody time."

"You don't say." Judith felt cold despite the sun.

Andrew nodded as if he was the martyr suffering Cassandra and not the other way around. "I know it's really different from the way that you did things with Cass, but if you could support her in being a stay-at-home mum, she'd really appreciate it." He offered Judith a smile as if he hadn't just verbally smacked her across the face. "Cass and Emily mean the world to me, and I would really like to have you in our lives."

Was that a threat Judith heard underneath his mild words? She thought so. "This is my Uber," she said as the sedan pulled up to the curb. She wasted no time getting into the car, throwing the crutches on the floor by her feet. "Please tell Cassandra that I'll call her later," she said.

"Of course. Bye, Mum!" Andrew banged on the roof of the car to send it on its way. Judith flinched at the noise. In the hideous stir of emotions boiling in her head, she was shocked by how much guilt she felt. She had spent two years resenting that Andrew for taking her daughter from her. It was awful to realize how much Cassandra had wanted to leave.

Andrew was quite decent to you, I thought.

Andrew had been decent to her. He'd said all the things she wanted Cassandra to say. Could she have been so very wrong about him as a partner?

She had to listen to Marigold's cackling all the way home.

NINE

WEDNESDAY BROUGHT WITH IT ANOTHER HOT, DRY DAY, just like all the other hot, dry days Judith had seen since her arrival in Adelaide. Not a drop of rain had fallen, and she was getting tired of always dusting the fine yellow pollen that drifted through the open windows and coated every surface.

Though her ankle was healing well, she had been feeling awfully flat and knew it wasn't just the unchanging weather. Moping was a waste of time in general, but being a moping invalid was just the worst. On the few occasions that she had ventured outside her house to get the mail, she'd managed to avoid Martha, though not Martha's constant stream of visitors. From breakfast to late in the evening, there were cars parked in front of the Thompsons' house and the sound of voices and laughter coming from their backyard.

Judith wondered if Marg, Bev, Chantal, and Cate would ask why she wasn't joining them for their ladies' lunch today and what Martha would say. She would be very surprised if Martha was honest with them about the racially insensitive comments she'd made. Or maybe the women would think Judith the rude one, like Andrew and Cassandra had?

Some of those cars are very fancy, Judith. They can't all be bad sorts, Marigold remarked.

"Oh, Mother, stop it. You always thought wealth equaled intelligence, and it's just not true. People need to prove themselves in their actions, not their purchases."

Maybe you'd have kept that wonderful husband of yours if you hadn't always berated him for being successful.

"Terry's a selfish ass," Judith murmured as she limped to the front of the house and peeked through her screen door to see Chantal's Toyota four-wheel drive pull up. She could see that Chantal had brought her baby son, Eddie. Perhaps she had a pediatrician she could recommend.

A navy BMW parked in front of Chantal's SUV. Judith felt a sad twinge when she saw the neat figure of Bev at the wheel. It was hard to imagine that someone as refined and kind as Bev would agree with racist views.

Terry always said that if jumping to conclusions was an Olympic event, then you'd be a gold medalist, Marigold whispered. *Oh, he's a rascal, but he always had your number, Judith.*

Judith felt a familiar flush of humiliation remembering how Terry and Marigold would gang up, calling her "Saint Judith the Stern" and teasing if she tried to share any stories about the camps.

She knew that it would be childish to drag Bev into the argument between her and Martha, so without thinking too much about it, she stepped out onto her porch and told herself to just go and get the mail.

Bev was still sitting in her car when Judith made it to her front gate. She could see through the windshield that Bev was talking on her phone. She decided to give it a minute and then go over to say hello. If Bev asked about the tiff, then Judith would tell her side of the story. Slamming the mailbox door closed, she felt her heart rattle and her hands begin to tremble.

Still on her phone, Bev spotted Judith and waved from inside the car. Judith waved back, but felt stupid hovering by her empty mailbox and baking in the hot sun. She looked about to find another purpose and noticed a small pile of supermarket bags had been left at the gate at number 16.

"Well, that's no good," Judith scolded the invisible fool who'd left the shopping out. Martha had mentioned that her neighbor had problems.

Still, Martha probably told everyone that Judith had problems too, so that didn't mean much. She limped along the pavement, thankful she could walk on her cast without needing her crutches so much anymore. Inside her neighbor's white picket gate, she picked up the four bags. The name on the address sticker was Gladys Mulroney.

Judith made her way up to her neighbor's front door. There were two squares of very green grass on either side of the path and a border of dwarf rosebushes interspersed with rosemary plants along the fence. Framing the porch steps were two huge white pots with manicured Buxus balls. A beautiful camellia tree shaded the same spot. Paul had done such a nice job, and Judith wondered if he might do her garden too. The thought sent an electrical charge trembling through her.

She put the bags down on the pollen-dusted tiles of the porch. She knocked at the security door, then rang the brass bell with its old-fashioned twisty mechanism. She knocked again. She really hoped there wasn't any ice cream or meat in the shopping. To hurry this along, she decided to risk shouting, "Gladys, it's your neighbor, Judith, from number eighteen."

Listening hard, she heard faint noises inside the house. She wished she knew what problems Gladys had. Perhaps she was having trouble getting up, which meant Judith should go around to the back door.

She took a step back and craned her head to check the street. Bev was just now climbing out of her car, calling out to Chantal, who was bent double over her little boy, holding his hands as he staggered to the front gate on his own tiny feet.

There was a rattle of a lock, and Judith's head turned to see the door open a crack. "What the bloody hell do you want?" The voice was creaky and could've been a man or a woman. Blinded by the sunshine, Judith couldn't see a face in the door gap—the only thing she could tell was that the person was shorter than her. She looked down.

"Hello, Gladys, my name is Judith Drainger, I live just—"

"You live in Mary's house," Gladys croaked. "I hear your damn shouting day and night."

Judith frowned. "I'm sorry, I hadn't realized. I suppose I'm actually on the phone quite a lot—"

"And got your bloody windows open, don'tcha? Bloody Mother this, bloody Marigold that."

Judith felt her cheeks heat with humiliation and wanted more than anything to back away from the person who knew her secret. "Right, well, sorry. Look, I found your shopping sitting by the gate and thought—"

At her words, the door was yanked open, and she could finally see Gladys behind the security screen door. She was tiny, no taller than Judith's shoulder, and had a face like a withered potato. Milky brown eyes glared out from under a heavy brow. Thin strands of white hair stuck out from her head in a halo, revealing a crusty scalp. She was wearing a full-length nightgown with brown stains down the front. The gnarled fingers of her hands were folded in on themselves with arthritis. "Give it here, you thief!" Glady's screech was like a slap. "Give it!"

"It's all right." Judith felt her old instincts rearing up in a sensation akin to relief. This was clearly a very fragile woman who needed help. She knew to lower her voice and say, "I wasn't stealing your shopping. I was bringing it to you. It's all right, Gladys."

Gladys growled, her folded fingers unable to flip the catch on the security door. "You stay there, you thief!"

Judith held the shopping out with straight arms, though it made her elbows hurt. "I'm not leaving. This shopping is still yours."

Finally, Gladys squeaked the door open. "Well, don't stand there like a bloody ninny," she croaked. "Carry it into me kitchen." She turned and shuffled off down a dark hallway.

Judith hesitated for just a moment before she crossed the threshold. The smell of rot and old urine hung like a fog and only got worse as she moved further into the living room, making her eyes water. And it wasn't only the smell—the mess was just awful. Piles of newspapers, magazines, clothing, books, vinyl albums, and shoe boxes lay stacked in every available space. On the couch was a pile of filthy crocheted blankets, bundled like a nest. Was it her bed? Judith didn't have time to wonder. Gladys had stopped at the kitchen door and was glaring at her again.

"Don't you touch anything, busybody," she snapped, pointing with a curled fist. "Don't take nothing from me, neither. I hate thieves. Hate 'em!"

Judith followed Gladys into the kitchen and found one source of the hideous odor—the sink was full of old, empty cat food cans. Trying to hold her breath, she looked for a space to put the groceries. There was no surface that wasn't already covered with dirty pots, dishes, and general filth. She found a fridge, then realized that the door was open and the light was off. A ragged tea towel hung on the handle.

"Doesn't your fridge work?" Judith realized why Gladys's voice was just a croak when her own rasped with the stench in the air. "You've got cold things here."

"Put it down, busybody." Gladys pointed at the floor. "Put it down and get yourself out of here."

Judith did as she was told, turning on her heel and making a beeline for the front door. She needed fresh air or she would vomit. Outside, she held onto the porch post and gasped in deep breaths.

"You looking at them?"

Judith jumped. She hadn't heard Gladys come out behind her. In the sunlight, she could see Gladys's skin was yellow with advanced jaundice, and blond whiskers sprouted on her chin. "Look at 'em. Busybodies and thieves. There's the chink lady."

Judith followed Gladys's gaze to Bev in Martha's front garden, where she was smiling and swinging Eddie around in her arms.

"Please don't use that disgusting word," Judith ordered, wondering why not even gossipy Cate had mentioned the extent of Gladys's problems. "Bev is of Asian descent."

Gladys rubbed a hand against her nose, making it red. "Then look at that fatty girl—wassername—Chantal? She'll eat everything. Eat that baby if you let her." She cackled.

Judith knew a piece of work like Gladys was best ignored, or the attention would only feed her negativity. "Right, you're being horrible, so I'm leaving. Goodbye, Gladys."

"It's greedy, isn't it?" Gladys screeched louder as Judith walked away. "Greedy. So happy-happy. Thief! There's no happy left for the rest of us with a big greedy girl like that around. Oi! You big bag of sticks, you listening to me? Oi, Sticks?"

Bev and Chantal were both staring when Judith made it to her own front gate. She waved at them, not quite sure what to say with Gladys still shouting at her back.

"You all right, darl?" Bev asked, then came right in and hugged Judith without waiting for an answer. "You just had a run-in with the Wicked Witch of the West."

Judith could still taste the stench of urine on her tongue. She hugged Bev back before letting her go, embarrassed to feel tears sting her eyes. "She's very unwell, I think."

Chantal's expression scrunched in sympathy, her blue eyes filled with tears. "That poor old thing, and she's got no family to look after her except Paul and Martha. Paul is her great-nephew or something. She's a bit scary, but she's had a hell of a life, and now she's really losing her marbles. She almost never comes out of her house."

"Yep, she must really like you." Bev chuckled, and Judith was relieved to hear the undercurrent of kindness in her voice. "Normally she just yells at everyone from behind her door."

"I know how to handle the mentally ill—" Judith coughed as the tears threatened to humiliate her. "Sorry. I'm tired of surprises. Moving here, and not being settled, and everything is so new all the time..." She gestured vaguely at her house. "I'm tired—I mean, today."

"Aw, darl!" It was Chantal's turn to surprise Judith with a hug, enveloping her in a cloud of floral perfume. Judith felt little baby hands gripping her T-shirt and pulled back to see Eddie grinning up at her.

"Hello, sir." She poked his tummy, and he giggled, making Chantal and Bev laugh, too.

"Come on in for lunch, eh?" Bev suggested, and Judith wanted so badly to go inside and surround herself with the comfort of these nice women. If only there wasn't her fight with Martha in the way.

"Actually, I have to... I've got something on the stove. Tell Martha I said—said hello. Oh, drat this pollen!"

As Judith hurried back to her house, she was relieved to see that Gladys had disappeared. Inside her own front door, she dragged in deep breaths, enjoying the pine-scented floor polish she'd used just that morning. Limping to her old but spotlessly clean kitchen, she got herself a glass of water. Unbidden, Martha's words came back to her about there being plenty of people to help in her own backyard.

She felt an unfamiliar sourness curl low in her gut and realized, with some surprise, that it was shame. Gladys needed help desperately. However, she would suck an awful lot of time and energy from the poor saint who stepped up for the job. From experience, Judith knew it would only take hard work to set Gladys to rights, and she was good at that.

Still, she shuddered at the idea. The hoarded filth would take weeks to clean out, and no doubt Gladys would replace it daily.

You'll keep your nose out of that one's business, Judith.

She pressed her lips together, and her gaze drifted to the open window that overlooked the side of Gladys's house. She yanked her phone out of her back pocket. For goodness' sake, she really needed to break the habit of talking to Marigold. Desperate to connect with someone real, she tried the only number in her call history.

Cassandra didn't pick up.

She had already sent several texts inviting Cassandra and her family to Sunday lunch, hoping that a lunch two Sundays in a row might start a routine that would turn into a tradition. Of course, Cassandra was probably just keeping her phone off in case the baby ever went to sleep, so Judith didn't particularly think she was avoiding her. After all, it was clear that her text messages had been read.

She bustled over to the fridge, having a sudden urge to check that the light was working and it didn't need a clean-out.

Yet again, her mind ran over the complicated conversation with Cassandra from the weekend, and she remembered to be grateful that she hadn't let her temper run away. Poor Cassandra had idolized her two-faced grandmother, and it would break her heart to know how much Marigold had disapproved of her. Better to let sleeping dogs lie. Terry, on the other hand, was a hypocritical beast. He could never stand Marigold.

What? Terry adored me! Marigold interrupted. *He always bought me the most exquisite birthday presents.*

"I bought you those presents! Me. I did it!" Judith felt the rage bubbling close to the surface and rounded on the Queen Anne shelf. "Terry only ever signed the sodding card! He was furious whenever I left for a mission, knowing you'd run straight over to Belgravia and move in. He called you his jailer! I was the one who did everything to make you happy, so why was Terry more important? Why does no one ever see what I do?"

Judith! Lower your voice, Marigold whispered.

Her hands were on the varnished wooden shelves, clutching hard, her knuckles white. Thankfully, triage came to the rescue, packing away the sadness, the panic, the agony of heartbreak, leaving only a calm, cold numbness.

Through the dining room window, she could hear a lawn mower somewhere nearby. Everything was fine. It was a typical suburban Wednesday. Normal. No reason to be upset. No reason to feel anything at all. The only mystery was why she couldn't stop the tears spilling down her cheeks.

"I should get back to work," Judith reminded herself as she blew her nose. "There's still so much to do. Best get on with it before I go under it."

TEN

WEDNESDAY EVENING, THEN ALL DAY THURSDAY AND Friday, Judith limped through a deep cleaning of her house, cataloguing repairs and all the painting that needed to be done as soon as she could arrange it. By the time Saturday morning rolled around, she felt she had well and truly earned a lazy day. Her treat was to take a cup of tea to the living room and sit down with laptop in hand, ready to while away the hours online shopping. A large black-and-white bird, like a British magpie but bigger, flew down to her back porch and peered through the screen door. It made a beautiful noise, like a warbling laugh. She ignored it. The cheeky thing was probably looking for scraps, not her company.

The magpie warbled again, and she realized it was the only sound she could hear. The Thompsons' backyard was strangely peaceful for a Saturday. Of course, Gladys's yard was always quiet. Judith stared down into her terra cotta-colored tea. She didn't feel quite ready to begin helping Gladys yet. Not only because once she started, she knew she couldn't stop. It was that nursing another difficult old woman just felt too close to how she'd spent most of last year. Marigold had taken so much energy and time and patience. It had been six months since she'd died, but Judith still felt a tingle of exhaustion whenever she remembered walking through the automatic doors of Our Lady of Grace hospice—their *shoosh* noise your first warning that this was a place of quiet endings. The walls in Marigold's ward were painted a fleshy salmon pink, and her room had smelled of dried roses and vinegar.

Judith shuddered. No, Gladys could wait a little longer.

She returned to flicking through websites and debated buying custom wardrobes to take the burden of fiddling around with ready-to-assemble furniture off her shoulders. She had the money, after all, though the profligacy made her hesitate.

Mrs. Marigold Henley, widow to a listless pharmacist, had been thrilled the day Judith brought Terry Drainger home for tea.

You must mold the man, Judith, Marigold had instructed her over and over. *Terry is from old money. Wealth always makes the children lazy, but when his grandfather dies, you might get the terrace in Belgravia! Just think of it, Judith! Think of all that . . . security.* Marigold had manipulated and coerced Judith into dating Terry long past the moment she wondered if they really should be together.

Certainly Marigold had been right about one thing: while Terry had never been a good student, he had found a new academic focus with Judith at his side, working hard to impress her with a law degree. Meanwhile, supported by his family money, Judith had enjoyed the freedom of working for nonprofits without needing to earn a salary herself.

She added a lovely cedar armoire to her cart. Then deleted it.

It was strange that Cassandra had thought her parents were in love. Was Terry ever happy, she wondered as she sipped her tea. He had been more married to Marigold than to her. Judith never made a secret of the fact that she judged him for going into corporate tax law instead of social justice, just like she knew that he resented her for her volunteer work, always asking when she'd get her halo in the mail. God, he was such an ass!

She patted her chest, her heart beating triple time. She reminded herself that their marriage had been put to bed. Dredging up old memories wasn't going to help anyone.

Best get on with it before you go under it, Marigold whispered.

The magpie warbled cheerily at the back door, and Judith didn't feel her spirits lift so much as she shoved them higher. "I should look at doing something with this garden," she said. "It's only small—how hard could it be?"

She was out in the garden, measuring things under the watchful eye of the newly named Mr. Magpie, when Cassandra called to apologize about Sunday lunch. Judith pushed the phone so close to her ear it hurt. She listened intently as Cassandra explained that they were already expected at Andrew's auntie's house for lunch and really couldn't get out of it as it was a "bit of a tradition." Emily was wailing in the background, so Cassandra couldn't talk for long.

After the call, Judith went inside to her laptop on the kitchen table and tried to cancel the big supermarket delivery due that afternoon. She'd ordered $60 worth of lamb racks and a $40 bottle of shiraz to go with them. It was an extravagant waste now. She was still trying to navigate the website when her phone rang. Thinking it was Cassandra wanting to change plans again, she picked it up immediately.

"Hello, Judith? It's Terry."

Judith's stomach felt suddenly hollow. "Terry. Yes. Hello."

"Yes. Just calling to ask how it's going? Over there. In the colonies." He coughed. "Ha!"

"It's lovely." Judith looked out her back door at the withered lawn. "Very green and hot. Sunny, you know."

"Sounds wonderful. Miserable here, of course."

"Of course." Judith was sure that Terry had a point to make. He charged hundreds of pounds for his time, so he was usually very stingy with his words.

"Look, I won't dillydally." She could just imagine him pacing, waving irritably at someone to turn down the television while he was on the phone. She wondered who was sitting on the couch, keeping quiet for him. "I've been speaking to Cassandra, and she's quite upset. Now, I'd thought, with you moving there, things might be rather, well, better between you both. I calmed her down, of course, but I was hoping that you might make more of an effort with the baby and that dentist."

Judith felt the hollow space fill with a fiery ball of anger. "I'm sorry to have disappointed you, Terry."

"Oh, Judith, don't be like that." He sounded exasperated. "I love Cassandra very much, and one day I'd like to have a conversation without her complaining about you the whole time."

Terry wasn't an emotional man, which was how he could manipulate those who were. Judith knew he had no interest in her relationship with Cassandra, and she had learned from long, painful experience that he was just warming her up for something else.

"I wanted to let you know that I've accepted an offer on the Belgravia terrace, finally." He paused. "Got a good price for it, though not as much as you'd hoped. I had to be realistic in this market. How's your job hunting going?"

And there it was. He probably thought she'd be too upset over his comments about Cassandra to focus, but Judith heard Terry's attempt to sabotage her financial future loud and clear.

"You know my half of that money is my only income for the foreseeable future, Terry." Judith kept her temper with an effort that made her sweat. "And yes, you were meant to discuss it with me first. How much did you accept?"

"Now, Judith." Terry's tone was resolute. "We loved this old house, but it wasn't exactly fit for the modern market—"

"How much?"

"You'll get your due, don't worry." After bossy, Terry always went to patronizing. "It's all in the paperwork that the lawyers drew up. Fair's fair, and all that."

"How much, Terry?"

"I'll send you all the details today. You do have internet at the house, don't you? Look, must dash." He paused. "It was good speaking to you, Judith."

"No it wasn't." Judith hung up because that was how they did it—Terry got what he wanted, and she got the last word. Dropping her phone on the table, she sank back into the dining chair.

If she had been a maudlin twit, it might have been a good time to cry. Especially the sort of maudlin twit who upset her only child and drove her away without meaning to. Maybe if she'd been conniving, she would have made more of an effort with that Andrew and used him to get through to Cassandra. And poor Emily.

"She certainly seems to be feeding Andrew better than she feeds the baby," Judith murmured and felt her worry deepen. "Here I am wanting to save Cassandra from Andrew, when maybe it's Emily I should try to save from Cassandra. Yet how? Everything I say she takes as a criticism. For heaven's sake, I'm no Marigold!"

Despite the sun streaming in her windows, Judith felt cold. Leaving the crutches, she limped outside again. She stood beneath the baking-hot sun and let it dry her suddenly wet eyes. Mr. Magpie swooped down onto the roof of the garden shed. His claws clattered on the gutter as he edged along, head cocked, as if to get a better look at the woman trying not to weep in her dusty backyard.

No use crying over spilled milk, Judith, Marigold whispered. *There's always someone who's got it worse.*

Judith closed her eyes, visions of the camps flashing under her lids. It was always when she was feeling low that the memories clamored loudest to escape the box that she kept them in.

No, this nonsense needed to stop! The past was the past, and she had a new home now.

Yet in her suburban backyard—so far from London and the refugee camps of northeastern Kenya—she was more lost than she'd ever been. "It's so easy to be a good person when everyone around you wants something you can give them. It's so much harder to help a daughter who can't bear to look at you," she whispered to Mr. Magpie, in case he needed to know. He warbled back a long, lyrical song that Judith thought held a critical undertone.

"I hope you aren't talking about Gladys," she warned him. "I'll get to her when I feel a bit more myself."

But now Mr. Magpie was shuffling along the gutter, angling to look inside the house. He squawked a warning, and Judith heard a loud knock at the front door. When she saw who it was, she quickly clomped her way to meet him.

"Paul! What a nice surprise." Fingers trembling, she struggled to unlock her screen door.

Paul ruffled his short, sweaty hair with a dirt-crusted hand. His eyes flicked up to Judith's face and then back down to his boots. He mumbled, "Sorry to bother ya. Martha says you're welcome for Sunday lunch." Done, he turned to leave.

"Sorry, pardon, I didn't quite catch that," Judith said. She really hadn't, his accent was so thick.

Paul looked pained at having to repeat himself. "Sunday tomorrow," he enunciated, showing straight, pale yellow teeth. "She says you're invited to lunch."

Judith couldn't tell if Paul's cheeks were flushed or just sunburned. "Oh! Lovely! That's very kind of you," she said as he turned his broad back again. The miserable shroud of loneliness hovered at her shoulder, waiting to descend if another person walked away from her.

"Paul, could I just borrow you for a minute, please?" she called, and when she saw the warm glint in his eye, she felt an answering surge of heat ripple through her body. She stepped backward, and he followed her into the house. She didn't have to coerce or beg—he just came inside. Paul was a beautiful man, much more handsome than Terry, and he was *here*.

She knew her bedroom door was open and that if he looked over her shoulder, he would see her unmade bed. Would that excite him? She'd seen it in the camps and knew how fast these things could happen between men and women.

Don't give the milk away when you want the man to take the cow, Marigold admonished.

"Would you like to yard the look?" Judith spluttered, then forced herself to speak slowly. "I mean, look at the yard? Well? This way, please." Instead of to her rumpled bed, she led the beautiful man to her wretched backyard. They stood in the shade of the porch and gazed out over the brown lawn. Paul stood so close that the hairs on her skin were touching the hairs on his skin.

"Mine's such a mess, and your yard's so beautiful," she said.

"I work on it." Paul's voice was gruff and low. "You can't leave a yard. It'll die in a minute."

"I know how that feels," she said. "I know how it feels to be left." Her breath came through struggling lungs as she drowned in Paul's cobalt-blue eyes.

Paul sniffed and pinched his nostrils, then wiped his fingertips on the side of his shorts. "You just need time—for the yard, I mean."

"Yes, the yard." Did she imagine Paul's interest waning? The first wave of adrenaline had already petered out, and she craved another. Was he waiting for her? She reached out, and they both looked down at her index finger touching his thumb. She had never seduced anyone before. Was this all it took to have a married man? Her wayward thoughts slipped to Terry and wondered how many women had reached out and touched his hand, knowing he was married too. Paul wouldn't want this to be messy, would he?

His fingers slipped around hers. His hand was rough, the palm callused. Judith imagined the feel of it on the delicate skin of her thighs. A muscle jumped along his jawline. Was it a symptom of his own nerves? How many times had he done this to Martha before her? She felt a stab of sadness, as though the deed had already been done. As though she were already stamped with a red letter A.

If you play with fire, you will get burned, young lady, Marigold hissed.

Paul leaned forward. When his lips brushed hers, they were dry. "We gotta be quick. I need to get the outside tables washed down," he murmured.

Washed tables? Judith remembered that she was a grown woman and not a craven fool. She stepped backward, pulling her hand free. "Honestly, Paul, it's probably not a good idea. I mean, you are married." She raised her chin, ready to defend her "play yes, say no" behavior.

He only shrugged. "Another time, maybe?" As if he was talking about a loaf of bread instead of Judith's moral compass.

Who cares about morals! Judith's heart skipped a double beat with happiness. Why did it feel so good that he still wanted her, though she had just rejected him? Maybe she was more attractive than Terry ever gave her credit for.

She followed Paul to her front door and stood on the threshold as he stepped off the veranda without even a goodbye. She couldn't let him leave like that, though. "So, what time tomorrow, Paul?" When he glanced over his broad shoulder, he was clearly wondering what she meant. She felt like giggling. Who knew she was such a flirt? "For lunch, of course."

"Round one o'clock," he said, walking back to his own gate.

"Shall I bring anything?" she called.

"Nah, she'll be right." Paul flashed her those radiant eyes before slinking down the side of his house, heading to the backyard.

Judith stepped back and watched the door close softly on its repaired hinges. Paul really was very good with his hands. She made it all the way to her dining table before she realized that lunch with Paul meant lunch with Martha, too.

Why would Martha want to invite Judith to lunch after their terrible argument? Judith wandered back out to her yard. And why send Paul? Did she think Judith wouldn't say no to him? Had she noticed his flirting? She felt her heart bump and raised a hand to her chest. Did Martha want revenge? She considered Martha with her round face, unfashionable glasses, and thick thighs. She just didn't seem the revenge-seeking sort. It was probably more likely that Martha had extended an olive branch.

Judith decided she would accept it in good faith. After all, she could also be accused of being a little closed-minded sometimes. She wrapped her arms around herself, remembering the sensation of Paul's dry lips and let herself feel desirable for a long moment before shaking it off. A little flirting and a kiss did not make an affair. Though if she wanted it with anyone, it would be with Paul Thompson.

ELEVEN

AT ONE O'CLOCK ON SUNDAY, JUDITH MADE HER WAY to Martha and Paul's, carrying an expensive bottle of shiraz in a string bag and a bouquet of yellow gerberas that she'd bought for her own table but was happy to gift. Leaving her crutches at home, she stumped over the uneven pavement and was already sweating through her white guipure lace blouse when she knocked on the door.

"S'open!" Martha's voice came from the depths of the house.

Judith froze. With her hands full, she couldn't very well turn the handle. Yet her hostess had instructed her to come in, and she was determined to be polite. She saw her salvation coming out of a room while still buttoning up his short-sleeved shirt.

"Hello, Paul!" For goodness' sake—she instructed herself to calm down and stop shouting. "Would you mind getting the door for me, please?" Paul finished his last two buttons and opened the door. "Thanks so much," she gushed.

Taking off her single shoe, Judith took in all of Paul. He walked in a cloud of Old Spice cologne, and his hair was still wet from a recent shower. His shirt was pale blue with darker blue checks, his shorts a clean pair of blue cargos. Did he get dressed up for her? If so, my goodness. She handed him the bag of wine, and Paul's gaze didn't rise from her chest as he took it.

"Am I late?" she asked, knowing full well she wasn't but needing to pull Paul out of his tongue-tied state. She followed him down the short hall. All the doors were closed except the one he'd exited from. She peeked inside and saw a room with a single bed, an ironing board with a cooling iron on it, and a window covered with a cheap venetian blind. She wondered if Paul ever slept in that bed. The sight of the neatly folded sheets gave her strange urges.

"S'truth, Paul," Martha was shouting as the two of them entered the dining room. "How long does it take to shower? Oh, Judith, you're early!"

"I'm sorry, Martha," she said, wincing internally at the criticism and proffering the gerberas. "I always forget that being on time is being early in Adelaide." She laughed too loudly. "I'll have to remember to be late next time."

"Well, there's a bit of crisis, you see," Martha said, wiping her hands on an apron with *What's the Magic Word?* written across the chest. "Paul, you going to get Billy?"

"The kid said he'd get himself here," Paul muttered and headed to the backyard. "I'm getting the extra chairs out of the shed."

"What's the crisis?" Judith asked. She was always great in a crisis.

"Well, I've got fourteen people coming, and I've roasted two legs of lamb for them," Martha said. "Muggins here"—she pointed at herself—"forgot that I'd invited the Reynoldses to lunch as well. They have two teenage boys who are going to eat me out of house and home. And I've completely forgotten to make the gravy."

"I have a decent pile of lamb racks in my fridge," Judith said, "and my mother taught me how to make proper gravy."

"Oh, love, they'll be perfect on the grill." Martha wiped steam from her thick-lensed glasses. "Give us your keys, and I'll go get them." She pointed at the roasting pans sitting on the stovetop. "You get on in there and get your gravy going!"

Judith warmed at the invitation to enter Martha's sacred space. She leaned into the moment. "Martha, about the other day—" It was too late for that quiet word because the Reynolds family had let themselves in the house, shouting their greetings from the hallway as they took off their shoes: Steve, Linda, their teen boys, Jesse and Jordan—wet hair dripping—and the baby, Keenan, full of giggles. Linda apologized profusely for being on time. The boys'd had swim practice at the public pool close by, and they hadn't wanted to go home and come back again.

After introducing her guests to each other, Martha left to fetch the lamb racks, and Judith's fear of awkward silences was dispelled by Linda, who pounced on her immediately, demanding the when and why behind her move from London—Linda's mother was from Cornwall, and she'd been to London twice. Steve extolled the virtues of South Aussie vineyards while pouring drinks for the ladies, a lovely Skillogalee rosé from the Clare Valley. Apparently, a place that was like nowhere in the world, and Judith simply must visit. Under such pleasant duress, she promised to take a weekend once her new car arrived and she finally got her ankle cast off. Linda promised to come with her so they could make a girls' weekend of it. Judith had never been on a girls' weekend. Goodness, these people were so friendly! And so pushy! She flushed with the pleasure of it all.

More guests arrived and let themselves into the house, greeting each other with shouts and laughter.

Even on Martha's return, Judith felt like, if not exactly the guest of honor, certainly an interesting curiosity. There wasn't a moment that she wasn't engaged by someone who had a dozen questions about her travels and her background.

"Paul spent a bit of time in Africa," Luke said. "Course, he doesn't talk about it much, but he doesn't talk about anything much."

Luke Graham was a balding thirty-something, with a low-hanging beer belly and a great laugh. He was married to a very slim blonde called

Tilly who had given Judith a tight hug and lots of compliments on her lace blouse. "Paul likes to be a mystery man," Tilly said.

Judith silently agreed. She'd been watching Paul on the periphery of the party, pouring drinks and fetching bags of ice from the deep freezer in the garage. He'd had to barbecue the lamb racks, and even though the three other men gravitated to the hot grill, beers in hand, they'd spoken more to each other than to him. Paul was lonely, and she felt a renewed kinship with him, a man who acted like a stranger at his own party.

She took a chance when Paul passed by with a bottle of wine in hand, leaning in closer than she should have. "This wine is lovely, Paul," she said. "One of your favorites?"

"I just pour the stuff." He twisted the bottle so she could read the label.

She reached out and ran her fingertips over the back of his hand. She was ridiculously gratified to see that certain flicker of warmth light his eyes again. It was only a moment, then he blinked and moved away.

As fourteen people sat down to eat around two o'clock, Judith marveled that Martha had ever imagined her guests would go hungry. There was a huge feast spread out over the dining table set for the adults and two card tables set up for the children in the living room. She was offered a chair at the head of the table that gave her leg space to straighten out—and a nice view of Paul too. She was happy when Tilly sat next to her and immediately launched into a diatribe of self-loathing about how many pre-lunch snacks she'd eaten. Tilly was probably in her late twenties and very pretty. She wore her blond hair down and played with it constantly, moving it over one shoulder, then the other, twisting the ends between her red-painted nails.

"So how do you know Martha, Tilly?" Judith asked, offering a jug of gravy that she herself had declined.

"Martha is my foster mum," Tilly said as she passed the gravy on and piled cucumber sticks onto her plate. "What I mean is, she was my foster carer for the last two years I was in the system." She smiled, rueful. "I was a bit of a ratbag, but she got me off the drugs and kept me in school. Martha was the only one who never gave up on me. She's always had a houseful of kids, but she's only got Billy now. He's a real hoot, that kid—we all love Billy."

"And Paul was like your dad, I suppose." Judith couldn't help but try and shine a light on Paul's almost invisible presence in Martha's house.

"Paul's always worked away." Tilly lowered her voice. "And when I lived here, he *didn't*," she added, as if it was significant.

Judith felt a stab of jealousy and then dismissed it as irrational. Tilly would've been far too young for him anyway. "It must have been hard on Paul to be away from the family for so long," she said, defending him as she would have defended herself for the same choices.

Tilly glanced over at Martha, who was serving salad to the collection of kids, making them all groan and laugh. "Well, he was away from this family," she replied so quietly that Judith had to strain to catch it. "Because he had his African woman then."

Judith thought she must have misheard and turned the conversation to lighter topics.

The meal progressed so nicely, and there was so much noise and action, that no one commented on Judith and Tilly skipping dessert, as they would have at a formal dinner. Judith was having a wonderful time, and after three glasses of rosé, she was embarrassed but delighted when Luke asked for her scariest story of working in the refugee camps.

"Oi! Bit of shush, everyone!" Luke shouted, and the adults all swung their gazes to Judith. "Cheers, Judith, come on, give us your best worst one."

She didn't even have to think. One day stood out head and shoulders above the others. She quickly unpacked it from the locked box of her memories and cleared her throat to begin. "It was 2015, I was in a camp called Ifo, in Dadaab—that's northeastern Kenya. It was right at the start of the wet season, when the mud and mosquitoes in the camp could just about drive you crazy. Lots of volunteers were getting sick with a fever, and we had starving refugees flowing in from flooded farms and drowned settlements. This one particular day, I was feeling edgy because no boys had attended school, and then in the evening, the camp was strangely peaceful. I probably don't have to tell you that a refugee camp is always frantic, especially with an influx of newcomers.

"This night was so quiet that I went to find the administrator on his sickbed. The poor man was delirious with fever, so he couldn't help much, but he told me to be ready for trouble. I just knew something was on its way. I could feel it in the air, and I could see it in the faces of the newcomers—it was a fresh fear." Judith took a breath and was disappointed to see that Paul had slipped away from the table.

"The raid happened the next day, just after the children had finished their morning snack. I heard the screams coming from the other side of the camp and rushed them all inside. Our schoolhouse was just a single room with concrete block walls and an iron roof. All morning I'd had the students building a heavy barrier for the plywood door, using my teacher's desk and nailing bits of scrap wood over the windows. And thank God, because the rebels were disorganized, but were they ever desperate! They'd armed themselves with machetes and long fishing knives and were looking for boys for their army and girls for their camps."

Judith paused and took another deep breath. All the attention was on her—even the teen boys, Jesse and Jordan, were silent, eyes round, hanging on her words. "Outside the schoolhouse, the howls and shouting were hysterical, and we could hear the rebels smashing at our doors and windows. I had the kids cuddled under a fort of desks and chairs and told stories to keep them calm—stories of my childhood in London, Winnie the Pooh, just anything. Then I sang all the nursery rhymes I knew until my voice was hoarse. We had a bit of water, but I'd forgotten to bring snacks for them. I felt so bad about that. Some of them only came to school for a square meal. It felt like a week, though it was really three hours, when I heard my friend Jurgen shouting that it was all over. I opened the door, and there was a mob of crying, screaming parents. Just to see their faces when they found their children . . . "Judith drifted off for a moment, the memories too close:

"You're a bloody saint, Judith." Jurgen had grasped her tightly in his arms, his breath hot on her ear. "A goddamned bloody saint." And it hadn't been a joke.

Judith hadn't wanted to be a saint. In the moment, she would have done anything not to be stuck alone with those children in that stuffy little schoolroom, thinking she would die being stabbed with rusty machetes. Those were not the thoughts of a saint, regardless of what she'd achieved. Only later, when Jurgen told the other volunteers the story as he stitched up the wounded, did Judith feel a teaspoon of pride—then quickly tempered it by looking into the eyes of all the victims whom she hadn't been able to help that day.

"Jesus, Judith, you're amazing!" Luke raised his beer bottle in her direction, and she quickly wiped a hand over her cheeks, smiling back at him. "No way I'm telling my story about stopping a carjacker on Rundle Street now!"

A huff gusted out of Judith, taking the tears with it. She smiled when the rest of the table cracked up, the laughter a release after her harrowing story. Tilly squeezed her in a one-armed hug. "Cassandra's so lucky to have a brave mum like you."

Later in the evening, when Judith offered a dozen times to help with the dishes and cleaning, her efforts were kindly rebuffed. Saying good night to her still-busy hosts, she hobbled home around nine o'clock and was planning to sit on her back step with a cup of tea and stare at the night sky. She turned on all the lights in the kitchen and was so unprepared for the intruder standing inside her open back door that she just stared at him, blinking. He was young, maybe early twenties, and was holding a screwdriver against a laptop—*her* laptop. In his other hand, he carried a paper grocery bag, heavy with unseen objects. He hadn't covered his face. In a camp raid, that would mean he planned to kill any witnesses, but in this sleepy suburb, Judith hoped it meant he was simply inexperienced.

In her mind, she felt the separation of logic from panic as quick as a wink. She needed to act quickly and aggressively to overwhelm the intruder. She sucked in a breath and screamed from the bottom of her lungs. On pure instinct, she followed the man out into the backyard when he ran. He'd made it to the back fence when she let out another almighty scream.

A head popped over the fence from Martha's side, shouting, "Judith!" Then "Billy!" Then "Martha, it's Billy at Judith's!"

Billy froze at hearing his name, just for a moment. Encumbered by his bounty, he threw the laptop and the bag over the top of the fence, getting ready to swing himself up after it. In a flash, Paul had leaped his own fence. Dodging the lemon tree, he shot through the garden and grabbed Billy's leg just before it disappeared over the pine palings. He dragged the boy to the ground and wrestled him into an awkward hold, his forearm pushing on the back of Billy's head.

Judith finally thought to run and turn on the outdoor lights. She could hear the shouting in the Thompsons' yard and the shrill calls for Martha to hurry. She approached Paul and Billy. At second glance,

Billy appeared younger than early twenties, probably no more than late teens, still with a smattering of acne on his cheeks. His hair was dark and matted with sweat at his brow. His jeans had rips in the knees, and his Converse sneakers didn't match. As the boy struggled to get upright in Paul's grip, his big brown eyes looked right back at her. He seemed more uncomfortable than properly scared.

Martha came running down the side of Judith's house and into the backyard, shouting "Billy!" She stood barefoot on the dead lawn. "Judith, are you all right?" She grabbed Judith's arm. "He didn't hurt you, did he?"

"No, no, I'm fine," she said. It'd been a while since she'd had to scream like that. Her whole body felt raw and hot. She wrapped her arms around her chest, wishing they covered more of her.

"C'mon, Mum, I'm never gonna hurt anyone." Billy sounded genuinely offended as he hunched under Paul's arm.

"Cuz that's all you'd need, Billy." Martha was furious. "An assault charge! You want to go back to juvie?"

Back to juvie? Judith hugged herself tighter.

"He grabbed a bunch of stuff from her house," Paul said, his gaze on the back of Billy's head. "Looked like a laptop too. He chucked it over the fence. Probably broken now."

Martha planted her hands on her hips. "That true, Billy? You stole from our neighbor Mrs. Danger?"

Billy squirmed in Paul's grip. "Yeah," he grunted.

"Say it," Martha commanded. "You know you need to own your behavior, Billy."

"I stole from our neighbor," Billy said, his voice breaking. "I'm sorry, Mrs. Danger."

"Yeah, you're sorry," Martha agreed. "And you'll be working to replace anything you broke tonight." She took a deep breath, her expression showing dread at what she had to say next. "I don't mind telling you, Billy, I am rotten with anger right now. You want Paul to take you to the police station? Do you?"

Billy stayed silent, his eyes on the ground.

"You know if I tell the police you ran off, they'll take you away from me," Martha said, pushing.

Billy scuffed at the grass with his filthy sneakers. "Don't let 'em, Mum," he pleaded.

"It's not going to be my choice one of these days." Martha's tone was still severe, but her eyes were glassy with tears, and her jowls trembled. "Now. D'you want to act like a civilized human being and come have some dinner?"

"Yeah," he mumbled.

"You heard him, Paul." Martha deflated with relief. "There might be some lamb left for you, then it's pajamas and bed, Billy. We'll talk properly tomorrow."

That was it?

The thief went home for dinner. Judith couldn't quite believe what had just happened. Robberies in the camps had been treated far more seriously, with much harsher consequences for the perpetrators. All right, so this wasn't the UNHCR—it was a suburban family with a wayward teen. She had no idea why, but it felt like the moment for the police to be called had just passed her by.

Paul released Billy from the headlock and marched him down the side of the house while pinching the back of his T-shirt, prepared for the boy to run again. Judith was still trying to wrap her head around it all when Martha grabbed her in a hard embrace, elbows clamped against her ribs.

"Thank you, Judith, and God bless you." Martha's cheek was wet.

Though she'd been Billy's victim tonight, Judith knew she wasn't the only one. Her heart broke for his disappointed foster mum. She led Martha to the top step of the porch. They both sat. "Can I get you a stiff gin?" Judith asked, craving one herself.

"I don't drink, love," Martha said, still managing to convey an air of judgment despite her upset.

Judith sat on the edge of the step next to Martha. She listened to the exclaiming voices next door as Billy made his appearance at the dinner party. More than one head popped over the fence to check on Martha. Judith gave Tilly a little wave to let her know Martha was all right.

"Billy's a ratbag, but he's come from worse," Martha explained, fishing a wrinkled tissue from her sleeve. "If he can just get away from his old life, he's got a real chance to make it, you know." Holding her glasses, she dabbed at her tears with the tissue. "He's only sixteen, but one more criminal charge and he's back in juvenile detention until he's eighteen. Then it's adult prison. He's a sweet boy, and there'll be no coming back from that. I've seen it before." She was wringing the damp tissue, white fragments falling into her lap like snow.

"What makes you think he won't run away tonight?" Judith asked, concerned about Martha's faith in this boy criminal.

Martha sighed. "My cooking, maybe? Or a warm bed after he's been sleeping rough?" She tucked the shreds of tissue back into her sleeve. "I don't always know what will work. I just have to try everything, you know." She leaned against Judith, just for a moment, then climbed to her feet, all business again. "Thanks for not calling the police, Judith. Billy must've given you such a fright, and for that, I'm sorry."

"He's only a kid," Judith said, adding a shrug to complete the show of nonchalance. "I've seen tougher than him."

Martha sighed gustily. "Yeah, I guess you would've," she said, then headed home without another word.

Judith went inside and pressed the back door shut with both hands. She examined the locks and checked every window. There was no sign of forced entry. She stuck chairs under the front and back door handles for good measure and got ready for bed like any other night. It was only when she was brushing her teeth that she realized Billy must have stolen her house key from Martha's during the afternoon. She wanted to text Martha to make sure it had been found, then realized she didn't have Martha's phone number. Cassandra did, though. She shook away the thought. Her daughter had enough on her plate without Judith involving her in tonight's drama. Cassandra adored Martha and didn't need to know the strange choices the woman made in her life. Judith could protect her from that.

It was a long time before Judith could get to sleep, even with the wine making her head feel fuzzy. Her crush on Paul suddenly seemed so very ridiculous and contrived now that she lived in a world where the neighbor's boy could rob her in the night and then go home to a roast lamb dinner.

TWELVE

EARLY THE NEXT MORNING, JUDITH WAS STILL DRINKING her first cup of tea when there was a knock at the front door. It was Billy. He was holding her laptop, now sporting a large dent, and the paper shopping bag. Giving Judith a quick wave, Martha watched Billy from her front veranda, arms crossed over the rainbow on her sweatshirt.

"Mrs. Danger, I've come to apologize for my behavior," Billy said. He handed her the paper bag and laptop. "You probably shouldn't've left these outside last night. The dew could wreck your laptop."

That was ironic coming from the thief. "It's Drainger, actually, not Danger," Judith said and checked the bag. She saw her collection of silver plate picture frames and a handful of colorful bead necklaces made by a friend in Dadaab. "You wouldn't have got much for this stuff." She willed her heart to stop racing at the sight of her home invader. For goodness' sake, he was just a boy. A young teenage boy, in fact. A silly boy.

Judith, he's a criminal! Marigold was unforgiving. *His sort always turns to crime. Oh, it just makes me sick!*

His sort? Judith trembled as a hot surge of hatred for Marigold's ignorance coursed through her.

In the bright daylight, Billy wasn't even that tall, probably three inches shy of Judith's five foot ten. His shoulders were skinny but square and tapered to a narrow waist. An unruly bunch of dark brown curls hung over his forehead and down the back of his neck, but the area above his ears had been shaved in a fashion Judith thought could only be called a mullet. She could see a pimple on his neck that was still bleeding where he'd picked at it. Clearly Martha had cleaned him up for his apology. He was wearing a black T-shirt, sharp creases ironed over the shoulders, and straight-leg blue jeans. Even his mismatched sneakers had been given a wipe-down.

Billy returned her gaze. "I heard you were from England and thought you'd be rich," he said, the words delivered with chagrin at his own stupidity. "You've got nothing but that laptop, though."

Judith leaned against the doorframe, glad her antiques and crystal were still packed in boxes. "Well, you would've had better luck with my ex-husband in London," she replied. "He got all the money in the divorce."

Billy chuckled. "Sorry for stealing your junky stuff," he said. "And sorry your ex-husband cleaned you out too. Guys suck, eh?"

Judith's eyebrows flew up her forehead, and she couldn't help but fall back into the role of the teacher she used to be. "Not all of them," she said. "I've met some real princes in my day—and some who were simply diamonds in the rough."

His smile grew, making the apples in his cheeks shine. "Are you quoting *Aladdin* at me?" he asked. "I used to have a thing for Princess Jasmine once."

"Well, Aladdin started off as a thief and turned into a prince."

"He got a genie, though," Billy said, shifting his feet apart and crossing his arms over his chest like he was enjoying the debate.

Judith really wasn't sure how she felt about this young man being so audacious with her. She nodded over at Martha, still watching them from her veranda. "Looks like you've got a genie too," she said. "Martha will give you all the wishes you want, Billy—like staying out of juvenile detention."

Billy shook his head, disagreeing. "Martha can't stop helping people. It's like a disease with her, you know." He hefted his smile back into place. "But the old girl said I have to do jobs to pay you back for the damaged laptop. We can't afford to buy you a new one."

Judith could afford a new laptop, and she was pretty sure she didn't want Billy in her home ever again. He seemed like a bright boy, but to give him a second chance was a leap too far. Just as she was trying to decide how to respond, a massive green trailer truck pulled up in front of her house. The name of the lovely gardening website, Bunnings, was written on the side. The driver got out holding a folder. "Mrs. Drainer?" he shouted over the noise of the truck's engine.

Judith met him at the gate, thinking to rectify a mistake. Sure enough, her correctly spelled name and details were on the invoice, and she'd already paid for the delivery of a terrifyingly long list of items.

The driver clearly didn't have time to waste with a conversation about her buyer's remorse. He opened the truck doors and lowered the back end. Using a tiny, noisy forklift, he unloaded an enormous pallet. Huge bags of soil and fertilizer and tall piles of turf squares were deposited on Judith's driveway, and the forklift went back into the truck for yet another pallet.

"Well, here's your start, Billy," Judith called out to the boy leaning in the shade of her porch. "Your first job will be to help me get all this stuff into the backyard."

Billy went to introduce himself to the delivery man. "Billy. I'm helping Mrs. Drainger," he said.

"Pete." The man shook Billy's hand and winked. "She's lucky to have you, son. I just saw the cast on her foot."

It looked like hot work lugging the turf-laying supplies and equipment, including a wheelbarrow and a lawn aerator, into the backyard, even with the help of the tiny forklift. She served the two thirsty workers the fancy Italian mineral water and cookies from her canceled lunch to make herself feel useful.

"You got some quality turf there," the delivery man said as he smothered a burp caused by the soda water. He was wearing the same kind of green cotton shorts and shirt as Paul but didn't look nearly so good in them.

"Thank you," Judith said.

"If you don't lay it today, " he said, "then keep it damp and covered for tomorrow."

Judith was surprised. "Can't I leave it until the weekend?"

"It'll all die in the heat if you don't put it down now." He said this like it was something she should have known. He climbed back in his truck with a cheery wave at Billy and trundled off.

Judith thought maybe she should have read the instructions as well as the shopping list on the gardening website. Billy was sitting on her front step, trying to fish the lemon slice out of his empty glass with a finger. "How do I lay turf?" she asked him.

He shrugged. "Dunno."

"I guess I can google it," she said. "Can't be that hard. It's just a bit of lawn."

"Still going to be tricky with your cast," he added.

Judith quietly swore, making Billy laugh. "Is that the worst word you know?" he asked, squinting up at her.

She huffed. "Not hardly, but I didn't want to burn your ears."

He laughed again. "All right, see you later, Mrs. Drainger. Glad I could help today." He handed back the glass and went home next door, as if he'd set everything right.

Judith hobbled inside with Billy's empty glass and put it in the sink. Going out to her backyard, she cringed at all the turf glowing greenly in square piles. "No time like the present," she announced and headed straight back inside to make a cup of tea. The newly opened package of cookies lay on the counter. They were pretty, with pink icing and a streak of jam down the middle, all covered in dried coconut. The name on the package was odd: Arnott's Iced VoVos.

Judith wondered if everything was set right with Billy. She pressed the memory of last night like a bruise. She really needed to get that key back from Martha, at any rate.

A leopard doesn't change its spots, Marigold warned her.

Judith had the package of cookies in her hand, hovering it over the rubbish bin, when she heard voices in her backyard. What now? She stumped back out to the yard and found Paul on his knees in the dirt with a measuring tape in hand, Billy holding the other end of it, and Martha counting the turf tiles.

"There's not enough for the whole yard," Paul said. "She'll still cover a bit of ground."

"Hello!" Judith waved to get everyone's attention. "What's going on here?"

"Judith, Paul is going to teach Billy how to lay turf," Martha explained. She took an Iced VoVo from the package clutched in Judith's hand.

"It's a hot day." Paul frowned at the vulnerable grass. "Like burning money not putting it in the ground now. I'll show young Billy how to start, then he'll finish it himself."

"You hear that, Billy?" Martha's tone was severe. "This is expensive turf, so you do a good job for Mrs. Danger."

Billy grinned and helped himself to three cookies. "I'm a street rat, remember, Mrs. *Drainger*? I'll improvise."

"Don't get smart, kid," Paul growled at the same time as Martha said, "Billy, watch your manners."

Billy grinned wider at the trouble he'd caused, and his white teeth flashed. Judith felt a giggle bubble up somewhere in her chest, then it slipped out as a full-throated laugh. "He's quoting a Disney movie," she said by way of explanation to his annoyed foster parents.

"Yeah, it's our inside joke, isn't it, Mrs. Drainger?" Billy's eyes sparkled, and she smiled back.

"Being a smartarse," Paul grumbled and returned to measuring the yard.

"I've got a cake in the oven," Martha said. "Just send Billy home when he's done enough for the day, Judith." She shuffled off in her rubber clogs.

True to his word, Billy worked the rest of the day side by side with Paul, then they returned bright and early the next morning to finish off the new lawn. They were almost done by lunchtime, when Martha delivered a large platter of sandwiches cut into triangles along with three thick slices of pineapple upside-down cake. She couldn't stay to eat with them—she'd promised Chantal she'd babysit Eddie for the afternoon.

Judith studied her backyard. Instead of the ratty lawn, now she had a bright square of green with a wide border of bare dirt. She couldn't work out if it looked better or worse.

"You need a row of flower beds there." Paul pointed his cheddar-cheese-and-relish sandwich at the ugly edges of the garden. "Put some railway sleepers in or a treated pine border, fill it in with soil, and plant some color. Me, I like agapanthus. Green leaves all year and nice purple flowers in the spring and summer."

Billy was hovering over the sandwiches, checking all the fillings before taking one in each hand and putting another on his lap to save for later. "Agapanthus." He snorted. "Sounds dangerous."

Paul glared at Billy, looking less like a movie star and very much like a man who knew how to hurt someone when they annoyed him. It made sense, though. He would've had to be tough working in the diamond mines, and Judith thought now was a perfect chance to ask him about it.

"Gardening must be a big change from mining," she said, her tone bright to dispel the tension between the two males.

"Tore up the earth most of my life," Paul muttered. "Nice to put something back in it."

Judith was touched. She'd guessed Paul had hidden depths. It also showed he was capable of guilt, she reminded herself for no good reason.

"Do you miss it?" she asked. "Africa, I mean. I miss Kenya so much. At least Adelaide has the same dry heat, but it's the smell I miss. Not the smell of the camps, of course. Ha ha! No, not that. The smell just before sunrise, that special scent of cold desert. It's sort of a salty, medicinal kind of smell." She paused, embarrassed to have revealed so much in such a desperate tone. "I'm sure you know what I mean. That, and having a real job, of course."

"Plenty to do here," he said and took a big bite of sandwich.

"Oh, yes, of course. I'm retired now too." Judith rushed to draw parallels between them. They'd never really talked before, and her imagination needed more fuel to keep the crush burning. "Like I said, I worked in northeastern Kenya—in the Dadaab region of the Lagdera District—but I did one mission in Nairobi City. Where were you?"

Paul's eyes creased in a squint. "Angola."

"Oh, I never went there," Judith said.

"Africa's a big place."

"Was it all desert in Angola?" Billy asked, alight with curiosity. "Did you see lions or elephants?"

"Saw a leopard outside the fence once, but too much noise and people for it to stay close to the compound. You go on safari if you want the Big Five," Paul managed to say before his voice rasped away into silence.

"The Big Five? What's that?" Billy asked.

"The Big Five are elephants, rhinoceros, buffalo, lions, and leopards," Judith replied. "They're typically what all the tourists want to see when they go on a safari."

"Did you ever do a safari, Paul?" Billy prodded.

Paul was done talking about Angola. "You finish off now, Billy. Water it all in good again, and bring the lunch plates back for Martha."

Raising a finger to touch the brim of his cap in farewell, Paul walked away down the side of the house. The back of his green shirt was dark with sweat, and Judith couldn't help wishing Billy hadn't been there that afternoon.

"That's the most I've ever heard him say," Billy said. "He must really like you, Mrs. Drainger."

Judith tamped down a smile and shook her head. "Paul's just being a good neighbor."

"Bonus, he left his cake!" Billy reached out, then remembered his manners. "You want to share the last piece?"

"Why do you think Paul is so shy to talk about his past?" she asked, to herself more than Billy.

"Because he was a real shit to Martha in the old days," Billy replied. "He used to come home all drugged up—heroin, I think—and drinking heaps of booze. Then Martha would look after him, dry him out, and send him back—or he'd just leave. Not sure which."

Judith was as shocked by Billy's nonchalant tone as the information. "Who told you that?"

"All the other kids I've met at Martha's, but Tilly mostly," he replied. "She hates Paul for what he did to Martha in those days. Once Paul gave Martha a bad STD—chlamydia, she said—because he was, you know, screwing around and that."

Judith wanted to sigh with disappointment. She knew exactly what sort of man Billy was describing. She'd seen hundreds of them. Men with foreign cash in their pockets ready to buy on the cheap what they could and take by violence what they couldn't.

"Poor Martha," she murmured, because it was the right thing to say. Honestly, though, if what Billy said was even half true, why had she put up with such a scoundrel all these years?

Billy held out a smushed bit of cake. Judith shook her head.

"Don't eat much, do you?" he remarked. "You didn't take a sandwich, either."

"I had a big breakfast," she said, still lost in her thoughts.

"Do you have what Tilly has?" he asked.

"Hmm?" Judith returned her focus to the boy next to her.

"Anorexia," he said. "Tilly's real mum got so fat that she couldn't even get off the couch. Tilly said she was too fat to get in a car even, and they needed a truck to take her to the hospital. That's how she ended up with Martha, getting fostered." He tilted his head, seemingly unaware that this was none of his damn business. "Now she never wants to eat in case she ends up like her old mum."

"What? That's not me!" Judith scoffed.

"Do you think you're fat?" he persisted. "Or do you just hate food?"

Judith was alarmed to see the sparkle in Billy's eye was now more of a canny glint. He'd spent all this time on his repentant sinner act to butter her up. This boy casually asking her to bare her soul was the same boy who'd thought she'd be rich because she was British. Martha hadn't domesticated him yet—he was a clever predator, and he was still wild.

"I'd better let you get back to it," Judith said. "I'll wash these dishes for Martha." She even managed a quick smile for Billy.

When she went inside and shut the door, her hands were trembling.

THIRTEEN

THAT WEEK, JUDITH THOUGHT ABOUT BILLY A LOT. SHE thought about him when she heard voices out on the street at night, when she went to the bathroom and forgot to lock the back door, when she sat in her backyard with a cup of tea and heard him trying to convince Paul to take Martha away for the weekend. She thought about Billy so much it frightened her, and that was confusing.

In the camps, Judith had kept her guard up, slept lightly, and was prepared for trouble at any time. This one South Australian teenager was shaking her harder than all the starving gangsters in Dadaab hustling for survival. In a refugee camp, there were clear reasons to go after fresh water, food and shelter—and to fight savagely to keep them. Here in the beautiful suburb of Goodwood, Billy had food when he wanted it and a lovely home with the Thompsons. Judith was pretty sure he didn't have to worry about intestinal parasites in the tap water he had easy access to or medical care if they did crop up. What Billy wanted was more. More than he had now.

The real problem was that Judith no longer lived in a tent with a locked trunk containing clean underwear and blankets she was happy to share, nor did she live in a palatial London terrace house with Fort Knox-style security. Now she had a simple suburban home filled with things that could be taken away from her.

So she did what she always did. She lined up the problems and fixed them, one by one.

It was Thursday afternoon when the locksmith was finishing up the work to secure her windows with sturdy screens and replace the locks on both her doors. It didn't make the cottage Fort Knox, but it was a comfortable compromise. She was out on her front veranda being handed her new keys when she saw Billy exit Martha's house. The sight of a man dressed in a black-and-gray uniform, the Lock It Up logo on the back, attracted his attention, and he came sauntering over to her gate.

"Hi, Mrs. Drainger." He squinted at her in the bright sunshine. "You getting all the locks changed, eh?" He started swinging the gate with his foot, the squeak of the rusted hinges loud and irritating as it moved back and forth.

Judith had a great poker face. She'd been complimented on it by her colleagues and criticized for it by her family. She was confident that Billy wouldn't know how anxious seeing him smiling at her gate made her. "It finally hit the top of my to-do list," she said.

"S'pose you'll want to give Martha a spare key in case of emergencies." He walked up the garden path. "I'll give it to her for you." He held out his hand, and Judith could see his clever gaze reading the reluctance in her body language.

"I'll take it to Martha myself," she replied. "It'll give me an excuse to pop over and see what she's baking today."

Billy laughed, white teeth shining. "She made lamingtons. I'll be sure to tell her to save you a big one—I know how much you like cake." Still chuckling to himself, he made his way out the gate and turned in the direction of the shops.

There was no way Judith was going to let him have the last word after that comment. "Shouldn't you be in school, Billy?" she shouted. Billy just raised a hand in a backward wave, and Judith knew he was still laughing at her.

"Bloody poofter." The Lock It Up man had sandy hair and the red nose of a habitual drinker. His gray shirt collar had a ring of sweat around the top. He nodded at Billy's back, a scowl contorting his mouth. "That cheeky shit wanted your key for nothin' good."

"Sorry, what's a poofter?" Judith asked, though she was sure she could guess and it was already making her blood boil.

The man sniffed. "It's another word for them gays," he said, pleased to be of service. "You can tell by the haircut, yeah? My day, we used to sort 'em out one by one."

"So 'poofter' is a nasty term for a homosexual person?" Judith felt her poker face slip.

The homophobe rolled his eyes at her. "Just a piece of advice," he said with a huff. "A woman on her own might want to keep her distance, that's all."

Judith felt a thrill of fear. How did this creep know she was on her own? Her fear morphed quickly into fury as she checked the name on the invoice she'd been handed. "I'll be sure to educate myself, thank you, Mr. McNamara," she snapped. "I'll also be sure to let your boss know that he has a nasty homophobe working for him, making inappropriate comments to female clients." Mr. McNamara got into his van, but Judith was too angry to leave it at that. "And I'll have you know that boy is my neighbor, and he's a lovely kid!" she shouted even as the van engine drowned her out.

Still shaking with anger, she watched the Lock It Up van until it reached the end of Rowntree Street and turned the corner. She stomped inside, clumping the plastic cast hard with every step, and sat down at the dining table. Snapping open her dented laptop, she wrote a letter to the locksmith company and then checked it three times before getting up to make a cup of tea. She drank it while sitting bolt upright on her couch, before returning to her laptop to read the letter again. Judith found sleeping on it impossible, though she had learned her vitriol often clouded the issue in letters of complaint. Which was why she cut a few of the more personal insults about Mr. Tyson McNamara's upbringing, then pressed send.

Satisfied that a wrong had been righted, she relaxed in her chair and returned to thinking about Billy. She'd never been one to doubt her own instincts, and he definitely set her alarm bells ringing. So why didn't Martha see it? Was she just too keen on being a saint to recognize the devil she'd let into her house?

She went to her kitchen and stood at the kettle without turning it on. She wondered why this situation with Billy was so unsettling. Yes, he was a troubled boy. But Rowntree Street was his home, and Judith was the interloper here. She decided she should learn more about his situation before she condemned him forever like that hideous Mr. McNamara had. She was profoundly annoyed that she'd even had to remind herself of this. Who was she turning into?

She carried the kettle to her spotless sink and turned on the tap. As the water sputtered, her thoughts turned to another soul who needed compassion. Poor Gladys could've died in the night, and Judith hadn't even checked on her, though she knew that fragile woman needed every kind of help there was to give. How could she be so selfish to stay away when the remedy for Gladys was simply Judith caring enough to take out her garbage and get the fridge fixed?

Oh, Judith! Marigold whispered. *That nasty little woman won't even remember you helping her, so there's simply no point in it.*

Judith got a tea mug from the cupboard and felt her heart thump heavily at Marigold's words. Questioning herself like this made her feel weak and ordinary, feelings that she'd worked hard all her life, in dangerous countries with dangerous people, to avoid.

The electric kettle clicked off, and she poured steaming water into the mug. At the very least, Judith thought she should share her concerns about Billy with Martha. After the break-in, she was sure Martha would understand if she explained she'd rather not give her the new key. Then she would go on over to Gladys's and make a start on cleaning the . . . make a start somewhere.

Feeling solidly on the righteous path again, Judith left the tea and prepared for her conversation with Martha, exchanging her sweaty T-shirt for a clean one and rolling on more deodorant. Her lipstick stayed capped, though. There was no need to go overboard for a woman who wore sweatshirts with cartoons on them.

She made her way next door, confident now without her crutches. The front door was open, so she knocked on the black mesh security door and waited. There was a radio playing pop tunes somewhere deep in the house. She knocked again and waited some more. She began to lose a little of her fervor but decided she couldn't leave now. Martha simply must hear her thoughts on Billy. Though it went against her upbringing, she decided to take a leaf out of Martha's own book.

Judith, no! Marigold whispered, aghast, as Judith turned the security door handle. The door was unlocked, so she put her head inside.

"Hello, Martha! You home?" she called out. "It's me, Judith." She stumped into the hallway, kicking off her shoe and leaving it near the door. She wondered if Paul was in, and the thought came with a thrill of anticipation. She walked through the house and felt emptiness where Martha's energy usually filled the space. The kitchen smelled like toasted coconut and coffee.

Hearing the tinny sound of a motor, she followed the noise out to the backyard. A shirtless Paul was trimming the already immaculate edges of his lawn. Standing in the doorway, she watched his sweat-sheened back ripple with muscle as he moved the machine backward and forward over the grass. His shorts hung low over narrow hips, and she saw a thin white stretch of underwear elastic.

He hadn't heard her, so the right thing was to turn around and go home, Judith told herself.

She stepped out onto the patio. "Hello, Paul!" she shouted over the noise of the motor.

Paul glanced over his shoulder, and Judith thought he didn't seem at all surprised to see her there. He touched a button, and the motor sputtered to a stop.

"Hello, Paul," she repeated, overly cheerful to cover her nerves.

He lifted his chin in greeting, eyes hidden by the shade of his cap.

"So sorry to intrude like this, I was looking for Martha." Judith didn't know what to do with her hands as she spoke, so she settled for putting them on either side of her waist, then realized that was what Martha always did, so she clasped them behind her back.

"She's not here," he said. "Gone to town to see someone in the hospital."

"Oh, no, I am sorry," Judith said, screwing up her face to reflect sympathy. "Is it a close friend?"

"All her friends are close." He lay the edge trimmer down on the grass at his feet. Pulling a small box from his pocket, he knocked a plastic lighter and a cigarette out. His shorts were hanging very low at the front.

"Oh, I miss that," Judith said with a high-pitched giggle that was embarrassing to her own ears.

Paul held the pack out to her, offering one. A wild surge of adrenaline sent her heart racing. It had been forever, and one wouldn't hurt, she promised herself as she walked toward Paul and the little white box. When she took a cigarette, she really hoped he didn't notice her trembling fingers. He held the lighter out behind himself in the direction of the garden shed.

"Better get out of sight," he said. "In case I'm spotted."

"Oh, I see, yes." Judith stifled a giggle as she followed him behind the shed. He had arranged a little private area with an old trellis screening the view from the garden. There was an old tree stump for a seat, a ripped-open beer can next to it full of cigarette butts marinating in filthy water.

"This is cozy," she said, grateful that her voice had returned to a normal pitch.

Paul leaned in with the lighter already aflame, and Judith put the cigarette to her lips. She inhaled. The glorious first puff warmed her taste buds and floated down her throat. For a moment, there was just the sour, malty taste of heaven, and she completely forgot the world. When she opened her eyes again, Paul was standing so close that she instinctively took a step back. He retreated too. She took another greedy drag on the cigarette. Head buzzing pleasantly with the hit of nicotine, she looked around at the narrow space and tried to remember when she'd had her last tetanus shot. The yard was beautiful and precisely organized, but back here in Paul's private space, it was ugly and a little dangerous. He blew out a puff of smoke that surrounded her.

Judith needed to giggle again. She was behind a shed, smoking a cigarette with a man who wanted to kiss her. When had she turned back into a sixteen-year-old? Paul was watching her intently, and she was old enough to know that the mood had changed between them. He leaned forward, and she stood still, letting his lips touch hers. This time, the adrenaline didn't fire like it should have. She tried to enjoy the tobacco-flavored kiss. Honestly, though, she felt more than a bit ridiculous. She put her hands on Paul's wide, muscular shoulders, his tangy body odor tickling her nose as she leaned into the kiss. She was still daring herself to lick his tongue when he moved off her mouth. His lips crawled down her neck as his hand slid under her T-shirt. His fingers pinched her nipple, making her gasp at the too-rough treatment.

Judith loved sex, more than her ex-husband might ever have thought, but it had to be sweet, and it had to end well for both parties. Being pushed against a garden shed with a hand yanking her breast was not what she wanted. Not when Paul was wearing an expression that looked more bored than enraptured. She realized she would have preferred to finish the cigarette that was now burning to ash on the ground by her feet.

Sod it! Judith stopped pretending to enjoy Paul's touch. He was, quite frankly, a terrible kisser, and she didn't want to do this anymore. At the moment of decision, she felt a sliding sensation against her ankle, cold enough to make her yelp. She looked down to see the too-long tail of a reptile disappearing behind the tree stump. "Snake!" she shrieked.

Paul only gave the stump a cursory glance before he moved back toward her face. She snapped, fear of the snake and disappointment with Paul coming out in a string of expletives as she struggled to escape the confined space.

"So you do know other swear words, Mrs. Drainger." Judith's head whipped around to see Billy peeking at them around the edge of the trellis. "The question you'll be asking is how long have I been standing here?" He chuckled. "The answer is—"

Paul was even quicker than the snake. He lunged and grabbed Billy, yanking him so Billy's shoulder hit the trellis and knocked it over. Judith cringed away from the fight but couldn't escape as the man and boy scuffled in the only exit. She kept waiting for Paul to stop. Billy's mouth was gaping, and he clearly couldn't breathe with his head jammed under Paul's arm.

"That's enough," Judith commanded. Paul's lips were sucked into a hard line as he worked at squeezing Billy's neck. "I said stop!" she shouted, and finally Paul looked up at her. His eyes were red around the cobalt irises. "He's just a kid," she said. "Let him go. Now."

Paul released Billy, shoving him into the shed hard enough to make the whole thing shake. "Are you all right?" she asked, but Billy was laughing even as he ducked away from Paul's half-hearted swing.

"You're so screwed, Paul." He chortled. "Poor Martha's finally going to kick your arse out, and I'm moving in for good."

"I didn't do nuthin'," Paul snarled, though his shoulders sank in a defeated way. "You little shit, Billy."

Shrugging, Billy turned and grinned at Judith. "I bet you're sorry too, aren't you, Mrs. Drainger?" he said. "I bet you're sorry enough to pay me to keep my mouth shut."

"Billy, you don't have to do this," she advised in what she hoped was a sensible manner. "This is between Paul and Martha."

"Wasn't it your tongue down Paul's throat?" Billy grinned. "I know Martha hasn't been giving our man Paul any action, but I doubt she wants her best friend, Judith, all in there. Now it's gonna cost you."

Judith found the strength to pull together her shredded dignity. "Look, there's a snake behind this tree stump, and I'm going to leave." She made her way around Paul and stepped up to where Billy stood in the narrow entrance. She endured his gleeful chuckle, determined not to be intimidated by this sixteen-year-old hustler. She wondered if she should stay to negotiate terms of blackmail but couldn't imagine it going well, so she left. Walking up the side of the Thompsons' house, she snuck back in the front door to retrieve her single shoe, and then stumped all the way to her own home. Entering the cottage, she shut the door behind herself and carefully locked it.

You silly girl! Marigold hissed.

Judith dropped her face into her hands and caught the first of the tears. "I'm so sorry," she moaned. "I am so, so sorry."

"Sorry" won't get you out of this one. Marigold's wrath was in full flight. *With the neighbor's husband too! Could you be any more common? No daughter*

of mine should flush her reputation away for a dalliance with a working man like that Paul.

"I know. I know." Judith stomped through the house to her living room, trying to escape her mother's accusations. "How could I have done that to Martha? She'll be devastated at his betrayal. I've broken their home."

Honestly, I would think when a plain woman marries such a handsome man, she'd be used to this sort of thing. Marigold had always been very callous in her opinion of "plain women." *Still, I never taught you to take what belonged to others, no matter how undeserving they might be.*

"Oh, Mother, stop being so hideous." Judith moaned and slumped down on the couch. "Martha has already suffered enough in her marriage, and I've just barreled in and made it so much worse. I live next door to them, for God's sake!" The guilt was like a living, breathing monster squeezing her heart.

Not even her triage could help her now.

Over the too-long hours of that afternoon, Judith tried and failed to compartmentalize the emotions caused by what she'd done. Every few minutes, she caught herself studying Martha's orange-spotted curtains through her own kitchen window. The light was on, so she knew the Thompsons were home. Of course she knew they were home—she'd heard Martha's car pull up just after six o'clock. Home from visiting a friend in the hospital to make a meal for Paul and Billy. Judith wondered if Billy would tell her right away. Did he hate Paul that much? Did he hate Martha after all she had done for him—or because of it? Poor Billy, who thought kindness was a disease and Martha was sick with it. Judith was terrified of how her life might change after this one terrible afternoon.

You made your bed with that man's sweaty body, young lady. Now you lie in it, Marigold hissed.

Martha would tell Cassandra, and Cassandra would believe the worst of her—that Judith had cheated on Terry and broken up their marriage too. She groaned as the guilt clutched at her again. Everything that had come before and everything in the future would be cursed because, just once in her life, she went after a man who wanted her as a woman.

A man who was someone else's husband, Judith, Marigold whispered. *Easy girls walk a hard road. I always told you that.*

FOURTEEN

MUCH LATER THAT EVENING, JUDITH SAT ON HER BACK step and watched the moon rise. The sky was a deep azure, covered in the dense cloud of stars that made up the Milky Way. A chorus of cicadas filled the air with rasping music. She could still taste cigarettes on her tongue, even though she was sipping a stiff gin and tonic. She wondered if perhaps she should just be done with it all and move back to London. Cassandra didn't want her or need her. Maybe Emily did, but Judith had made Cassandra too angry to listen to a word she said. She sipped her cocktail and burned with shame.

She heard voices in the Thompsons' backyard, but no matter how she strained her ears, she couldn't hear what they were saying.

God, Judith didn't even like Martha! In fact, she actively disliked lots of things about that woman, from her round owl eyes to her arrogant way of accepting compliments for being kind or generous. Compliments that Judith had spent her life rejecting. One should help just for the sake of helping, not for acknowledgment or appreciation, she chided Martha in her mind. Charity was both sacrifice and its own reward. Even if your loved ones hate you for leaving them behind to do the work that must be done. Judith gulped her drink. Even if they always had to come second when you left—

"Huntsman!" The shriek from Gladys's garden startled Judith out of her misery. She put down her drink and hobbled to the fence. Using her metal watering can as a step, she balanced on her good foot and peered over the pine palings into Gladys's yard.

"Gladys, it's Judith!" She looked around the manicured fruit trees and rosebushes but couldn't see her neighbor until the back porch light came on. "Gladys, are you all right?"

"Itssa man, in me house!" Gladys was standing on her porch, wearing a quilted bathrobe. Unfortunately, she wasn't holding it closed, and Judith had an unpleasant eyeful of naked octogenarian.

She wobbled a little on her watering can, thinking the poor woman must be having an episode of some kind. "Hang on, Gladys, I'll get the man."

As quickly as she was able, she stumped over to Gladys's front porch. She stood in the dark, knocking on the security door until a weak yellow light spilled over her head from above. The door opened a crack, and Judith heard a croaky, "Sticks, s'that you?"

Judith waved. "Hi, Gladys, I came to help you with the man."

"What man?"

"You said something about a man in your house."

"No man, you bloody idiot." Gladys threw the door open and started fiddling with the lock on her security door with folded fingers. "Itssa bloody huntsman."

"Right." Judith waited for the click of the lock. She could already smell rot and thanked the gin and tonic for diluting her senses a bit.

Gladys shuffled back as Judith followed her. "It's in me lounge."

Judith saw there was a big yellow stain on the back of Gladys's bathrobe. It didn't look wet, just old and filthy. "So, Gladys, this huntsman, is he—"

"There." Gladys pointed up into the dim corner of her living room ceiling.

Judith didn't quite know what she was looking at until the shadow moved, then she swore. "It's a spider," she said, and her heart gave a heavy thud. "Are you sure that's just one?"

"A big 'un." Gladys offered a rolled-up newspaper. "You try, Sticks."

"I hate spiders," Judith confessed, already knowing it wouldn't help her get out of this. "Maybe we should leave him there until morning. Maybe we could—"

Gladys struck her shoulder with the newspaper. It didn't hurt, but Judith had to fight the urge to slap her back. "Can't sleep with him there watching," she said. "He'll bite me."

Judith let out a long, deep sigh and accepted that she'd better just get on with it. She looked around the cluttered room. There was nothing stable she could use to stand on even if she wasn't wearing her ankle cast. That meant if she couldn't get up to the spider, she'd have to get him down to her. She felt sweat break out over her forehead and shuddered in advance of the act.

She searched the mess in the kitchen for a broom as Gladys followed on her heels with numerous warnings not to steal anything. She found it behind the door and risked opening the cupboard under the sink, only to find several empty cans of insect spray and a half-full can of hairspray. That would have to do. She was holding tight to both weapons as she returned to the living room. She looked up at the corner, and the spider chose just that moment to relax and stretch out his disgusting long legs, making Judith yelp and Gladys screech. She felt the newspaper nudge her shoulder.

"Go on, Sticks, I got no time for this."

Judith really wished she was on her back step finishing her gin and tonic instead of standing in her neighbor's horrid house, trying to sweep a spider off the wall. She felt Gladys nudge her back again, and it took all her willpower not to let fly with a mouthful of expletives. Instead, she reached out with the broom, waggling and batting at the hand-sized creature, before catching one of its legs in the bristles.

"Jesus, Sticks!" Gladys had backed up to the front hall. "You made him mad now."

"Where did it go?" The words had only left her mouth when Judith spotted the spider on the broom handle sprinting toward her. She dropped the broom with a yell and engaged the hairspray, waving it frantically over the last place she'd seen the creature. Only when the can was empty did Judith begin hunting on the brown carpet covered in brown stains for a brown spider. She spotted it, covered in hairspray particles, limping away to hide under a stack of ratty old magazines. She raised her navy suede slip-on and brought it down on top of the enemy with a disgusting yet satisfying stomp.

She turned to Gladys and raised the can of hairspray in triumph. "I did it!" she crowed. "I killed that huntsman!"

"Easy, Sticks, it was only a little fella," Gladys grumbled. "Get yourself gone. I want to sleep."

Still elated by victory over her own phobia, Judith thought she'd better take the empty hairspray can with her to properly recycle it. She had turned to leave when Gladys let out another shriek. "Thief, give it to me!"

She let the can be snatched from her hand. Gladys was snarling, her old potato face screwed up with hostility. "You thief!" she hissed. "You all want me stuff."

"No, I don't want your stuff, Gladys," Judith said, and it was only her finely honed reflexes that caught Gladys's hand before it could hit her. She lowered her head to Gladys's height. "Don't hit me, Gladys, or I will bring the spider back."

Gladys whimpered and cradled her fist when Judith released it. "You can keep your can tonight, but tomorrow, I'm coming over to clean up around here," she warned. "There might be spiders living in all this junk, and it's not good for you. Do you understand?"

Gladys nodded, then shook her head. "You can't take me stuff, Sticks."

"We'll talk tomorrow," Judith said.

She headed to the front door and rushed out, letting it slam behind her. Pulling in deep lungfuls of fresh night air, she stomped back to her own home. She was on her back porch collecting her warm gin and tonic when the empty hairspray can flew over the fence and rolled across her new lawn.

She frowned at it for a moment before she realized what it meant. "You're welcome, Gladys," she called out. "Anytime."

FIFTEEN

BY THE TIME THE SUN ROSE THE NEXT MORNING, JUDITH realized it had been one month since she had moved to Adelaide. Four short weeks and she'd already made a complete mess of her new life. It was no more than she deserved. Today she was ready to face the firing squad, come what may. She simply couldn't live another moment with the guilt of what she had done to Martha. Not even her triage system could stifle the overwrought emotions that sickened her conscience. Her moral compass only pointed in one direction, and it was down the hardest road: apologize to the woman she had wronged.

However, getting ready to leave the house brought one hesitation. Martha never visited Judith without a plate of food in her hands. Yet with no time to waste to make her confession, she didn't want to go and buy something at the Beans and Brew bakery. There were no flowers in her garden, just a green square of turf and an old lemon tree—with lemons! Gratefully, she stripped half a dozen and put them into a string shopping bag. The bag would be part of the gift—Judith had spotted Martha many times with plastic grocery bags.

Ready with her sordid story of betrayal and an unworthy gift, Judith slowly stumped next door. Standing on the Thompsons' porch, it was as if she'd gone back to the day before, when her heart had leaped at the thought of seeing Paul. Now it dropped away, and she quickly realized that she'd need a plan if he was home. Perhaps she could just invite Martha to come over for a cup of tea. Oh, then why had she brought the lemons?

Marigold tutted. *What a wicked web we weave.*

Judith knocked. She knew the door would be unlocked, but today she wanted to do everything differently. If she'd never walked into the house without an invitation, she would never have seen Paul half-naked, she never would've kissed him, and she wouldn't need to be here now with her dignity in tatters.

That's enough "woulds" for a forest, my girl. Marigold cackled.

Judith made her second knock hard enough to hurt her knuckles. Martha had to be there—she just couldn't carry this guilt another minute.

Just then, Martha stuck her head out of a hallway room. "Judith! Sorry, love, I had my music on." She came to open the door, inviting her inside. "This is a nice surprise. Everything all right?"

Though nothing would ever be all right between them again, Judith held up her gift. "I thought I'd bring you some of my lemons."

Martha looked at the bag and back at Judith. She blinked. "Just give me a sec, and I'll be right there."

She stumped to the doorway of the room Martha had disappeared back into. She watched her finish picking up the mess of men's clothes from the floor and off the single bed. "Is this Billy's room?" she asked, knowing it was nosy but trying to bring up the boy's name casually.

Martha snorted. "Billy's neat as a pin," she said. "This is Paul's room. Sixty-three going on twelve, if you ask me. Just now he's gone out to Bunnings to buy more gardening gadgets he probably doesn't need. He'd never dream of cleaning up first, so this is all left for muggins here."

Judith was shocked at Martha being so open about not sharing a bedroom with her husband. She would have been mortified if anyone had found out that she and Terry had separate beds. Ostensibly it was to have separate mattresses for their different back ailments. For goodness' sake, they hadn't even admitted to each other they didn't want to have sex again.

Martha was still complaining about Paul as she dropped the basket of dirty clothes in the laundry room next to the kitchen. Judith stood by the dining table, awkwardly unsure if she should sit. Unsure if Martha would even want her to after the confession.

She thought Martha gave her a searching look as she took the lemons from her hands.

"Shouldn't complain, though, should I?" Martha bustled off to the kitchen to put the kettle on. "There're others who've got it much worse than me. How about I make us an Earl Grey tea, and we'll use one of these beautiful lemons in it."

"That'd be lovely," Judith murmured. She finally took a chair as she waited for Martha to settle with the tea things. Martha heaved a grand sigh as she sat down opposite her. Wondering how best to open the conversation, Judith took a sip of tea. The delicious combination of bergamot and fresh citrus made it impossible to speak until she'd swallowed an ocean of saliva.

"Is this about Billy?" Martha asked, and Judith realized the prattle about Paul's bad habits had been to cover her anxiety. "What's the ratbag done now?" she asked, clearly bracing herself for bad news.

"Martha, how long have you known Billy?" Judith asked, stalling.

Martha squinted like it was a trick question. "He came to me maybe six months ago," she said. "His mum's gone, and his dad's in and out of the hospital. He lives with his uncle when he's not here."

"Billy just comes and goes when he feels like it?"

She frowned. "Not when he feels like it, when the social worker goes round and makes him come back here. Billy's got some little cousins who live in the same house, and I know he worries about them. I try and help, give him clothes and toys for them when he goes back, but it's probably not enough."

"Have you met his family?" Judith asked. "Do you know if these cousins really exist?"

Martha took a sip of tea and looked Judith squarely in the eye. "Did Billy ask you for money?" Judith shook her head. "Did you find some of your pain pills missing?" She shook her head again. She'd checked her medications, and they'd all been there on her nightstand. "Because he won't take the bottles," Martha explained. "He'll just take a handful from each. It makes you think you're going crazy or taking too many, but it'll be him."

"He hasn't been inside the house since that night he broke in," Judith said. She paused. "Yesterday I changed the locks, and he asked me for a new key."

A blind fool could read the resignation on Martha's face. Judith softened her tone. "I didn't give it to him, and I wanted you to know, well, why I don't think I should give you one while Billy lives here."

Martha picked up her cup, gripping it with both hands, and put her lips on the rim. "And that's all it is?" she asked.

"Lovely tea," Judith murmured and gulped her cowardice away with the next swallow. "Actually, there is something I need to tell you, and it's . . . well, honestly, it's about Paul and Billy and . . . mostly me, actually."

Martha held up her hand for silence. The skin of her palm was dry and chapped in the creases. "Judith, I need to show you something." She rose from the table, and Judith followed slowly behind her into the living room, dread dogging her footsteps.

Martha sat on the beige faux suede couch and patted the seat cushion next to her. Judith sat, despising the low-key melodrama of the moment. Couldn't the woman just scream and slap her like a normal person?

She reached to a side table hidden by the puffy arm of the couch and picked up a large, square picture frame, holding it in her lap. Judith sat and dutifully gazed at the picture. A tall, grave-faced Angolan woman was holding two children dressed in brightly patterned fabrics to her side with one arm. With the other, she balanced a baby on her hip. The baby looked about ten months old, with curly, light brown hair and big, round eyes. He was very pale compared to his brother and sister. Next to the rectangular family photo were three little round photos of the children: the big kids—now grinning teenagers—and the baby, now grown into a handsome boy.

"This is Naomi. When she met him, she knew Paul was married with a family of his own in Australia." Martha's voice didn't shake, but her hands holding the frame did. "She got into his bed and even talked him into moving off the mining base to live with her. Her own husband had run off, you see, and her father had cast her out. She was all on her own and had two kids to feed but no way to do it. Then she finds this stupid white man with a pocketful of money and a man's needs." Martha looked up at her, and Judith held her breath, shocked.

"Naomi got pregnant, maybe hoping that a baby would keep Paul with her, and it did—for a time. Then one day, he moved back on base, leaving her and the baby in the dust. It must've been a few months later she sent me this picture and a letter telling me that she'd had my husband for two years. Said he was spending all his pay on heroin and brothels in the shanties near the mine. She knew about me and our three kids in Adelaide and wanted half of his paycheck every month, or the next time he was back in Angola, she'd find him wasted and have her brothers kill him."

Judith pressed her lips together. She knew the world that had forced Naomi into taking such a godawful risk on a drug-addicted miner. She understood the sort of man Paul was to have taken advantage of a woman in that situation. Her gut roiled in protest to think that she had allowed herself to fantasize about him, press her lips to his, when he represented everything that she hated. For goodness' sake, even Billy had warned her!

But even through her own self-loathing, Judith could hear that the story of Naomi and Paul was being recited in a way that suggested Martha told it often enough to have the rhythm paced quick and tight for her listener. The owl eyes blinking behind thick glasses were keenly searching Judith's gaze for the sympathy she was owed—the pity she felt she deserved.

"Paul knew Naomi had told me everything, so he came back from that trip wrecked. He hit the booze hard and was mean with it, verbally aggressive with the kids and me too. He wasn't interested in getting better, and I couldn't help anymore. So I kicked him out. He ran back to Angola with his tail between his legs, as I knew he would." Martha tapped on the photo with a stubby finger. "Judith, my guilt ate me up. I knew Naomi didn't have my choices. Maybe she'd need him so bad that she'd let him do anything if it meant he stayed? What would he do to her kids and their son?"

Martha wiped her eye, though there wasn't a tear there, and Judith wondered if it was the moment to say something. But what? Offer her condolences for having such an awful husband with a secret second family. Or apologize because Judith had tried to sleep with him too. There were no words that worked, and Martha wasn't finished anyway.

"In the end, I told the mining company he was in trouble. Bless 'em if they didn't go and force him into rehab on his next break. I controlled the money anyway, so I made sure to send Naomi and the kids a third of his check every month." She raised her chin. "She had three, but I had my three kids too, plus Chantal and Tilly here. I'm sure you know that a dollar stretches a bit further in Angola than it does in Australia." This time Judith knew the pause was to let the gravity of Martha's generosity wash over her. This was her cue.

"Of course," she rushed to agree. "Martha, you did a wonderful thing, helping Naomi like that."

Martha put the photo down on the table again. "Paul's son has grown into a beautiful big boy, and Naomi tells me he's really good at math. Her eldest daughter got into university this year too. I'm glad I could help with that."

Judith reached out but didn't quite touch Martha's shoulder. "What you did would've meant the world to Naomi."

Martha nodded, agreeing. "I'm telling you all this because you called me racist once, and I don't normally let things like that bother me, but you worked in all those refugee camps with the death and danger. I'm just a housewife ready to set another place at the table if a kid needs it." Her tone was humble, though her gaze pierced right through Judith. "I might not know how to be politically correct sometimes, but I love kids, Judith—black, brown, or white. Whether they're my blood, or off the streets, or my husband's accidents, God bless 'em all. The world is a lonely place when your family doesn't love you. It can make a person do crazy things just to get noticed."

Judith felt her heart shrivel in her chest. "Martha, I have to tell you—"

She still wasn't sodding finished! "Billy's all alone, Judith, and s'truth, he reminds me of Paul at the same age." She reached for another picture frame. It was a wedding photo clearly taken in the eighties. A petite Martha was hardly recognizable, wearing a brunette beehive and a white lace maxi dress with billowing sleeves. Paul, so much taller than his young bride, was dressed in a brown suit with wide lapels and a brown tie. He had a daisy in his buttonhole to match the tiny bouquet clasped in Martha's hands. Neither bride nor groom was smiling.

"I grew up with Paul on the end of my street, you see," she continued, and again there was the telltale note of worn repetition in her voice.

Judith had already guessed who the hero of this story would be and tried not to begrudge Martha the credit. "I was just a moony-eyed kid, and he was a handsome mechanic with a big grin and the gift of the gab. I was even there at the church when he married Denise Watson after he'd knocked her up. They were only eighteen. In those days, he worked on the train lines and made a good living. Poor Denise was a bit of a girl about town, and she left him after the baby was born, putting it up for adoption.

"My mum used to send me over with a cake or a casserole to feed him after Denise left. I always say it was my apple crumble that made him marry me." Martha chuckled, then quickly became solemn again. "It was my dad who went over to him with the beers and whiskey. Paul never really drank much before that." She raised her gaze to stare into her beautiful, lush backyard. "He'd always been such a hard worker and handsome as hell. Even with a young family, his future had looked pretty bright—before Denise broke his heart and my dad got him addicted to the booze."

Martha surprised Judith with a sob. "If I can save Billy from the same fate as Paul, it'll make up for it, you know." She sniffled. "Paul's not a perfect man, Judith, but he's trying really hard to be good now. He still makes mistakes, o'course. Sometimes by hiding a bottle of booze from a barbecue or falling into the wrong woman's bed. Because I know how he got to be like he is, I can forgive him." She blew her nose and managed to look both resigned and proud. "I can't be angry with a weak soul for making mistakes. It wouldn't be fair."

"So, Billy told you—"

"Billy lies for attention." Martha's plump hand pressed down on Judith's bony knee. "Billy also lies because he wants to watch me leave him, like everyone else in his life has. Even when he's telling the truth, it's sometimes for the wrong reasons. I can only teach him love by showing him forgiveness. Just like I try to do with Paul. Just like I do with all my kids—and everyone else."

Martha knew, and she *forgave* her? Judith was shaken to her core. Her own eyes boiled with tears until, drop by drop, the heavy flood released. She threw her arms out and clutched Martha's face to her shoulder. She grieved hard for the selfish thing she'd done to this kind woman. Martha truly had a heart of gold.

Though overwhelmed by emotion, Judith was unaccustomed to crying like this, and her tears stopped suddenly, like a tap was turned off. She let go of Martha and searched for something to wipe her streaming nose.

Martha noticed Judith's need through her own tears. "Wait there, love. Tissues are in the kitchen." She heaved herself out of the couch and fetched the box.

Judith didn't recognize herself as she mopped her cheeks and nose. She'd just confessed to a hideous crime and been forgiven by the wronged party. And she'd cried in public. Triage didn't arrive, so she had to come up with her own solution. "I'd better go home," she croaked. "But, Martha—"

Martha squeezed Judith's hand and helped pull her to her feet. "S'all right, love, we've cried enough today. Best get on with smiling again."

Judith didn't know how to accept forgiveness. She'd never asked for it before. She hadn't even known that you could ask for it. "Please, I really should—I mean—about Paul, I'm so very sorry, and thank you."

Martha chuckled. "All your manners in one mouthful, eh? Look, Judith, I've got Chantal and her family coming for dinner tonight, and I still need to go shopping for bits and bobs." She hesitated. "Only it's just—what do you want to do about Billy? I can tell the Department of Child Protection not to send him to me the next time. You're a woman on your own. You've got just as much right to a quiet life as Billy does."

The truth poured out of Judith before she knew it. "I'm a grown woman acting like an idiot," she said, "and Billy needs you. He deserves his home, too."

Martha heaved such a sigh of relief that Judith felt even more despicable for not only kissing Martha's husband but wanting to cause trouble for her foster son, too.

"I'll get out of your way if you're busy." She quickly stumped through the house to the front door. She paused on the threshold, needing to say something to encompass the gravity of what she was feeling—the hideous guilt, the profound gratitude. She opened her mouth, determined not to make a mess of this poignant moment. "Your Anzac biscuits were delicious, Martha. I would've eaten them all if I didn't—if I wasn't like this."

No, she'd messed it up again.

Martha seemed to understand anyway. "Water under the bridge, love. I'll see you later, eh?" She opened the door to let her out.

On her way down the front path, she heard Martha call out, "Good afternoon, John! How are you?" Still dazed, she followed Martha's gaze. Just across the street, she saw a flash of red trousers as someone hurried along, dragging a little brown dog. Forgiveness was for everyone. Even inconsiderate dog owners. She carefully stumped home again.

SIXTEEN

IT WAS EARLY THE NEXT DAY, SATURDAY, WHEN JUDITH decided she had to get out of the house and do something normal like get a coffee at a café. After sending yet another carefully worded text to Cassandra and watering the new turf, she picked up her crutches and swung her way down Rowntree Street toward the shops. She managed quite easily, resting weight on her healing ankle more now.

When she arrived at Beans and Brew, she was surprised to see that every table in the café was occupied, even the ones sitting in full sun. With a Londoner's practiced eye, she assessed who had just sat down and who might be paying the bill and getting ready to leave. Sadly, all she saw were half-drunk lattes and open newspapers.

Not quite believing it could be so busy, she swung her way inside and almost hit a waitress balancing plates of avocado toast and poached eggs. "Any chance of a table for one?"

"Sure, grab any free seat," the young waitress said, cheerily unhelpful. "It'll probably only be a forty-five-minute wait."

"Oh, sod it," Judith muttered. She turned when she heard her name called.

"I thought that was you!" Bev was smiling and leaned over to kiss Judith's cheek without stepping from her place at the front of the coffee line. "No point trying to get breakfast here. You've got to be up at dawn for that. I'm just getting our coffees—let me order for you too."

Judith looked up at the bewildering handwritten blackboard menu above the coffee machine on the counter. "A regular latte, thank you, Bev."

Feeling very much in the way of the busy servers, she edged outside after letting Bev know where she'd be. Finding a little spot of shade, she wondered how she was going to carry her coffee cup and crutches home at the same time, then decided it didn't matter. She was out of the house and getting coffee with a potential friend like a normal person and not a home-wrecking hussy.

Wiping sweaty hands on her cotton pants, Judith felt yet another lurch of guilt and reminded herself for the hundredth time that Martha had sincerely forgiven her. It just felt very odd. She supposed she was waiting for the other shoe to drop. Could Martha really be that much of a saint? Billy broke into a house, and she gave him a hot dinner. Judith broke into her marriage and was given a hug. It was too hard to fathom, and maybe she should stop trying.

Intrigued by the locals of Goodwood, Judith distracted herself by watching the procession of nicely dressed people arrive and study the café tables before grumbling and moving on again. Only a few bothered to ask how long the wait would be. A couple of older women in leggings and rugby tops with the collars popped approached Judith, asking if she was in the queue for a table too.

"I'm just waiting for coffee," she replied. "My friend is getting it." The word sounded a little stilted, but it felt nice. The women wished her a good morning and left.

"God, it's a zoo in there!" Bev exclaimed as she came out holding a cardboard tray of coffees and a brown bag already soaked with melted butter. "We better get these home before they're cold. Are you happy to come with me, Judith?"

Judith realized that Bev had extended an invitation to come to her home. Her T-shirt was already damp with sweat, and she wasn't wearing lipstick, but then again, neither was Bev. "Thank you, that would be lovely. Do you live far?"

Bev only lived a few blocks away from the café. Judith estimated a twenty-minute hobble back to her own house. Perfectly doable.

The street to Bev's house was narrower than hers, the sidewalk littered with dead leaves and thin sheets of eucalyptus bark that got caught up in her crutches. Just as she was getting tired, Bev stopped at a house with a rather grand wrought iron fence, the driveway lined with the ubiquitous lollipop rosebushes. The large bungalow was dark stone trimmed with red brick and white woodwork. Bev's navy-blue BMW was parked in the paved driveway, and a man dressed in an old polo shirt was on his knees weeding around the pavers. His smile was bright when he spotted Bev and Judith.

"There she is, my lady wife!" He climbed to his feet, brushing dirt off his pants. "If you'd taken any longer, I would've had to do some real work."

"Ha!" Bev offered the tray of coffees. "Don't let me interrupt the pretense."

Judith smiled, uncomfortable. She really didn't want to meet any more husbands right now.

"Michael, this is Judith—she's just moved into the Phillips' old place, next to Martha Thompson," Bev said. "Judith, this is my incorrigible hubby, Michael."

"Ah, dear Martha Thompson, our very own self-made saint," Michael said gravely. "How is she doing with her eternal back ailments? Foisted any foster kids onto you yet, Judith?"

Bev rolled her eyes. "See, I told you—incorrigible."

Judith forced another smile as she was ushered through the front door. Bev indicated she could leave her crutches by an antique coatrack in the entryway. Narrow batik carpets covered the pale wood floor of thehall, and the white walls were lined with art like a gallery. Family portraits were interspersed with intricate sketches and watercolor paintings, all framed in black wood, looking stark but very elegant in the sun-drenched space.

They passed a haunting portrait of magnolias painted in ghostly shades of green and gray. "That's a Monica Hall," Bev said. "She's a local artist. Ridiculously talented. I'll take you to her gallery opening next week, if you'd like. My whole book group's going."

Not an art expert by any stretch, Judith couldn't help thinking the melancholy painting didn't quite gel with Bev's cheerful nature. Still, an invitation to an art exhibition was wonderful; the sort of thing friends would do together. Judith controlled her delight behind good manners. "Only if it's no trouble."

"Of course not," Bev assured her. "The more the merrier."

The long hall led them to the polished concrete floors of an open-plan kitchen, dining, and living space. There was a T-shaped bar in the middle of the room, the long side set as a dining table, and the short cross served as a kitchen counter. The yard glowed greenly beyond floor-to-ceiling sliding doors. Judith could see a neat, rectangular pool off to the side and rattan outdoor furniture set around a firepit.

When invited, Judith perched on a high stool at the kitchen counter. "Bev, you have such a beautiful home."

"It's all pretty new, actually," Bev said as she dished toasted banana bread from the paper bag and handed Judith a slice along with her latte. "Not the house—that's a hundred years old—but I redecorated a couple of years ago when our youngest moved out. Finally got the white leather couch of my dreams now no one's around to wipe their football boots on it."

Michael was leaning against the kitchen counter and took a piece of banana bread. "Hey," he said. "You know I've offered to do that for you many times."

Judith felt shy laughing at Michael's jokes. He was in his late fifties, with wide shoulders and only a small gut pushing out the bottom of his polo shirt. Short, salt-and-pepper hair receded off his forehead, though his bushy eyebrows seemed to be trying to make up for the lack. She saw a bright yet neutral curiosity in his eyes as he studied her.

"How many children do you have?" Judith asked, then saw the family photo on the fridge.

"Two," Bev said. "Scott just turned twenty-three in January. Phillip would have been twenty-five this June."

Judith felt the hairs on the back of her neck rise. Bev smiled and said with practiced ease, "We lost Phillip in a car accident four years ago."

"I'm so sorry," Judith said and meant it, deeply. Those melancholy magnolias made sense now.

Bev shrugged like it was an easy thing for her. "I know he hasn't left us yet, not really. That's why we keep his photo on the fridge, to remember to talk to him."

"It's where he spent most of his time," Michael added. The joke felt rehearsed, yet he was looking at Bev with an expression of such exasperation and profound affection that Judith felt her eyes start to prickle.

"I still talk to my mother," she blurted, then felt foolish. "At least—well, there's an antique shelf I inherited from her. It was her favorite piece of furniture, and I'm sure it can, you know, listen to me. Ha ha! Knowing Mother, though, I think it was that Queen Anne shelf she followed to Australia and not me at all." She shut herself up with an effort.

"When did she pass?" Bev asked gently. She reached out and touched the counter near Judith's hand, close but not invasive.

"Last year, September," Judith said. "She was nearly ninety and had been sick for a year or so. She hated that, so it was more of a relief for her when she went. I mean, I hope it was."

"Well, there's nothing wrong with keeping our loved ones close." Bev chuckled. "God knows why I keep talking, though, Phillip never listened to me when he was with us!"

"How are you finding the move to Adelaide, Judith?" Michael asked. "I imagine it's a little rowdier here than boring old London Town."

Bev rolled her eyes and smiled indulgently. Judith relaxed, knowing her sarcasm wouldn't be misinterpreted in this house. The conversation flowed, and she laughed often, delighted to make both Michael and Bev laugh too. Her coffee was cold by the time she took the last sip, and she decided to leave her new friends before she outstayed her welcome. Michael offered to drive her home, but Judith declined. Caffeine had given her the jitters, and she looked forward to finding her way, exploring this new part of her suburb.

Bev hugged Judith goodbye at the door, and Michael walked with her to the front gate. He was already complaining about the weeding again. Judith was unsure if she was meant to hug him, so she stood at a distance that would make it awkward, just in case.

"So lovely to meet you, Michael," she said. Her face ached from smiling, and she finally understood Cassandra's feeling of instant belonging with these Australians.

"It was really nice to welcome you to the neighborhood," Michael said. "You were right to dodge her gardeners' society, but it'll be nice for Bev to have you as fresh meat for her book club. Look out for those women, though—they are literary savages, eh?" He paused for her laugh as he crossed his arms, then uncrossed them, finally wrapping his hands around the iron stakes of the fence that stood between them. Michael had something else to say. Judith started praying that Martha hadn't gossiped about her short-lived predilection for married men.

"Just a piece of friendly advice?" His mouth twisted apologetically as he waited for Judith's nod of permission. "Get rid of the Queen Anne shelf. It's not good for either of you to cling to the past." He quickly waved a hand as if to rid the air of his words. "Anyway, that's my two cents. Tell me to bugger off, if you like."

Judith was shocked. Personal advice about mourning her mother was not something she would ever expect from a man she had just met. Especially a man as funny and charming as Michael. She should be furious as such interference. "Bugger off, Michael," she said.

"That's the spirit!" He chuckled, sounding relieved. "I hope we see you soon, Judith. I promise I don't normally give philosophical advice." He turned back to his gardening, suddenly engrossed in finding dandelions between the paving stones.

As she swung herself home, Judith reflected on her success at getting closer to Bev. She had liked the woman instinctively and now respected her calm grieving. It had clearly become a natural part of Bev's life and something she was comfortable with sharing. Michael's support for his wife was also remarkable. They were a couple very much in sync and possibly still in love. Despite knowing their pain, Judith felt a sting of jealousy. She had lost her mother, walked away from her husband, and been rejected by her only child. She was all alone in the world.

Her crutches caught, and she stumbled on the pavement. A single sob ripped from her chest. She leaned against the eucalyptus tree nearest her and let triage shove all those soft, sad feelings back into their boxes.

There was no need to be dramatic.

After all, Judith reasoned, she still had a chance to make it up to her beautiful Cassandra and Emily—for that she should be incredibly grateful. They really needed to get past this tiff about the divorce and be the family she knew they could be. She just had to try harder, that was all.

SEVENTEEN

JUDITH SPENT THE REST OF THAT SATURDAY FINISHING her photo collage project and keeping too busy to notice her daughter's unresponsive silence. Unfortunately, Sunday already felt too long by nine o'clock, and by noon, it felt positively eternal.

Sitting on her back step, drinking a glass of ice water, Judith smelled the Thompsons' barbecue. She hadn't been invited to Sunday lunch again, and that was just fine. She didn't feel at all ready to face Paul after their mutual humiliation—or Martha, for that matter. Mr. Magpie flew down from his tree and perched on the fence dividing the two properties. Head tilted, he warbled loudly at the Thompsons' guests, flapping his wings when someone shouted at him to "Shoo, you dirty great bird!", only looking back at Judith as if to say, "How rude!"

"Leave them alone," she said. "They deserve a break."

"Why're you talking to that bird?" Billy appeared from the side of her house, giving her such a start she splashed herself with ice water and yelped.

"Sorry," he said, grinning.

Judith didn't really mind. It was a very hot day—near thirty-six degrees Celsius—and her cotton pants were already drying. What she did mind was Billy coming over uninvited. Her expression set poker-hard as she regarded the teenager who had menaced her life.

Billy's amusement melted away, and he looked as uncomfortable as she felt. He scuffed the edge of the new turf with his sneaker toe. "Um, I guess I owe you, like, an apology or something, Mrs. Drainger," he mumbled, eyes on the dirt. "Like for blackmailing you and that."

"Oh, give over, Billy." Judith had no patience for this boy anymore. "Stop pretending you're sorry, and tell me what you really want."

He looked up at her from under a fringe of curls. "All right, if we're gonna be straight with each other, I'm sorry I tried to scam you. It was stupid, and I should have guessed it wouldn't work anyway. You're a goody-goody, like Martha. When you came over the other day, she didn't know I was in my room. I heard you and her talking about . . . everything. Even a bunch of stuff I didn't know about Paul and why Martha wants to help, you know, me. It made me feel . . . " He crossed his arms and gazed at Mr. Magpie, confused. No, not confused, thought Judith, the boy looked exhausted.

She shifted over on the concrete step, making room for Billy if he wanted it. He did. Dropping next to her, he let out an almighty sigh. Elbows propped on knees, he cradled his face in his hands. "I'm just sick of always being the arsehole," he said. "Sure, when I've done something to deserve it, but not when I'm trying to do the right thing."

Judith remained silent.

"Like what I did to you, that was shitty, but you were doing something shitty too," he explained. "Not to me, but to Martha, so you deserved me coming at you. When I robbed you, that was me being an arsehole. But not really, if you knew why I wanted your stuff."

He darted a glance at Judith, maybe to check if she was still listening. She was. "I was going to give those frames to my auntie. She lives in a house with a bunch of my family, and she never has any nice stuff—the kids are always nicking it or breaking it. I thought—nah, it's stupid." He wiped an eye with the back of his hand. "I nick stuff to give to my family, and they still hate me. They think I'm an arsehole because I'm living with a rich family, like I'm betraying them instead of making them look after me. No matter what I give 'em, they always think I'm not giving them half as much as I've got. Like I'm lying to 'em! Shit." He sighed again. "I just hate always being the arsehole."

Judith thought of Cassandra and Terry. "So do I."

Billy's dubious expression made her smile. Sod it. The boy had gotten under her skin again. "Do you want to come inside for a drink?" she asked, and Billy followed her into the house. She gave him a glass of soda water with ice and the half-full package of Iced VoVos that was still in her cupboard.

Billy wandered, trailing crumbs around her dining area and then into her living room. "You've made the house look really nice now."

"Sit down, Billy. It feels like you're casing the joint," she said, only half-joking.

"I wouldn't do that again, Mrs. Drainger," he replied, running a finger along the spines of the books on her shelves. "The police would come straight for me with the record I've got." Judith had nothing to say to that. "What are these?" He had pulled out a couple of brass plaques mounted on wooden shields. "Awarded for Distinguished Service—I didn't know you could get prizes for being a goody-goody."

She took the plaques from him and returned them behind the books. "They aren't important," she said, seeing that he had already moved on to her photo frames.

"You look happy in these photos." He studied the collage she had made. A primary school–aged Cassandra with Judith. Judith and some refugee kids from the camp Ifo 2. Another of Emily wrapped in a blanket. "Did you help them over there in Africa because it was easier to help people who don't look like you?"

Judith frowned, feeling her defenses shake under the insulting question. Though if she hadn't known any better, she would've said that Billy was genuinely curious, maybe even trying to puzzle her out in a way he couldn't do with Martha. "I went to Kenya because it's where I felt the most useful. More useful than I'd ever felt in my life." She sat down on the couch, gripping her glass of water with both hands. "I felt a profound connection with the people and their beautiful country. Don't ask me why, because I've got no answer for you. It was just whenever the plane landed, and I stepped foot onto Kenyan soil, I was . . . home. Because even though what the people were suffering was terrible, it made me feel good to help. I wanted to be with them and lighten their load in whatever small way I could. I was so useful there."

"And when you'd had enough, you ran home to your rich husband." Billy cocked an eyebrow at her. "Until you wanted another holiday in a refugee camp."

Judith winced at such cynicism in so young a man. "I could only ever get a visa for a three-month stay. Then I had to stay in the UK for three months before I could go back again. I loved the work, I loved Kenya, and I miss it terribly—like I've lost an arm or a leg. I don't feel the same without it in my life. It was just so easy to do the right thing there." Out of breath, she put a hand on her chest to still her thudding heart.

"Must be weird not belonging to the place you love," Billy said. He looked away, maybe to give her a moment to compose herself.

Judith wasn't normally a spontaneous woman. She couldn't have explained why she did it. She dug out her key chain from her jeans pocket, detached the house key, and handed it to Billy. He took it, wonder blooming in his expression.

"I accept your apology," she said.

Billy tucked the key away in his jeans pocket.

"I've also got some pretty vases and painted bowls I don't need," she said. "You could take them for your auntie."

Billy frowned, suspicious of such a windfall. "What do you want for 'em?"

"To be free," Judith said. "Free of the bad memories that come with them."

Billy's face relaxed in a grin. "So I'm doing you a favor, then?"

"Billy! Billy!" The call came from next door.

Both Billy and Judith went outside to answer it. Billy cupped his hands around his mouth and shouted, "I'm here, Mum, next door with Mrs. Drainger."

Paul's head popped over the fence and looked at the two of them, eyes narrowed. "You all right, Jude?"

She felt her stomach twist at the sight of Paul. "We're fine," she said. "Just having a chat."

Martha's head joined Paul's, though Judith knew she'd have to stand on their backyard bench to be seen. "You all right, Judith?"

"They're having a chat," Paul answered her.

"Aw, that's lovely, you two being friends!" Martha's face lit up with delighted pride. "You're such a good boy, Billy. Now come home and have your dinner." Paul and Martha dropped out of sight.

"As long as I haven't robbed or beaten you, she thinks I'm a bloody angel," Billy muttered, exasperated.

"Martha's your genie—you should appreciate her," Judith said. "Now off you go, and give her that key, street rat."

"Thought I was your diamond in the rough, Mrs. Drainger." Billy smirked as he wandered over to the fence, reaching to grab the top and swing over.

"Well, you're making me feel more like Jafar, so sod you!" she said.

Billy laughed so much he had to attempt the jump twice before he got his leg over the top. It was Judith's turn to chuckle when she heard Martha scolding him for not walking around the fence with proper manners.

As Judith swept up the cookie crumbs from her floor, she wondered if she had really forgiven Billy for breaking in. And had he really forgiven her for kissing Paul and hurting Martha? Was life to just go on like before, and she didn't have to do another thing to earn their friendship? Honestly, she felt as confused as Billy at the purity of Martha's forgiveness. She didn't believe in karma because she'd seen too many bad things happen to innocent people, but she did believe in quid pro quo. She decided to keep a sharp lookout for the next time that Martha might need her—right after she fixed things with Cassandra. Oh, and Gladys could do with a visit, too.

Satisfied with her plan of action, she allowed herself a night of tea and television as a treat, enjoying the relief of a calm conscience as she watched old comedies. It was nice after the confusing interactions of the weekend to quietly be on her own, all alone.

EIGHTEEN

JUDITH WAS CLEANING HER BATHROOM AT MIDDAY on Monday when she heard a knock on the front door. She braced for the usual "Coo-wee, Judith, s'just me!" so was surprised when there was a second knock, louder than the first.

"Cassandra!" Judith couldn't remember a time she had been happier to see her daughter. "What a lovely surprise. I had no idea you were coming by today." As she ripped off her yellow cleaning gloves, she noted Cassandra's beautiful face was pale and drawn. There were dark circles under her eyes, and she didn't smile when Judith lurched in to give her a stiff-armed embrace. She looked at Cassandra's hands, but there was only a blue Tupperware lunchbox. "Where's Emily?"

"Sorry to barge in, but I think we should talk." Cassandra didn't make that sound like a good thing. "We need to clear the air."

Judith stepped back. "Then you'd better come in. I'll make the tea."

In the end, Judith sat at the table because Cassandra insisted on making the tea. When she heard the microwave, she looked over. "What's that you're doing?"

"I knew you wouldn't have any food in the house," Cassandra said over the beeping. "Emily's been fussy all day, and I haven't been able to stop for a moment. Luckily Andrew got off work early so I could come see you."

"I was just over at Martha's last week," Judith said, pleased with her good news. "We are well over our tiff, and I think you were right, Cassandra. Martha is a genuinely lovely person, and Billy—"

"Mum, please. I don't need you pretending to like people to make me happy. It's fine, really." Cassandra put down the mugs of tea and dropped the box of hot food on the dining table. She threw herself into a seat and began stabbing at the contents with a fork. "I don't want to be rude, but it's just that . . . I haven't stopped thinking about our conversation the other Sunday about Daddy, and the divorce, and all of that."

"Oh, that." Judith sat back in her chair. Seeing Cassandra at her door looking so tense, she had prepared herself for a very different kind of confession. Maybe one that included needing her mother to help disentangle her life from Andrew's.

Cassandra lifted a forkful of noodles to her mouth, then dropped it back down again. "Do you know what really gets me about this whole situation?" She didn't wait for a response. "What really upsets me is that you always act like such a martyr all the time, Mum. Like you had to suffer through your happy marriage to Daddy. Like it was some sort of burden to have a loving mother who was kind enough to look after your daughter while you worked in Africa. Like having a family at all was just another chore. Why could we never make you happy?"

Shocked by the personal attack, Judith fought to stay calm. Cassandra was a sensitive soul, and she would probably appreciate hearing Judith's honest feelings. "I'm sorry you feel that way," she said. "I never meant for you to think I didn't love being your mother, because I do love it."

"And Daddy?"

Judith closed her eyes, took a breath for strength, and opened them again. Cassandra was still a child, despite being twenty-nine, so she couldn't say that Terry was an ass who never knew how to treat a woman. "Cassandra, you need to realize that your father and I are just people. We don't love each other, and we haven't for a long time."

"That's—that's horrible!" Cassandra's hands turned to fists on the tabletop. "How can you be so selfish, Mother? It's not just your marriage we're talking about—that's our family!"

"I suppose I've had a long time to think about it." Judith reached for the Tupperware box. She smelled ginger and garlic and raised a forkful of stir-fried noodles, catching bits of mung bean sprout with it. She took a bite.

"So that's it? You get to break up our family, and it's because you've had a long time to think about it?" Cassandra pushed back her chair and began pacing the length of the dining table, studying Judith as though trying to recognize her. "Look, Mum, I'm trying very hard not to blame myself, but how can you deny that without me in London to keep the family together, you tore it all apart? I leave for Australia to be with the man I love, my grandmother dies, and then you decide to divorce Daddy. To top it all off, you move to Adelaide so you can play at being a grandmother. Is that how you think a family should work?"

Judith couldn't answer with her mouth full. Anyway, Cassandra clearly had a plan for how this conversation was going to go and intended to get it to its destination.

"I know you're going to leave again, so don't deny it." Cassandra turned and paced in the other direction. "I'm sure you won't be able to resist all the traveling you can do in Australia without needing a doctor's note. You've probably already researched the underprivileged communities you can help instead of just boring old me."

Judith swallowed the noodles. "What do you need help with, Cassandra? Tell me."

Cassandra's chin went up as quick as the wall she'd built between them. "I didn't mean help *me*," she said. "I meant you should want to just . . . sorry. It's your loyalty I'm talking about, Mum."

Loyalty? "Loyalty!" Judith's voice was a squawk. "Cassandra, sit down, and let me tell you exactly why I didn't come home the night you were attacked. You're a mother now, and I know you'll understand."

Cassandra didn't sit. Judith continued anyway.

"It was a Thursday evening, when the survivors had begun flooding into the camp after the LRA—that's the Lord's Resistance Army—massacred a village over the border in southern Sudan. It was the first time I'd seen such atrocities up close. I was at the end of a mission, already tired of the blood and heartsick from seeing the hunger in my students' faces every day. As the injured began to pile up, I was given charge of a line, mostly young women, and told to triage their injuries. The ones who'd fought back had been badly beaten, the others who'd gone quietly had lesser injuries, and they all had this . . . hideous despair in their eyes." She took a breath, needing more air for the memories that she'd locked up tight until today.

"I spent all night writing descriptions of their injuries: the positions of knife wounds, presence of anal bleeding, or internal pain. The survivors just kept coming, all night, all the next day, and the next. All in pain, all needing every bit of help the team had the strength to give."

"I called you on Saturday morning," Cassandra whispered.

Judith nodded. They both knew the next part of her story. Her eighteen-year-old daughter sobbing on the phone, so hysterical that it had taken Judith a long time to even understand what Cassandra was trying to tell her. The attack on her way home from the pub in Soho. No, she wasn't in any pain; she'd had drugs in the hospital. No, she wasn't alone; she had Daddy and Grandmother with her. No, she wasn't afraid; both the men had been caught and charged.

"When I took your call, I had a thirteen-year-old girl in front of me, an orphan," Judith said in the formal tone she used when giving reports.

"She had deep lacerations on her breasts, her vulva just a pulpy mess from gang rape, her belly distended by a six-month pregnancy. And—"

And Judith had triaged her own daughter's pain right away. She'd chosen to stay on in the camp, to help the girls in front of her. She had gone home to London the following Tuesday, knowing no one in her family would ever check up on the lie of the military coup causing flights to be canceled.

Judith ached to wipe the tears from Cassandra's freckled cheeks, wishing she had a better explanation for why she was such a wretched mother. "I am loyal, Cassandra," she whispered. "It's just that I'm loyal to those who need me most."

"That's never going to be me, is it?" Cassandra held up two hands to stop Judith's denial. "You've always lived your life your way and never listened to anyone, but now . . . " She was breathing heavily, sweat streaking her temple. She looked down at the Tupperware box. "God, Mum, did you eat all of that?"

Judith was just as surprised that the box was empty. "It was delicious. Did you make it?"

"Yes, I did." Cassandra crossed her arms like she didn't want to be pleased by the compliment. "I've never seen you eat that much, ever."

"I didn't know how well you could cook." Judith thought she'd better say her piece quickly while Cassandra was getting her breath back. "Look, I moved to Adelaide because I know how hard it is to be a stay-at-home mother. Maybe you think I was terrible, but I am trying to be a good grandmother. I want to support you and see Emily properly thriving and—"

"Emily's fine!" Cassandra was shrill again as she grabbed her handbag off the table. "You don't get to make me feel bad for not doing things your way. Do you understand?"

Judith didn't but still said, "I understand, Cassandra, really I do." She stood up when Cassandra slung her handbag over a shoulder. "You need to know, my girl, that I've changed my whole life just to be here for you, and that should mean something."

"Oh God, you aren't listening!" Cassandra seemed horrified to repeat herself. "What I mean is that you're coming with too little, too late, and—" She braced herself with a deep breath. "Mum, I'm sorry, but I really think you should go back to London. Where you belong."

Then she left.

Judith only sat down when she heard the front gate squeak closed. Still holding Cassandra's Tupperware box with shaking hands, she scraped out the last noodle with a fingernail and ate it. Outside Mr. Magpie was having a warbled birdy conversation at her back door.

There's no fool like an old fool, my girl, Marigold chided.

"Then we make a fine pair of fools," Judith said.

Don't look at me, Judith, Marigold hissed. *It's not my fault that you raised such an ungrateful daughter. You spoiled Cassandra. I told you that creative arts school was a waste for a girl with her lack of imagination—*

Judith leaped out of her chair so quickly she stubbed her cast on a table leg. Crying out in pain, she took the Queen Anne shelf in both hands and shook it hard, all the new frames falling to the floor. "I'm doing the best I can!" she shouted. "Why am I never good enough for anyone?"

"Mrs. Drainger?" She heard a voice call from outside. "You right? I heard shouting."

Judith was too emotionally frazzled to be surprised by Billy at her back door. Instead, she picked up the two mugs of un-drunk tea and limped out to join him on the back porch, though she knew she must look a fright with her wet cheeks and red eyes.

"It's a little ironic, don't you think?" she said. "My home invader now trying to be my protector."

Billy's concerned expression morphed into a snarl. He held his hands up in mock surrender. "Hey, I heard a lady screaming at you, then I find you talking to yourself like a weirdo. It's not my business if you want to act like bloody Gladys."

"Take the damn tea, Billy." Judith thrust the mug so tea almost sloshed on his white T-shirt. He took it. She sat on the back step, and he followed, sitting right next to her.

"Mrs. Drainger?"

"No," Judith said. Then, "There's nothing to talk about. No matter what I do, Cassandra thinks I've been—an arsehole."

"Shit. I know that feeling."

"It's awful. I'm awful."

They sipped their tea in silence, and Judith ran over all the accusations Cassandra had leveled at her. She had never shouted at Judith like that before. Even as a teenager, she had only ever sulked and sniped. Was that because she'd never found the words to tell Judith what she felt? Judith, the distant mother, who made her daughter feel so unloved?

Her heart curled up into a hard little ball. She knew too well how it felt to have a mother who was never satisfied with—or God forbid, proud of—her daughter. She had never been brave enough to ask Marigold to leave her alone when she was alive, or now that she was dead. At least Cassandra had the raw courage to tell her own mother to get lost. She felt the tears prick her eyes again. Leaving Cassandra would also mean leaving Emily with a mother who was blind to her problems. Should Emily have to suffer because Judith was too obtuse to find a way to communicate with Cassandra?

This was an emotionally complicated situation, and now even Billy knew Judith wasn't good at emotionally complicated situations.

THE SELF-MADE SAINT

At that moment, an empty cat food can came flying over the fence and landed next to the Hills Hoist.

"Oi!" Billy shouted. Judith lay a hand on his shoulder.

"Thanks, Gladys, kind of you!" Judith shouted.

Billy's eyebrows couldn't be any higher, so Judith explained, "She must've heard Cassandra and me. The can's a gift."

"She's bloody nuts," Billy said.

Judith only shrugged.

"Thanks for the tea, Mrs. Drainger." Billy got up, set his half-drunk cup carefully on the concrete step and backed away. "I just wanted to say, no offense, I think it was your kid who was being the arsehole in there. I heard most of it, and I reckon she sounded like a spoiled brat. No offense."

Judith shook her head. "My poor girl. I was never really there for her. Too busy off trying to be a self-made saint, apparently. It's made her very angry with me."

Billy shoved his hands deep in his jeans pockets. "The world's got plenty of angry kids, I reckon," he said finally. "We probably need a few more people trying to be saints." He made his way to the side of her house. "If it matters, I think you're all right, Mrs. Drainger." Then he left.

Oh, the cheek on him! Marigold whispered. *How dare he compare himself to Cassandra.*

"He wasn't," Judith murmured. "He was letting me off the hook, one arsehole to another."

Judith, such common language! Marigold sounded appalled. *Watch your manners, or you'll slip down to Billy's level.*

Judith levered herself to her feet, holding both tea mugs, and stumped back into the dining room. She glared at the disheveled Queen Anne shelf and whispered, "Fuck off, Marigold."

NINETEEN

THE NEXT MORNING, JUDITH STOOD ON HER FRONT porch, sweat already trickling down her spine, the air drying out her lungs. She was starting to fantasize about gray clouds, heavy rain, and deep puddles. Today the heat felt especially intense, crisping her skin in the few moments it took to swing along the garden path to her mailbox and find the fresh pile of dog poop by the fence.

Exhausted after spending all night going over things in her head, she was nevertheless relieved to have a plan. She loved Cassandra, and she loved Emily. However, she hated her house and, after seeing her daughter's beautiful home, knew Cassandra would never have agreed to live in something like this old cottage anyway. So she would sell it and use the money to buy something much nicer, even if it was further from Cassandra's house.

Maybe later she would take Cassandra's advice to go. Back to London and her old life in the city. Or better yet, Kenya. She might be able to find an Australian doctor to help her fudge the paperwork. If poor little Emily got a clean bill of health, the standards had to be pretty lax here.

Right now, Emily's needs came first.

Still, there was a lot to do just to get started. Judith went online to see how to sell the ugly cottage. After a very quick search, it became apparent that every house for sale in her area had beautifully landscaped yards, alive with blooms and an immaculate lawn.

First things first. She had to start by fixing up her yard and then interview real estate agents.

Then your house will be just like Gladys's, Marigold whispered. *Pretty on the outside and ugly on the in.*

Judith refused to answer that. Anyway, one of the benefits of being truly alone was that she didn't have to run her idea by anyone and listen to their complaints. She could do whatever she wanted.

Only because Cassandra doesn't care, Marigold warned. *Shouldn't you set that girl of yours straight? How dare she speak to you—*

"I'm going to sell the house with your shelf in it if you don't shut up!" Judith shouted. She felt a movement of air, like a door had been closed behind her. For a moment, the silence was total. Slowly the normal inside sounds filtered back—a fly buzzing on the ceiling, her fridge humming, and a car with a very loud engine driving along Rowntree Street.

She resisted the urge to ask her mother a question just to test the depth of the silence. Instead, she went to the kitchen and made a cup of tea. Her Fitbit beeped, revealing a low number of steps for the morning so far. She felt guilty about becoming so unfit with this wretched cast on. Out of habit, she grabbed her phone, and it confirmed there were no messages from Cassandra. Then she checked the calendar for her next doctor's appointment to get this cast off. She noticed another appointment and cursed—the new car was being delivered today.

A few months ago, there had been a meeting with Terry's lawyer. The purchase of a new car had been part of the divorce agreement, as Terry hadn't wanted to share his custom-made automobiles. Judith's car was supposed to have been a perfectly ordinary Volvo sedan, but she'd gone online after a few too many glasses of red burgundy and decided to upgrade it with all the bells and whistles. Now, standing in her shabby kitchen, she felt rather stupid taking possession of such an expensive car. She didn't even have a proper garage to store it in, for goodness' sake.

As if on cue, there was a loud knock at her door, and another immediately after it. The double knock felt particularly aggressive Judith was frowning when she opened the door to a handsome young man sweating in a tight gray suit. He held a black leather folder and a black fob on a shiny keychain. "Mrs. Drainyer?" he asked and offered his hand to shake. "Good morning, I'm Leo Trimmer from Volvo."

Judith opened the security door and stepped out to join him on the porch. "It's Drainger, actually." She shook his sweaty hand. "I suppose you're here with the car."

"Not just any car, Mrs. Drainger." Leo Trimmer swung his arm out to encompass the shiny red Volvo parked out front. Another young man in a white shirt and black pants was polishing a spot on the window with his sleeve. "You have a top-of-the-line S60 with all the whiz-bang features." She could see the lust in his eyes as he gazed at the car. "She's a beaut, isn't she? No one ever gets all the features, so it was heaps nice to have a model fully fitted. The boys down the shop were all sorry to see her go." He handed over the black fob and folder. "You probably want to jump in her straightaway."

"Well, there is this." She gestured at the cast on her foot. "I'm afraid my driving days are still a week away."

The young man seemed inordinately disappointed. "Looks like we'd better park her for you, then," he said. "Where're we going?"

She flapped her hand at the front yard. "Just park it here, I suppose, next to the house on those runners."

Leo stepped off the porch, assessing the concrete runners with their patches of wiry couch grass and oil stains. "You don't have a garage for it?" he asked, perhaps hoping one would appear from the air. "If only you'd said before, then I would've brought you a car cover. Sitting out in the sun like this, you'll damage the leather. Excuse my French, Mrs. Drainger, but bird shit is going to really affect the anodized paint job."

Judith didn't have a chance to answer before they were interrupted by the sound of shouting coming from Martha's house and her security door swinging open. Judith and Leo Trimmer watched as a tall blond man stormed out, only to stop in the middle of the front yard and look back at the house. He was tan and muscular, wearing a blue tank top that Judith knew Australians called a wifebeater, and his jeans had seen better days.

"You always take his fuckin' side!" the blond man shouted, spit glistening in the spray of his anger. "You know I'd pay you back, Mum. Christ, I thought you'd understand!"

Martha appeared on the porch with Tilly and Chantal close on her heels.

"You watch your language, Peter!" Tilly shouted, her thin face red with anger. Chantal looked terrified. "Mum doesn't deserve—"

"She's not your fuckin' mum." Peter stabbed a finger toward Tilly, his other hand curled in a fist. "She's mine, and if she doesn't give me that money, I'm in a lot of bloody trouble. Don't you care about that, Mum? Don't you care about me, cuz I'm not a fucking freeloader like your bloody heart kids?"

"Peter, enough." Martha sounded weary. "Don't speak to the girls like that. If you've got a problem with your dad, then talk to him."

"Talk to Dad! That's a fuckin' joke, and you know it." He turned to wrench the front gate open. On his way to the rusty Holden Astra parked out front, he glanced at Judith and Leo Trimmer both gawking at him. Judith thought she could've been looking at Paul thirty years ago.

"The new neighbor's a chick, eh?" He tossed a sneer over his shoulder at Martha. "Has Dad fucked her yet?"

Judith felt her heart lurch and heard Leo Trimmer murmur, "Jeez, mate, ease up."

Peter yanked the door of his car open and folded himself inside, then revved the motor and took off with a screech of bald tires.

Rowntree Street stood in a moment of silence before the birds started chittering again and a faraway dog could be heard barking in anger at the rude disturbance.

Judith gave Martha a half-hearted wave, but it was Chantal who waved back. Both Tilly and Chantal had an arm around Martha as they led her off the porch and over to Judith. She was terrified that she would be next in the firing line, presuming that Martha had told Tilly and Chantal about her kiss with Paul.

"It's all right, girls," Martha was saying. "I'm fine." When she got close, she gave Judith a wet-eyed smile. "Hi, Judith, sorry about that." She sniffed, and Tilly handed her a tissue. "That was my Peter. He's a bit of a hothead and never got along with his dad. O'course, they fight—effing and blinding at each other—but it always ends up being my fault. Hello, who's this?"

Judith's throat was so choked with fear that Leo Trimmer ended up introducing himself and shaking hands with the three women. Tilly still looked livid with anger. She raised an eyebrow at Judith, and in that instant, Judith was sure she was going to attack. But no, Tilly was nodding at Martha in a gesture that told Judith to keep talking, act normal. Could it be that the young women really didn't know?

"Leo's delivered my new car." Judith coughed out the words. "He was just heading off."

"After we park it for you first, Mrs. Drainger," Leo corrected her.

Desperate for any distraction, Judith noticed Billy walking down the street. He was carrying a backpack over one shoulder and wearing a school uniform, gray trousers and an untucked white shirt, his black-and-gray-striped tie all askew. She waved at him with her whole arm, but his eyes had already lit upon the shiny red Volvo parked on the street.

"Billy, why aren't you at school?" Martha asked as he threw his backpack on the ground by her feet. "You promised you'd go every day now."

"I had a bunch of free periods after lunch," he said, grinning. "And I missed you, Mum."

"Oh, get away! You've got the gift of the gab, Billy," Martha said, already charmed.

"We've just had Peter here causing trouble," Tilly told him.

Judith sucked in a breath and waited for Billy or Tilly to reveal her hideous secret as well, yet Billy's attention was on Martha, assessing her.

"He's an arsehole at the best of times, Mum," he said, growling a little. "You all right?"

"Language, Billy," Martha admonished. "Peter just got Paul's temper is all. Now, Judith here got some good news today, looks like."

Billy took the hint. "New car, Mrs. Drainger?" He whistled with admiration. "She's a beaut."

"Will it have to be parked outside?" Leo Trimmer asked, as if begging for a solution from a fellow male.

"I'll tell Paul to let you park it here," Billy offered, all business. "He's only got his old Mazda and Martha's Nissan. I'll put the Mazda on the street, the Nissan in the driveway, and then your Volvo can go in the garage."

"Oh, Billy, that's a good idea," Tilly said. "Paul would probably be grateful if someone nicked that old junk bucket, anyway."

"No, he wouldn't," Martha corrected her sternly. "That Mazda's got a lot of sentimental value to Paul."

"Did you conceive any kids in it?" Billy asked.

"Billy, you cheeky thing!" Chantal laughed, along with Tilly. "Don't be disgusting."

Martha only rolled her eyes, but Judith felt her lungs squeeze at the mention of Martha and Paul's sex life.

She had to clear her throat a couple of times before she could say, "The car will be just fine in the drive. I'm planning on getting a garage built very soon, as it happens." That wasn't a total lie—it was right at the bottom of her to-do list.

Billy jumped the hip-high fence between the houses. "I'm Billy." He held his hand out to the young salesman.

"Leo Trimmer." Leo shook Billy's hand firmly. "Let me just get Kevin to bring her in while we work out where she can live." He waved to the other young man on the street and then ushered Judith and Billy back to the shade of the porch.

"So, what've we got here?" Billy asked as Kevin drove the car carefully onto the runners. "Did she get the hybrid engine? Or is this the T5?"

Leo walked Billy through the luxury features of the car, both near salivating over the huge wheel rims. Judith stood behind Billy's shoulder and was glad he was there to think of all the questions she wouldn't have known to ask about a hybrid engine.

There was some paperwork to sign, and then the young men from Volvo left in an older-model station wagon with the company logo on the side, still gazing lovingly at her new car. On her return, she found Billy sitting in the driver's seat, hands stroking the mesh inlay on the dash and inhaling deeply.

"That new car smell really is beautiful," he said, dreamy.

"It's a shame you can't drive it yet," Tilly said to Judith. "Nice car like that."

"It's a bit fancy for me," Martha said with a sniff. "Who needs a computer in the dashboard?"

Judith also thought the computer screen was a bit over the top. "As long as it gets me from A to B, I'll be happy," was all she said.

"Speaking of which, Judith," Martha said. "Chantal has just asked me to look after Eddie next Wednesday afternoon, after our ladies' lunch." Judith didn't understand why that might involve her and cocked her head to the side. "So I can't take you to your doctor's appointment," Martha clarified. "I wrote all your appointments down in my calendar. Chantal only just asked me today, so I thought I'd check with you and see if Cassandra could take you instead?"

"Sorry, Judith, Eddie's only happy with Martha, so I can't leave him with anyone else," Chantal said. "But if you're stuck, maybe you could take Eddie to the hospital with you for the appointment?" Though her expression showed she'd prefer they didn't.

"Oh, no, Chantal, it's fine," Judith said at the same time that Martha protested about taking the baby into a hospital when he wasn't sick already. "But Cassandra has a baby too, so I can't ask her. I'll just get an Uber—it'll really be no trouble."

"What in the hell?" Billy shouted so loud his voice squeaked. "Why would you spend money on Ubers when you've just dropped a bomb on this car?" He got out of the red Volvo, and only then did Judith see he was holding a second key fob. "I'll drive you to your appointment, Mrs. Drainger. In fact, I'll drive you anywhere you'd like, anytime, starting right now. You know, I passed my permit test with flying colors, and I need to drive lots of hours with a licensed driver for my logbook anyway."

"Billy, that's really kind of you," Martha said. "That'll be a real help to Mrs. Danger until she can drive herself. I'm sure she'll be happy to sign off some hours in your logbook. It's win-win!"

Of course Billy didn't have his license—he was only sixteen. Judith understood right away what a big favor she was doing by letting him get behind the wheel of her new car.

"I'd love to be your chauffeur," he added. "How does that sound, Mrs. Drainger? You want to buy me a hat and monkey suit to drive you everywhere?"

She refused to be cowed by Billy's suggestion that she was somehow demeaning him by letting him give her a lift. She felt a flare of anger but tempered it with humor to match him at his own game. "Of course, if you think I should get a licensed chauffeur, then I should probably do that, Billy." She looked him directly in his brown eyes. "One who doesn't need his learner logbook signed."

"I'm just kidding!" He flashed a smile with a lot of teeth. "It'd be a pleasure to drive this car—I mean *you*—around, Mrs. Drainger."

"Cheeky boy," Tilly said with a chuckle, and Chantal giggled. They were clearly both besotted with their young foster brother.

Martha was nodding, looking proud. "I love that you're taking responsibility for a neighbor you wronged, Billy."

Billy tried to arrange his features into a contrite expression, but Judith noticed his hand massaging the napa leather of the headrest. "I'll do my best, Mrs. Drainger."

Judith decided to cash in right away. "If you aren't busy this afternoon, I could use some help at the garden center."

"The one in Oakland Park?" he asked hopefully.

Judith laughed. That one was miles away. "The one in Kent Town should be fine." She grinned at Billy's disappointment. "Much more helpful if we have to do two trips," she added.

"And you said you weren't rich." He tutted, shaking his head at her.

She shrugged. "The car is actually a gift from my ex-husband."

Billy hooted. "Some gift!"

"He got to keep the Aston Martin, though."

He winced like he'd been punched in the gut. "This car is a barely acceptable piece of crap, then," he said. Judith chuckled again. Tilly and Chantal giggled, and Martha scolded him.

This boy was really too charming for his own good, Judith warned herself. Then again, he also hadn't told anyone her dirty secret, which showed great character. She didn't feel like examining why he would keep her confidence like that. The point, as she saw it, was to accept the silence silence with gratitude and move on.

"As well as doing some gardening chores with me, I'll be happy to give you as many driving lessons as you want, Billy," she announced. "On one condition."

"Anything!"

"You go to school five days a week." She held his gaze so he'd know she was serious. "For the whole day. I don't care how many 'free periods' you've got. Deal?"

He took a long moment, then nodded. "Deal."

"Oh, Billy, you're a lucky boy! And we get to save all that money on driving lessons for you." Martha ruffled his hair as he reluctantly picked up his schoolbag and shuffled up the path to the front door, grumbling about having to do homework if he was going back to school tomorrow. Martha gave Judith a double thumbs-up and followed him inside as Chantal and Tilly called out their goodbyes.

Back in her own silent kitchen, Judith made herself a cup of tea, her ears pricking at every sound next door. "Poor Martha getting shouted at by her son," she muttered. "At least I could lighten her troubles with Billy today." She had to wonder if Martha would spend all night thinking about the horrible things her son Peter had said to her. It was odd, maybe even mean-spirited, but Judith felt less alone with her problems with Cassandra knowing Martha was right there with her.

And despite Judith's talking aloud, Marigold still had nothing to say.

TWENTY

JUDITH SPENT TIME IN HER YARD EARLY IN THE week, measuring and planning and staring and imagining what could be. She'd bought lots of magazines on gardening in the arid South Australian climate and was immediately overwhelmed by all she had to learn before she even started putting anything in the dirt.

Wednesday afternoon, she attended her second ladies' lunch at Martha's. Paul wasn't home, and no one mentioned him. It made it easier for Judith to relax and chat with Bev, who was the head of a local Gardeners' Plant Rescue Group, a club devoted to saving unwanted plants from residents in the neighborhood. An avid gardener, Bev encouraged her to be creative and try anything that struck her fancy, especially hardy desert flora, which did very well in South Australia.

"You'd be amazed what you can get out of soil if you put a bit of love in," Bev said, hands waving and bracelets tinkling. "You should really come along to a meeting, Judith. We rescue plants and trees from all over the area and organize sales to raise funds for our local charities. This next sale is for a women's shelter. It's a wonderful cause, and we could definitely do with someone of your boundless energy in our ranks."

Judith was reluctant to commit herself to something that frankly sounded a bit twee. "Actually, Bev, I'm going to be busy with Gladys for a while. Between Cassandra and Emily, the house, and things—I've got a lot on my plate already."

"I'll be there, and we have cake at our meetings!" Bev was surprisingly stubborn. "The other ladies are really lovely, and we even have a couple of handsome single gents who come regularly too. It'll be good for you to make some more friends in the neighborhood. Go on, you'll love it, Judith, I promise."

Judith was going to put her foot down about this gentle bullying when Bev said, "It'll be nice to have someone who knows how to run a team with me. I can get a bit frazzled with all the vote taking and paperwork and things."

Oh! Bev needed a helping hand, not a friend. Why didn't she just say so? "All right, then," Judith agreed. "I can't promise I'll come every time, but I'll do my best to help you get organized."

"Are you still talking about your plant group, Bev?" Cate asked, butting into their conversation. "Because you won't get *me* there, no thanks!"

"Don't worry, Cate, I know you're a lost cause." Bev rolled her eyes behind Cate's back, and Judith worked hard not to smirk. Bev didn't want everyone to join her group—she had picked Judith especially. Deep in Judith's rickety heart, that felt . . . nice.

Judith hadn't mentioned her plan to leave Rowntree Street—it was no one's business. Yet at the lunch, she began to feel a little guilty. Perhaps it would be polite to tell everyone that she was moving so no one put too much energy into helping her with the cottage's yard? Luckily she was saved from having to make any sort of announcement when Billy wandered into the room and made a beeline for the food.

"Billy, you ratbag, I thought you were staying at school all day," Martha scolded, even as she handed him the jam and cream for his scones.

"I went to school but left early because I've got to take Mrs. Drainger to the doctor this afternoon to get her cast off," he said through a mouthful. "We should go pretty soon—and bring your gold coins, Mrs. Drainger. It's bloody expensive in the parking lot there."

"Language, Billy." Martha frowned and handed him another scone.

Judith had intended to slip out the door when she needed to leave, so she was quite flustered when all the women got up to hug her goodbye. Even Cate pressed her cheek against Judith's and made a dry kissing noise.

When Judith got into the passenger seat of her car, Billy had already buckled up and waited for her to do the same. It had to be said—he was an excellent driver. She appreciated how often he checked his mirrors as he slowly backed the red Volvo onto Rowntree Street and then carefully accelerated to a few kilometers under the speed limit. They hadn't reached the traffic lights at the end of the street when Judith spotted a figure wearing red pants and walking a little brown dog.

"John!" She spat the name like a curse. Did the man have no other trousers than those garish red ones?

"Who?"

"That man over there," she said. "He lets his disgusting little dog poop all over the street, but especially in front of my house!"

"Tell me what you really think." Billy chuckled, keeping his eyes on the road. "Want me to run him over for you, Mrs. Drainger? Because I'll do it!" She paused for a beat too long, and Billy laughed again, saying, "Let's get this bastard!"

She tried to protest when he turned at the intersection to follow John and his little brown dog, but her heart lurched with vindictive excitement. With a quick rev of the engine, the car came level with John, and Billy lowered his window. "Oi, John, over here!"

John paused on the street and looked around. Billy gave Judith a gesture to take it from there. She opened her door and was halfway out of the car when she called out, "Excuse me, John, I have a few things to say to you, and this time, you will not run away."

John looked at the car and then off down the road, his expression bemused. Pressing his large black sunglasses with an index finger, he addressed the nearest tree. "Hello, who's this? Can I help you?"

Judith gaped as realization struck her. "Oh, sorry, you're the wrong—wrong John. Have a nice day." She slipped back into the car, quietly closed the door, and buckled her seat belt. "Just drive, Billy."

He checked all his mirrors and pulled out from the curb. They didn't speak until he'd stopped at a red light. He coughed, then said, "So, John's blind then."

Judith cringed. "In my defense, that little terrier doesn't exactly look like a guide dog." She laughed, covering her mouth with both hands. "Billy, I told him not to run away."

They were both laughing so hard that Billy had to pull over again. Judith let the tears fall, crippled by mirth at what a fool she'd been.

TWENTY-ONE

THE NEXT MORNING, BLESSEDLY CAST-FREE, JUDITH armed herself with rubber gloves, garbage bags, and a bucket full of cleaning products. Uninvited, she marched over to Gladys's front door and twisted the old-fashioned bell.

There wasn't any noise inside, but she heard a muffled voice say, "Sticks, izzat you?"

Judith felt a guilt so profound it took her breath away. How many times had Gladys stood at this door waiting for her? "Hello, Gladys, it's Judith."

The door opened a crack, and Judith almost recoiled from the smell that leaked out. "Whatcha want?"

"I'm going to help with the spiders." She brandished her bucket. "Is that all right?" The door slammed shut, and she resisted the urge to sigh. Her plan was a long shot, and it was going to take time for Gladys to let her invade—

The door opened, and Gladys squinted up at her. Thankfully, she had a nightgown on under her filthy bathrobe. "Don't just stand there looking stupid, Sticks."

Judith didn't delay. "I'm going to start in the kitchen," she said. "You tell me what I can throw out and what you want to keep. I won't take anything without asking."

She bustled down the hall but froze in the kitchen doorway. In the middle of the linoleum floor was a pile of what had to be human feces.

"Best get on with it before you go under it," she whispered and reached for the rubber gloves. She picked up John's dog's poop every day, and really, a human was just another animal.

Thinking that helped her keep her gag reflex under control. Unfortunately, Gladys didn't make the cleaning any easier. She didn't want the back door opened to let in fresh air, nor did she want the window by the stove opened. "Spiders'll come in, idiot!" she shouted, and Judith had to pretend that she saw a big hairy one so Gladys would run screeching into the living room.

She had fifteen minutes to clean up the floor and tackle the mountain of festering cat food cans in the sink. It turned her stomach to think of this fragile little woman living on pet food and wondered who was buying it for her. She unearthed an electric can opener, which explained how Gladys opened the cans with her arthritic hands. The grocery bags she had delivered the other day were still heaped in a corner of the kitchen, untouched and heavy with cans and packages of human food.

She placed the garbage bag full of cans on the floor and dumped half a bottle of bleach in the sink, scrubbing away all the grime and rotten food.

"Izzit gone, Sticks?" Gladys yelled from the living room. "You killed 'im?"

"Almost." Judith wiped a forearm across her streaming eyes. "It's a big one." She cleared the broken crockery from the dish drainer into another garbage bag and cursed when a mouse jumped out and dashed away behind the piles of pans, newspapers, and old food containers.

"Spider?" Gladys screeched.

Judith knew it was cruel to keep the threat of spiders going, even though it was giving her some good cleaning time. "No, they're all gone, Gladys!" she shouted back. "I got them all."

Gladys poked her head back in the kitchen. Brow furrowed in her potato face, milky eyes scanned Judith and the empty sink. "You took all me stuff," she accused, quietly this time. "S'all gone."

Judith stepped in front of the garbage bags, hoping they wouldn't be noticed. "It was just rubbish, and now you have a clean sink," she said. "Do you want a cup of tea?"

Gladys looked confused by the question, and Judith was about to hunt down a kettle when they heard a shout.

"Coo-wee, Gladys, s'only me!" Martha came in the back door, her arms filled with foil food containers. "I got your Meals on Wheels delivery, love, and—oh, Judith!"

Judith had never been happier to see her neighbor. "Hi, Martha, I was just helping Gladys in her kitchen," she said. "Is that her lunch?"

Martha put the meal boxes down on the clean counter. "Look at your sink, Gladys!" she shouted at the little woman. "Judith did a good job, didn't she? All those nasty cans are gone, eh?"

"Shut up, yer old busybody!" Gladys growled. She turned to Judith, accusing. "You took me cans." She dove to the floor, and with one quick tug, the bag opened and cans were scattered all over. "You're all bloody thieves!"

Judith pressed her lips together as she watched Gladys kick the cans around her kitchen floor. The only silver lining was that at least she wasn't kicking them through her own poop.

"Aw, stop it, Gladys," Martha said, shaking her head dolefully. "You've made a big mess of your floor now."

Gladys's tiny body was stiff with rage. "I hate you and your sleazing husband. Put his sticky hands on me friend Mary. I heard 'em going at it in Sticks's shed. So loud! Then he made her cry, and she moved. Now I got no friends. 'Cept bloody Sticks."

Martha buttoned her lip and left through the back door. "See you later, Gladys."

Judith was aghast—Paul had sex with Mary Phillips in her little garden shed? God, now she'd have to knock it down. Cheeks burning with shame, she was gathering her cleaning supplies when she felt a touch on her arm.

Gladys tapped her with the filthy can again.

Judith took the can with trembling fingers. "Thank you, that's very kind."

Gladys shrugged. "You got me shit off of the floor," she said. "Watch out for Paul, eh? He likes 'em skinny."

"I'll be back tomorrow," Judith promised her. "Enjoy your lunch." She closed the back door behind her.

She found Martha waiting for her in Gladys's front garden, plucking dead daisies off the bushes. She thought it best to clear the air right away. "Martha, I'm so sorry," she said. "I've never heard her say that before."

"S'truth, you've got a heart of gold getting in there with that one," Martha said, ignoring Judith's apology. "Poor old thing's got more troubles than I can help her with these days. I do my bit getting her Meals on Wheels delivered to me because the delivery guy scares her, but she's not even eating it."

"It's not safe in there for anyone, let alone a woman of her age," Judith said, following Martha back to her gate. "She had groceries delivered the other day, and they got left out in the sun."

"That'll be that new young man with the Woolworth's deliveries who did that." Martha tsked as she opened her gate. "Want something done right, do it yourself, eh? Come on in. We've earned our teatime, I reckon."

Judith followed her into the house. Martha's air-conditioning was like a kiss from the gods, and she was too busy cooling down to panic when Martha presented a pile of lamingtons with two mugs of strong tea. The moment she smelled the fresh chocolate and coconut, her stomach rumbled so loudly in the quiet room that she took a cake just to silence it.

Martha settled across from her at the table, watching the first bite pass Judith's lips with an air of supreme satisfaction. "Now, let me tell you about poor Gladys and her troubles." Judith took another bite of cake and settled in for a long tale, probably starring Martha as the hero of Rowntree Street.

TWENTY-TWO

GLADYS DIDN'T OPEN THE DOOR TO JUDITH ON FRIDAY morning even though she shouted several times. She knew Gladys was in there because she was told in no uncertain terms to go away. With her intentions to help thwarted and a whole lonely day ahead of her, she decided to dig out her plans for the front yard and finally plant all the flowers she had sitting around in pots.

It was hard work designing a garden, and her progress over the weekend was much slower than she thought it should be, even accounting for the belting sun and parched soil. Also slowing her down was the multitude of neighbors who stopped by the gate to give their unsolicited advice and repeated suggestions that she wait until April to begin planting the seedlings and shrubs. Instead of sharing the truth about wanting to sell, she came up with a neat little speech about how she was embarrassed to be the worst house on the best street. Her stubbornness was rewarded in the week that followed by the same nosy neighbors bringing her rose clippings and daisy cuttings from their own gardens as well as their advice on how to care for them.

When the next Sunday rolled around, Judith was presented with a filthy gift from Billy—a plastic ice cream bucket full of worms. He only told her after she'd buried them that he'd nicked them from Paul's worm farm. They both had a good laugh at that.

Yet after a week spent watering the young frangipani tree and the various daisies and rosebushes she'd been gifted, Judith just couldn't find much joy in the bare soil between her neat lines of plants or the square of dirt sown with lawn seed. She decided to move on to other improvements.

It took another full week to organize quotes from housepainters and window furnishing companies between her afternoons spent cleaning out the worst of Gladys's filthy kitchen. Of course, that was only when Gladys opened the door or didn't immediately throw her out for any perceived theft. Cassandra didn't answer any of her texts or calls. So, in an act of pure desperation, Judith tried to pop in on Thursday morning uninvited. Though Cassandra's car was parked in the driveway, no one answered the door.

It was Friday morning of the following week when a friendly overweight gentleman, Mr. "Call me Harry" Foster, came to give Judith a quote on a new carport—like a garage but with open walls—and eventually upsold her to a proper garage, with a new front fence and gate to boot. The brand-new garden shed was her own suggestion, though it puzzled Harry. Hers was still decent, as far as he could see. Judith refused to take no for an answer.

Harry stayed for so long that Judith was obliged to provide tea and a tin of butter cookies as she perused the many catalogs of colors and finishes, hoping to match the new garage with the roof of the house. She had thought it would be a simple thing to choose roof paint, but Harry was surprisingly philosophical in his approach to color.

"Imagine you're walking down the street, say, back from the shops, and you're tired and a bit cranky." He lifted both hands to frame the image, and she saw sweat patches in the pits of his green-checked, short-sleeved shirt. She also noticed his shining hazel eyes. "Then, in the distance, you see it—your house. You hurry a bit because you want to be home. You get closer." He paused dramatically. "Close your eyes, and imagine yourself taking those last steps past your neighbor's house, to see your lovely, welcoming home. Now . . . what color is the roof?"

Judith thought of Cassandra's front door. She imagined the color of Emily's eyes. She remembered the spring sky over the camp in Kenya. She opened her eyes to Harry's expectant gaze. "Blue," she said. "I think the roof should be blue."

"The color of adventure!" He seemed ecstatic with her choice, and it made her smile to see a stranger so happy over something so little. "We'll do Mountain Blue for both the house and the garage roofs. Now, the fence and gate—you want that blue as well, Mrs. Drainger, or you think it might be a bit too much?"

She liked Harry's instinct. "Yes, let's find a different color," she said. "And please, call me Judith."

"Right, *Judith*." He bobbed his head, formally accepting the honor of her first name. "Should we try my little creative exercise again, or do you think that this lovely dark gray might work just as well?"

She was disappointed when Harry's phone alerted him to the fact that he had another appointment. She'd had an enjoyable morning with him picking siding and talking about the "atmospheres" of garage trim.

Judith, please! He's a salesman, Marigold chided in a whisper so faint it could've been Judith's own thought. *He didn't enjoy talking to you—he enjoyed selling you his time.*

She gave the Queen Anne shelf a warning glare, then showed Harry out. They walked to his car as he continued chatting about how much time she had to change her mind and when she could expect a call to have the guys come out to take measurements. Of course, Martha was out in her own garden deadheading the rosebushes and greeted Harry with full-blown curiosity as to the work Judith was getting done, because you couldn't say the old place didn't need it.

"You better watch out, Mrs. Thompson," Harry said with a chuckle and a wink. "Soon you might not have the prettiest house on the street." Martha blinked owlishly and then dropped her shears in a rosebush.

Harry offered his hand to Judith again. It was a strong grip, pleasantly so. "I'll be in contact very soon, Judith, and look forward to speaking to you again. Have a lovely rest of the day." His sincerity sent a blush to her cheeks.

Judith waved him off. "Gosh, the day is half gone," she said to Martha as she checked her Fitbit. "That appointment took so much longer than I thought it would."

"Well, I'm not surprised." Martha's tone held an odd note. "He was quite the charmer, wasn't he—Mr. Call Me Harry? What a cheek on him, winking at me like that!"

Judith could see Martha was, in fact, delighted with Harry and his wink. Yes, he had been very agreeable, but she hadn't thought of him as particularly attractive. He had a perfectly ordinary face—round pink cheeks, hazel eyes, and thinning brown-blond hair with a receding hairline. His teeth were stained pale yellow—probably from coffee, and maybe even cigarettes if the strong minty breath was a cover for his habit. He'd smiled a lot and laughed so easily that Judith had presumed he was younger than she was, maybe early fifties. His large, square hands and stocky fingers had fumbled the pages of his magazines and catalogs. She couldn't remember if he'd worn a ring, though she did remember his watch, a sturdy stainless steel type that Terry wouldn't have been caught dead wearing.

"Hello, Earth to Judith!" Martha was waving her hand. "I asked if you wanted to come in for a bit of afternoon tea? We missed you at our ladies' lunch on Wednesday, you know. Oh, and Bev said to give you the latest notice for the Plant Rescue Group. She told me she'd signed you up to man a stall with her at Sunday's charity sale, and you're not allowed to skip it. I'd go too if I didn't have so much to do, what with one thing and another, and my back's been playing up again, you know."

Judith followed Martha inside her house. She'd missed that week's ladies' lunch because she'd been on the phone with Andrew being told she shouldn't call anymore and to please wait for Cassandra to calm down and call her. He'd been nice about it, yet the conversation had left her feeling bereft and ashamed. Frankly, she didn't want to discuss it with anyone. Especially not with Foster Mother of the Year Martha Thompson. However, today she was peckish—her meeting with Harry had sailed right past lunch. Normally this wouldn't have been an issue, so she couldn't say why she felt so flushed and dizzy.

Had Harry actually been quite charming?

"I haven't seen Cass around lately," Martha called from the kitchen as she set the kettle to boil and got out plates and cups. "I hope everything's all right."

Maybe it was low blood sugar? Maybe it was thinking about a new crush while sitting at the dining table of the woman whose husband she'd kissed? Maybe she was just really upset that Cassandra had asked Andrew to call her. Judith tried to answer Martha but instead let out a loud and shocking sob. She dropped her face into her hands to hide the tears.

"Aw, love." She heard Martha set down the tea things and drop into a seat opposite her. "That bad, is it?"

Judith still wasn't very good at crying in public, so the tears stopped as suddenly as they'd started. She looked up to see Martha pushing a box of tissues at her, along with an iced coconut cake. She took a shaky breath, feeling as if her heart were rattling around her chest like a marble in a jar.

"Chantal says some days a slice isn't enough—only the whole cake will do," Martha said, handing her a fork. "Course, maybe she should swap to sandwiches instead of cake, but she's a beautiful girl, and she's still fighting a lot of her own demons every day."

The tears must have taken Judith's self-control with them because she snatched up a fork and carved out a chunk of cake. There was pink icing sprinkled with grated coconut on top and a line of berry jam sandwiched between the two layers of vanilla sponge. The fresh scent of butter tickled her nose. "It looks like an Iced VoVo cookie," she said.

Martha guffawed. "It does, doesn't it? They're my favorite biccies from a package."

Judith groaned around the mouthful of moist crumbs.

"Yep." Martha nodded, satisfied with her reaction. "I make a lovely coconut cake. I've actually won a few prizes for this recipe—once even in a magazine."

Judith ignored the bragging and took it for what it was: Martha reassuring herself she was good at making cakes that people enjoyed. "Maybe I could borrow the recipe from you?" Judith asked. "Maybe it will make my daughter want to stay in my company for more than five minutes." She braced herself, waiting for Martha's judgment.

Her neighbor let out a gusty sigh. "Girls are tricky," she said. "They want you to be there when it suits them and then to stay out of the way when it doesn't. They spend years trying to be like you to gain your approval or the exact opposite to gain your respect. Most of that time they spend angry at you for being who you've been their whole lives."

Judith felt her jaw drop. "Martha, you're exactly right." Her mind spun. "I turned against my mother to prove that a woman could be worth so much more than her polished furniture and a fat husband."

"I saw a photo," Martha admitted. "Your Terry was pretty chubby, wasn't he?"

"Yes, Terry's huge." Judith didn't want to talk about Terry. "And my beautiful Cassandra has a daughter and wants to do it with no help from me, which is the opposite of the way I raised her, between boarding school and my overbearing mother. I guess she never wants me to see her making any mistakes, so she pushes me away."

"Your daughter thinks the world of you, Judith," Martha said, licking icing off her fork and then putting it back in the cake for another bite. Judith didn't even blink. They were eating a whole cake. No rules applied here.

Judith wasn't sure she believed Martha. "I should have used triage to fix her," she murmured. "Being methodical instead of saying whatever came into my head."

"What's triage got to do with it?" Martha asked, confused.

Martha's curiosity was so gratifying Judith felt sure she'd understand. "I learned it in the camps," she began. "Surrounded by so much chaos and suffering, I had to pack my feelings away just to get through each crisis." She tapped the side of her head. "Overwhelming fear goes in one box. Useless horror in another. I put compassion in its own box too. You can't help people if you're crying all over them. Then I deal with one problem at a time. One by one by one." She was so pleased she'd explained her entire method properly that she took a big bite of cake as a reward.

Martha threw back her head, laughter shaking her belly and making her eyes water. Judith blinked at her neighbor's mirth, mystified.

"Oh, darl." Martha took her glasses off to wipe her eyes. "That's a cracker." Her smile wilted when she realized Judith was serious. "Judith, kids have problems, but they aren't *the* problem. Turn your feelings off, and straightaway a kid will think you don't care about them. Get all of those emotions out in the sunlight, I say, turn them up nice and loud, shout 'em if you have to. Kids love love, and we're all kids at heart, aren't we? There's no problem love can't solve."

Judith snapped her mouth shut, considering this. Being the person she was, she decided to test Martha right away. "I can tell the baby is malnourished, and Cassandra won't let me help her," she said.

Martha nodded. She was a mum—she'd seen it too. "What've you done so far?"

"I suggested the baby might have a lactose intolerance because of all the vomiting and colic." Judith took another bite of cake, swallowing before she added, "Cassandra told me to mind my own business and go back to London."

"Girls are tricky," Martha said again.

"Girls are tricky," Judith agreed. The admission made the burden on her shoulders feel that much lighter. "What would you say to her?"

"Me? If it was my girl?" Martha dug through the cake. "If I could see my advice wasn't wanted, I'd probably invite that baby over every chance I could and feed her up on good food. Then I could sleep knowing she was having at least a few square meals a week she didn't throw up."

Judith scratched at the pink icing with her fork. She had lost so much sleep worrying about getting Cassandra's permission to help Emily she hadn't even thought about being underhanded with it.

"Sneaky, that's the way to do it," Martha said, as if reading Judith's mind. "Pretend you care that she and Andrew haven't had a date night in a while and offer to take the baby. Book her a massage at one of those lovely Thai places, and take the baby. You see where I'm going with this?"

"It must be nice to have the right answers," Judith said, sounding more wistful than she meant to. "I know I've not been a perfect mother to Cassandra. I can't even work out how to fix the little problems, let alone the big ones."

Martha scoffed. "Forget being perfect, Judith. You know what drives *me* nuts? It's like Chantal has forgotten what vegetables look like!" She threw her hands in the air, cake crumbs flying. "I know I brought her up to expect meat and three veg on a dinner plate, but she doesn't give baby Eddie more than potato. It's all fruit custard and puddings. It makes me crazy to see him eating like that! No wonder the kid's a pork chop. Then I've got my poor Tilly, who runs scared from a cupcake like it'll bite her. I don't know—kids are all mad, if you ask me."

Judith felt a warmth in her hollow chest and recognized the feeling as camaraderie. "And you were a wonderful stay-at-home mum," she said. "Why wouldn't Chantal follow your advice?"

"Oh, I wasn't wonderful by a long shot," Martha said. "But I was consistent—that's the ticket with bringing up kids. I'm only human, you know."

The tines of Judith's fork hit the plate. Looking down, she realized she'd eaten half the cake.

Greedy girls are lonely girls, Marigold would've told her. But in that moment, Judith couldn't have cared less about the sin of gluttony when her granddaughter was going hungry every day.

Why on earth did she think that she needed Cassandra's approval to try to help Emily the way she knew was right? Tears flooded her eyes with no warning. She snatched a tissue from the box and blew her nose. Embarrassed by her wayward emotions, she got up from the table and took her tea mug and fork to the sink. "Martha, thank you so much for the cake," she said. "Now I better go home and call Cassandra to make sure I get Emily this weekend. Or at least keep calling until she picks up the phone."

Both women laughed, though it wasn't funny.

Martha followed Judith to the front door and then out to the gate. The trees were still in full bloom. Purple jacaranda blossoms littered the pavement, and those lorikeets chattered in the bottlebrush tree. It really was such a pretty street.

"Well, I guess I'd better get on with it," Judith said. "No time like the present."

"Yeah, but go easy on yourself," Martha said. "Let me know how it goes with Cass."

"Goodbye, and thank you for—" Judith hesitated. What could she thank her for? The time to cry, the cake, the life-changing advice? "Thank you for being a . . . friend."

"No point in saying goodbye," Martha said. "I'll just see you later." She gave Judith a casual wave, as if this was just a normal day, as if Judith hadn't just revealed her true self and showed Martha all her vulnerable, broken pieces over tea and cake.

Judith walked back to the cottage and made yet another plan. Tomorrow, after cleaning Gladys's kitchen, she would drop by Cassandra's unannounced again. Then, after a second thought, she sent a long text promising to come over to bring some daisy cuttings and an offer to babysit so Cassandra could plant them in her garden unimpeded. If she was being helpful, surely Cassandra couldn't say no.

TWENTY-THREE

SATURDAY MORNING, JUDITH HEADED OUT WITH HER heavy bucket of cleaning products, the long-handled broom, and a mop. Taking a moment on her shaded porch, she braced herself to withstand the sunshine for the short walk next door.

She was already at Gladys's gate before she saw the man hunched behind one of the large white pots in the front garden. She smelled the cigarette smoke and knew who it was before he raised his sandy-blond head.

"Paul." She was pleased her voice held steady, though her heart rattled. Dignity demanded she open Gladys's sodding garden gate and keep going to the front door, right past him.

Paul gave her a chin lift and took a last drag on his cigarette before tucking the butt under the wooden paling of the front step. Thankfully, his cobalt-blue eyes were stuck on Judith's orthotic sneakers and never rose to her face.

She knocked harder than she meant to on the front door. "Gladys, hello!" she shouted, ignoring Paul muttering behind her. "Hello, Gladys, it's Judith from next door!"

"Go round the back," Paul told her. "The old girl always leaves it open."

"Actually, Paul, I'm trying to respect Gladys's choice to let me in." Judith spoke over her shoulder without turning around. "It's important that she gives me permission." She banged loudly on the door a couple more times and shouted her name.

"Martha thought she was a bit off yesterday," Paul said.

Judith turned, only to see him flatten his lips and spit on the grass. She honestly wondered how she had ever wanted to kiss that mouth. "What do you mean, off?"

Paul shrugged. "Nuthin', I guess."

Judith shifted her heavy bucket to her other hand. "I suppose I can go knock on her back door, just in case."

He shrugged again. His eyes rose to her face, the familiar spark glinting. Was he serious? He couldn't possibly think she wanted anything to do with him ever again. She was furious with herself, and with broken marriage vows, and with Paul. The anger boiled, and she was overcome by a desperate need to wipe that smug sodding look off his face.

"I'm really sorry I ever kissed you, Paul," she said.

Unimpressed, he backed away toward the gate. "They all say that."

Did Paul just try to have the last word! Fuming, Judith watched him open the gate and tried to think of something vicious. "Martha's too good for you!" she shouted.

"They say that too." He might have been talking about the weather. She watched him slink home to his beautiful yard and Martha's endless forgiveness.

Adrenaline pounding through her body, Judith stood alone in Gladys's front yard, huffing and mentally trying to deny the undeniable. It was impossible. She embraced the truth instead. "What a couple of arseholes we are," she murmured. "At least I'll never make that mistake again."

Along the side of the house, she saw the nettles from her own wild yard poking through the fence into Gladys's neatly mown corridor of lawn. She went around to the back door and finally put her bucket down. It was cooler here on the tiny porch. A hibiscus tree filled with hot-pink blooms looked festive in the tidy yard. Judith knocked hard on the door. It bounced back on its hinges and sat ajar.

"Sod it." Just when she'd promised herself never to walk into another home uninvited again. Instead, she put her mouth near the gap in the door and shouted, "Gladys, you there?"

Silence, except for the buzzing of a fly against the screen door. Judith wiped her forehead with the back of her wrist. If only she didn't know that Gladys had to be in the house. She took a deep breath and told herself not to be a coward.

"Gladys, it's Judith. I'm coming in," she said and stepped into the kitchen. The quiet was like a filthy blanket pressing against her ears. She sensed it before she knew what it was. The feeling was too familiar and always odd at the same time. She rubbed her hand over her eyes. "Oh, Gladys, do I really have to do this for you too?"

Finding the pair of scabby feet sticking out of the nest of crocheted blankets in the living room wasn't a shock. Realizing that there was a violet-blue vein pulsing underneath the skin was.

Triage descended to pack away the panic and dread and fear. With shaking hands, Judith took her phone out to look up the number for emergency services. Zero zero zero seemed too easy, but she called it anyway, and it worked. Moving methodically, she opened the front door wide so the paramedics could get in. Afterward, she sat by the bundle of nylon blankets, clearing a space to find Gladys's hand and hold it.

Judith wondered who else she might need to call. Who would take care of Gladys's affairs? If Paul was her only family, that meant Martha would probably do it. The calm of triage was so stultifying that she nearly didn't register the little squeeze on her fingers.

"Sticks, I'm a goner." Glady's wheeze was soft, like the air coming out of a tire.

"I've called the ambulance, Gladys," Judith said, her own voice loud and rudely vital. "They'll be here to help you soon."

"Stupid, Sticks." Even with skin like crumpled paper and counting her last breaths, Gladys seemed to find the strength to be annoyed with her. "I'm gonna die."

"Well, we'll see about that." Judith's lips stretched in a smile she didn't mean because she couldn't very well cry. "The paramedics will be here soon." At her words, a siren could be heard in the distance. Oh, so that was what an ambulance sounded like.

The paramedics, Matt and Carrie, brought that competent bustle of action that gave Judith such a childlike sense of relief, that "thank goodness, the adults are here" feeling. There was a moment of confusion when Judith almost had a blood pressure cuff put on her, but she quickly confirmed that it was the woman buried under a mountain of nylon wool who was their patient.

Rowntree Street was empty of witnesses as Judith stood by the ambulance, watching Gladys get packed in the back. "I'll follow in my car," she kept saying, varying the volume to shout over Gladys's wails. "I'll be right there."

"Can you try to calm her down a bit for us?" Matt held out a hand to guide Judith in close to the stretcher. Of course she couldn't shirk her duty, not in front of these stalwart paramedics whose lives were all about mopping up the pain of their fellow man. She leaned in and took Gladys's folded hand in hers. "I'll lock up your house, Gladys," she said quickly, hoping she would stop yelping. "So the spiders won't get in. Then I'll meet you at the hospital, all right?" Gladys's mouth snapped shut, and she sagged back on the plastic stretcher pillow.

"You've got a heart of gold, love," Matt said, guiding Judith out of the way with his blue-gloved hands so Carrie could finish pushing the stretcher into the back. "See you at the Royal Adelaide, eh?"

The ambulance roared off. It didn't use its siren or lights, which seemed worse than if it had.

TWENTY-FOUR

JUDITH STOOD IN THE EMPTY WAITING ROOM OF THE Palliative Care Center at the Royal Adelaide Hospital. She had a view of the reception desk and watched the nurses padding by in their rubber clogs, holding manila folders and cups of tea. There was no urgent rushing here, no frantic orders shouted or white coats flying like in the ER. Palliative care was about a peaceful end. Gladys had a thick file here.

"Mrs. Dai-ner?" The nurse was all round curves barely contained by her pale blue scrubs. Her badge had butterfly stickers around the letters of her name, Patricia.

"It's Drainger," Judith said, not caring. "Please, call me Judith."

"Gladys is comfortable," Patricia said, and her smile said this was the best they could hope for. "She's asking for you."

Judith's sneakers squeaked loudly on the waxed tiles as she followed Patricia down a short hall and through a door labeled *Mrs. Mulroney* on a pink card in a plastic holder. The venetian blinds had been pulled back, and the sunshine was the only color in the perfectly beige room. An air conditioner breathed heavily on the wall, and a couple of machines beeped in a reassuring way. Gladys was still with them.

Her neighbor looked tiny in the hospital bed. Her little wrinkled potato head was sunk deep in a pillow, but she opened her eyes when Judith approached.

"Sticks," she whispered. "Sticks."

"Just come to the desk before you go," Patricia said, padding out on her soft shoes.

"Sticks, did ya see that fatty?" Gladys gasped. "She's gonna eat me."

"You know she won't," Judith spoke normally. This wasn't a library—it was the last room of a silly old woman who was about to die. "You've got to be nice to Patricia—she's the one who'll bring your dinner. If you say rude things, she might not give you dessert." Gladys looked so frightened by this that Judith felt bad. "I'm only joking, Gladys. You'll get your dessert."

"So tired," Gladys whispered, her eyes searching the beige walls. The beeping of the machines sped up a little. "Promise you'll stay till the end? Promise, Sticks, cuz you're all I got now."

It was the right thing to do, so Judith forced the words through her lips. "Of course, I'll stay right here." She let Gladys cry herself out, tears leaking into the wrinkles around her eyes. She didn't do more than pat her hand and make *shh* noises, but soon the beeping calmed and Gladys was asleep.

Her phone vibrated in the bottom of her handbag. Reaching in, she saw that it was Cassandra, and her heart lifted in her chest when she pressed the button. "Darling—" she whispered and didn't get any further.

TWENTY-FIVE

IT TOOK LONGER THAN IT SHOULD HAVE TO FIND A space in the Women's and Children's Hospital parking garage, all the way across the city in North Adelaide. Judith kept driving around the winding levels, gripping the steering wheel with white knuckles. Ready to explode with frustration, she finally swung her red Volvo into a narrow spot furthest from the elevators.

Leaping from the elevator, she strode up to the hospital's front entrance. She tapped her toe, waiting impatiently for the circular electric doors to slowly spin around for her.

For goodness' sake! What a slow, selfish, stupid sodding door!

Even her triage system was no match for the hurricane of emotions whirling in Judith's mind. She was completely at the mercy of the panic that rattled her heart and squeezed her lungs. "Where are they?" Judith muttered. "Where are my girls?" Finally she saw the sign she needed on the wall near the main reception desk.

When she rushed into the waiting room of the children's emergency department, she found Cassandra sitting in a corner, staring at the blue-and-white tiles beneath her sandals like she was reading them. Andrew was slumped next to her, chin in his hands.

Judith sucked in a breath, striving for calm in the tumult of her emotions. Yes, Cassandra and Andrew were clearly a mess. That didn't have to mean Emily was dying, just that they were new parents with a baby in the hospital for the first time.

"Mum!" Cassandra's shriek startled a man across the room holding a sleeping toddler. "You're finally here!"

Judith ignored the inference that after always being early, now she was late. She rushed to Cassandra, grabbed her elbows and gave her a little shake. "Tell me what's happened to Emily."

Cassandra spoke through her sobs, and it took a minute before Judith understood enough to repeat it back. "So, Emily screamed for a couple of hours after her nap, then threw up all over her bed, and you saw traces of blood in the vomit."

"I cleaned her up, and she passed out in my arms." Cassandra's voice was shrill. "She fainted, and I thought . . . I thought she'd—"

"She woke up again," Andrew said, joining them. "Then we brought her straight to urgent care."

"They took Emily for some tests," Cassandra said. She hooked her thumb at Andrew. "He felt sick seeing all the needles, so we came out here to wait for you."

"Yeah, it was a lot for me watching a nurse put needles in our tiny baby," Andrew clarified, staring hard at the side of Cassandra's head.

Judith ignored the tension between the couple and focused on her priority. "What do you need, darling?" she asked.

"This is what you do, isn't it?" Cassandra said, gesturing at the hospital corridor behind Judith. "You tried to tell me. I didn't listen. I'm a monster because now—"

"No, stop that," Judith said. "You did everything right, Cassandra." She stared into her daughter's sea-green eyes, willing her to believe it.

"My baby—" Cassandra's tears leaked down her flushed cheeks.

"Emily will be fine," Judith said. "You'll get her well again." She pulled Cassandra to sit on a blue-cushioned seat. Andrew sank down on the other side of Cassandra.

"I just feel so guilty." Cassandra's voice wobbled. "This is killing me."

"The waiting is the worst," Judith said. "As soon as you know what's wrong with Emily, you'll find a solution for her."

Cassandra arched a ginger eyebrow at her. "How can you be so sure?"

Judith tapped her chest. "I like to triage a crisis," she said. "First I pack away the fear and panic in different boxes, then line up the problems. I always start by tackling the worst problem first. Today the worst thing is not knowing what's wrong with Emily. How can you solve that?"

Cassandra opened her mouth, but Judith wanted to give her the answer.

"By asking questions," she said. "Don't let another moment of mystery go by. Ask everyone everything you need to know. Don't stop, even if people are annoyed. Be relentless. This is your problem, and you will solve it." She only stopped talking because she'd run out of breath.

Cassandra frowned. "That's just compartmentalizing your emotions," she said. "It's not really triage, is it?"

Flustered, Judith shook her head. "Maybe I didn't explain it properly. In a crisis—"

"Is that how you deal with me, Mum?" Cassandra snapped. "You put me in a line, deal with me one problem at a time?"

What? How was Cassandra getting this so confused?

Andrew surprised them both when he twisted to face Cassandra.

"Jeez, Cass!" he said, exasperated. "Your poor mum's just trying to distract you until we can see Emily. She's not trying to have a go at you. For God's sake, give her a break for once!"

Cheeks flushed, Cassandra looked from her husband to her mother, frowning at both of them.

Judith felt conflicted. On one hand, Andrew had taken her side, when no one ever defended Judith in an argument. On the other hand, he was bossing her daughter around again, which she hated. "I really didn't mean—" she began, then Cassandra reached for her hand and squeezed it hard. Judith took that as a sign to stop talking.

A lost-looking older couple had just entered the waiting area. Judith knew who they were when Andrew went to greet them. His mother was a petite woman with white hair set in neat curls. She was wearing a yellow blouse with cream linen slacks, and her little mouth was pursed tightly to keep in the tears. Andrew's father wasn't much taller than his wife, and he had much less white hair on his shiny pate. His round face was pale as he clasped Andrew in a bear hug.

Andrew gave a desultory introduction between his parents and Judith. "Emily, Robert, it's lovely to meet you finally," Judith said, rising from her chair.

Emily hugged Judith. "Thank God you're here, love."

"Oh, no, I haven't done anything," Judith said, deflecting the compliment.

"Cass said you can talk to the doctors with her." Andrew's mother dabbed at her eyes with a tissue. "You can get Emily the best care."

"You do understand I'm not a doctor?" Judith said. "Cassandra, what did you tell them?"

Cassandra was hugging Andrew's mum, crying on her shoulder.

"Just do your best, love." Emily gave Judith a watery smile over Cassandra's head. "That's all anyone can do, eh?"

Judith thought things were getting very maudlin now that Andrew's parents had arrived. She never could stand preemptive sadness. "Babies are tougher than they look," she said, trying to be cheerful. "You aren't going to lose your beautiful Emily now."

Andrew made an odd choking noise, and Robert pulled his son in for a fierce hug. Judith saw Cassandra's expression filled with such contentment surrounded by Andrew's family that for the first time, she felt ashamed for breaking up their own family. Not that Terry would ever have shown up at a hospital unless he was the patient. It hurt to admit, but honestly, they had never been a family like the Casters anyway.

THE SELF-MADE SAINT

A nurse wearing pale pink scrubs came into the waiting area. Her rubber clogs were squeaky on the shiny tile and then silent on the nylon carpet. Without looking up from her clipboard, she shouted, "Family of Emily Caster?"

"That's us!" Cassandra pulled Judith by the hand. Andrew had to be pushed by his mother to join them. The man was terrified, and Judith warned herself to be compassionate, no matter how much she wanted to tell him to buck up.

Without another word, the nurse led the three of them down a cold, bright hallway to enter the ward where Emily was being looked over by a doctor. The baby was asleep and had a heavy bandage on her hand hiding the needle of her drip, the metal IV pole looming over her. Judith thought she looked especially tiny on the giant hospital bed and was reminded of Gladys. The nurse asked everyone to disinfect their hands with the tub of blue antibacterial gel attached to the wall and then left them.

The doctor checking Emily's vitals was young, almost certainly a student. Her blond hair was worn in a heavy braid over one shoulder, and her white coat was spotless. Making notes on a clipboard, she checked her wristwatch before acknowledging anyone's presence. "Mr. and Mrs. Caster?"

Cassandra didn't correct the doctor on her marital status, only nodded. She pushed Judith forward as if using her as a shield. "This is my mother, Judith Drainger."

The doctor didn't smile or look in any way reassuring. Judith didn't like how frightening that seemed with Emily lying there. "Baby Caster was undernourished and dehydrated when she was brought in," the doctor said in a clipped voice. "It looks like a chronic condition, so I have some important questions for you."

Cassandra got in first. "The blood in her vomit?"

The doctor frowned. "The sample you brought in contained vegetables, probably beets."

"Yes! She'd had some for lunch." Cassandra let out a gusty sigh and shared a look of relief with Andrew. Judith felt her stomach unclench.

"How well does your baby eat?" the stony-faced doctor asked.

"It's tough," Cassandra replied. "She vomits after most meals, and she's very fussy when she does eat."

"Has she been like this since birth?" The doctor was writing notes again.

Cassandra, reacting to the doctor's cold manner, began trembling. "I took Emily to every checkup at the Early Childhood Center and with her pediatrician. I have all the files at home," she said in a small voice. "They all said she was little for her age but normal."

"She is smaller than she should be," the doctor agreed.

"Our pediatrician, Dr. Chubbins, said Emily was just colicky and that I should persevere with the formula—"

"And you didn't think to get a second opinion?" The doctor glared at Cassandra, silencing her. "It could be that your baby's been slowly starving. I want to arrange an MRI to check for any brain damage."

Cassandra made a strange, guttural noise like a wounded animal. She backed away from the doctor, her hands covering her mouth. Andrew scooped her under his arm, holding her tight.

Judith decided enough was enough. Here was another sodding doctor saying hideous, damning statements because of inexperience and personal judgments. Unaware that those statements could destroy a woman's career in volunteer work or a young mother's confidence in her parenting. She had stood aside and let Cassandra take the lead with this obnoxious doctor, but no new parent could handle being accused of starving their child, especially when it wasn't true. She checked the doctor's name tag. *Dr. E. Timmons.* No butterfly stickers.

"Dr. Timmons, we would appreciate it if you would go and find your attending physician, and we'll discuss Emily's case with them," Judith said firmly. She knew as well as Dr. Timmons did that they couldn't be denied the request. Muttering about wasting the physician's time, the young doctor strode down the ward, blond braid swinging down her back.

"Hey, Jude," Andrew whispered. "Maybe pissing off the doctors isn't the best move."

"If Mum says that Dr. Timmons is wrong, then I trust her," Cassandra whispered back, but the look she gave Judith told her that she'd better be sure.

Although Judith didn't want to take responsibility for Emily's medical care, she felt confident about this particular case. "Look, you two, Emily is underweight and certainly has a nutrition issue, but she isn't dying. That young doctor is just inexperienced and a bit of a jerk."

Dr. Timmons returned, accompanied by a calm, smiling doctor wearing a white coat with bunny rabbit stickers on the lapels. Judith had that lovely, relaxing, "thank God the adults have arrived" feeling for the second time that day.

"Good evening, Caster family, I'm Dr. Vivienne Chien." She shook everyone's hand. She quickly read the notes Dr. Timmons had given her. When she checked Emily over and approved her treatment, Dr. Timmons darted a smug glance at Judith, who bristled internally but held her poker face.

"Okay, I can see Mum and Dad are terrified right now." Dr. Chien turned her warm gaze to Judith. "So, Grandma, what would you like to tell me?"

"I think Emily is probably lactose intolerant or has a similar food allergy." Judith didn't feel it was necessary to mince words with Dr. Chien "I've worked in refugee camps for over a decade in northeastern Kenya, and I can tell the difference between malnutrition, malaria, and a baby not reacting well to the cow's milk formula we give out in the camps, which can upset a lot of them—and their mothers too. When that happens, we wean the vulnerable babies onto a goat's milk or lactose-free formula, and they usually begin thriving afterward."

Dr. Chien nodded. Speaking in a low, calm voice, she led Cassandra a few steps from Emily's bed. Judith supposed Cassandra was being asked all the vital questions only a mother could answer. Andrew hovered by the bed. He couldn't seem to look at Emily and kept his gaze on the back of Cassandra's head. Judith guessed seeing his daughter with tubes hanging out of her was still nauseating him. Luckily Cassandra had enough courage for the both of them and asked a hundred questions about their daughter's care. Judith breathed out a deep sigh, so proud of Cassandra that she wanted to pump her fist in the air.

Dr. Chien recommended that Emily stay in the hospital while they waited for blood test results, then try different milk formulas and a new antacid medication that might bring her some relief from the colic. She shook everyone's hand again and left to provide her excellent care elsewhere on the busy pediatric ward.

Still reflecting on how wonderful Dr. Chien was, Judith overheard Andrew ask Cassandra to write a list of things that Emily might need so he could go home and get them. Cassandra gaped, her eyes filling with tears. With Emily now out of the proverbial woods, Judith's concern returned to her own child. She wanted Cassandra to feel loved and supported by her partner, like they were a strong team, and that Andrew still trusted Cassandra to be a good mother—something Judith had never felt with Terry.

Judith moved with Andrew, and when they were far enough away from Cassandra, she touched his arm. "Cassandra will blame herself for what's happened," she told him quietly. "She needs you by her side right now." Obediently Andrew turned back to his little family. He wrapped his arm around Cassandra's shoulders, and she leaned against him as they held each other together.

"Everything is going to be fine, you two," Judith called from the door. When Cassandra didn't even look at her, she decided that she'd done enough. She left the ward, retracing her steps down the hall to the main reception area. She had just made it to the ridiculously slow rotating doors when she felt a hand on her elbow, yanking her backward.

"Where're you going?" Cassandra snapped. Her nose was running, making her top lip all red.

Judith dug a tissue from her handbag. "Darling, it's my neighbor. She's unwell, and I—"

"Your *neighbor*?" Cassandra was incredulous as she snatched the tissue from Judith and wiped her nose. "You can't leave me here with all this. What if I need you? Don't you even want to stay for moral support? Don't you think I—"

"Cassandra, Emily needs *you*, not me," Judith said. "You're not alone. You have Andrew and his dad and his lovely mother with you."

"But you're *my* mother!" Cassandra shrieked.

Judith decided that Cassandra didn't need to hear about Gladys's health problems just after she'd been so frightened by her baby collapsing. "Emily is going to be fine, and so are you," she said. "I wouldn't leave if I didn't have to." She turned on her heel and marched toward the rotating doors. In her mind, she was already planning how to handle the next crisis and hoping Gladys hadn't had to die alone.

Cassandra didn't shout, but she was loud enough that the nurse at the reception desk looked over, frowning. "There's always someone who's got it worse, right, Mum? Someone is always more important than me."

Judith stopped as a sudden exhaustion seized her bones. She realized nothing she did would ever be enough for Cassandra. She turned and faced her daughter. "Cassandra, go and do your duty for Emily, and for God's sake, let me do mine for Gladys."

"If you leave now, that's it, Mum," Cassandra said, her stuffy nose and reedy voice making her sound like an angry child. "I never want to see you again!"

"Oh, Cassandra." Too disappointed to even say goodbye, Judith walked away. Rubbing at her dry eyes, she tried to remember where in the vast hospital garage she'd left her damn Volvo.

TWENTY-SIX

THERE WAS A SOLEMN QUIET IN GLADYS'S BEIGE ROOM, broken only by the rustle of Judith turning the pages of her book. She had borrowed one from Kerry, the glamorous nursing unit manager at the night station. She was reading about feisty yet submissive women getting their bodices ripped by macho yet sensitive pirates. The story certainly passed the time. She had resisted checking her Fitbit to see just how much time, though. This wasn't the place to be counting minutes of life.

The dark of night had softened to the gray light of dawn as Judith finished her chapter. She heard the morning warbles of magpies out in the hospital garden. Tomorrow was now today. Her stomach growled, but she ignored it. It seemed wrong to avidly sustain herself while Gladys was drifting to a place free of appetites.

Most of her life, Judith had studiously avoided thinking about the afterlife or a waiting deity. Quite frankly, she didn't think it was any of her business. She'd seen enough death in her work to know that a body could pass away easily or fight the coming end. Either way, the moment afterward was always the same—peace.

She was still trying not to think about God when she heard the door open behind her.

"You all right, love?" Nurse Kerry asked, looking radiant with her red lipstick and pink scrubs. "D'you like the book?"

"It's a page-turner." Judith searched for something else to say. Kerry had been so nice, even sharing her carrot and celery sticks with her for a midnight snack. "I, uh, like the descriptions of the boat and sailing."

Kerry guffawed like Judith had made a risqué joke, then patted her shoulder and left again.

"Sticks?"

Judith sat up in her armchair, already close enough to the bed that she could hold Gladys's hand. "I'm here," she said. "How are you feeling?"

Gladys had mostly slept, but sometimes she needed reassuring before she drifted off again. "Sticks?" she whispered, her milky brown eyes blinking slow. "You think my two little babies are in heaven?"

"Of course, Gladys." Because what else could she say?

Gladys's wrinkles deepened until her eyes disappeared. "You think they're still angry with me?" she whispered.

"No, they'll be so happy to see you." Judith squeezed Gladys's folded hand. "It's going to be wonderful, I promise."

Gladys wiped the side of her face on the pillow. "I like your bullshit, Sticks."

Judith was still chuckling when Gladys drifted to sleep again. She sat back in the beige vinyl armchair, flipping up the footrest so she could get comfortable. She opened the book to the next chapter and wondered who was sailing the boat now that the captain had moved belowdecks with his female passenger . . .

"Sorry, love, don't want to wake you." Martha's voice had Judith sitting upright again. Disoriented, she checked the machines. No change. The light was bright outside, and the blinds had been pulled over the window to cover Gladys in shade. She figured it was probably midday now.

"Thought you could do with something sweet, so I brought biccies for your tea," Martha continued. She put a tinfoil container of Anzacs next to the tiny vase of hospital flowers.

Judith forgot to answer when she saw Cassandra standing in the doorway of the room. "Emily?" she croaked.

Cassandra gave her a wan smile. "She's all right," she said. "Better than all right. She went down for a nap in the nursery with no screaming, so the new antacid is working."

Excited by the news, Judith struggled out of her armchair, then hovered. She wasn't sure her hug would be welcome. Cassandra made it easy by coming into the room. "Is this your neighbor?" she whispered, her face creased with pity. "Mum, I'm sorry. I didn't—have you been here all night?"

"I know I look a mess." Judith smoothed her hair, feeling tufts sticking up at the back. "The nurses said I could shower, but I've not got anything fresh here and I wanted to wait. Wait for Gladys to . . . "

"Good thing I brought you your bits and bobs then." Martha slung a string shopping bag onto the armchair. Judith spotted a fresh navy-blue T-shirt and a stick of deodorant among the jumble.

To think that Martha had gone into her house, rifled through her belongings, and picked those things out from her personal drawers. She felt tears prick the back of her eyes. "Martha, you're a saint."

"Nah, just sensible," Martha said, smiling to accept the compliment. "How's poor Gladys doing?"

"Sticks?"

The three women froze, and Judith reached out to touch the folded hand resting on top of the blankets. "I'm here, Gladys," she said.

Gladys opened her eyes, and Judith saw the yellowish whites had turned pink.

Judith looked to Cassandra. "Go and get Kerry—she's the nurse at the station." Cassandra dashed from the room.

Martha moved to the door. "I've never been a favorite of Gladys's," she said. "I'll just hop out with Cass, all right?"

"All right," Judith said as Martha shuffled to the door. "Martha." When Martha looked back, Judith nodded to the doorway and out toward Cassandra. "Thank you very much."

Martha knew what she meant. "She needed a bit of a talking to," she said, chuckling. "But she's a good kid, Judith. You did well with her."

Kerry bustled into the room. Judith managed a smile when she saw Cassandra hovering in the doorway. "I love you," she mouthed to her daughter before Kerry closed the door.

"Sticks, Sticks, Sticks." Gladys moved her head back and forth restlessly. Judith squeezed her hand. Kerry checked all the machines and medicines going through the tubes into Gladys. She gave Judith a nod. They both knew it was time.

"Gladys," Judith said. "Can I do anything?"

Gladys's head rocking slowed, and her milky brown eyes looked past her. "Oh, there they are."

The beeping became one continuous noise, and Kerry turned it down so Judith heard the air escape Gladys's body for the last time. "Goodbye, Gladys," she said.

No change. Kerry turned off the beeping monotone. "All right, love?"

Judith's eyes were dry from the air-conditioning. Even without triage, or compartmentalizing, or denial, or whatever the hell it was that she did to survive this wretched life, the grief made her numb. Everything felt clear and normal. "Kerry, can I do something for you?" she asked briskly. "Anything at all?"

Judith was sure Kerry had seen every reaction there was to death, and she was adroit at comforting the living too. "I'd love a cup of tea, hon," she said. "Kettle's out in the nurses' lounge—you know where it is. Take those biccies with you, eh? We love an Anzac around here."

Judith detached her long, cold fingers from the still-warm hand. She picked up the foil box heaped with knobby brown biscuits. "Milk with one sugar, wasn't it?" Or maybe Kerry had never said how she took her tea. Judith went out to make it like that, anyway.

TWENTY-SEVEN

THE DAYS PASSED, AND JUDITH'S LIFE FOUND A NEW normal. Unfortunately, it was a normal that she didn't quite care for.

"So, are you sure you'll be all right?" Judith asked Cassandra on the threshold of her azure door. Emily had been home from the hospital for a few days, and Cassandra hadn't responded to any of Judith's inquiring texts, so here she was, visiting unannounced. She was relieved to see that Cassandra had lost that icy, terrified expression she'd been wearing at the hospital, though there were still dark circles under her eyes.

Cassandra rested her head on the doorframe, holding the bag of lemons Judith had brought her. Emily was sleeping in her crib in the living room, so Cassandra hadn't wanted a visitor because it might wake her. Anyway, Judith certainly wasn't going to insist on coming in just to see if Cassandra was following Dr. Chien's orders.

"Thanks for coming by, Mum," Cassandra said. "I'm sorry I can't be more welcoming."

Judith was already shaking her head. "It's more important to let her sleep, darling," she said. "I've got to go anyway. Martha's organized a little memorial in Gladys's backyard this afternoon, and I said I'd help set up. I just wanted to drop by to see if you needed anything."

"No, I've got it under control." Cassandra looked over Judith's shoulder at the shiny red Volvo. "I don't think I've said it yet—I'm sorry for your loss."

Judith couldn't quite think what she'd lost before she remembered. "Oh, Gladys was my neighbor, not a friend." She wished Cassandra would give her the chance to explain that day properly. "She needed someone at the end, and I was there. You know, it's really one of those things you have to just honor. I suppose if I ever ended up a lonely old woman with no family around, then I'd . . . " She couldn't finish.

Cassandra's gaze drifted back to her. "I didn't know what it would take to do that for someone," she said. "I thought you were really brave."

"Oh, no." Judith scoffed at the compliment. "The nurses did the real work. I just held her hand. I've seen enough death to know it's nothing to be frightened of, darling, especially in a lovely hospice like Gladys had. They made her so comfortable at the end. We should all be so lucky."

Cassandra blinked and seemed to come back to herself. "Of course. I can imagine it was worse in the camps."

"No comparison at all," Judith assured her. "In the camps, we had proper suffering."

"Of course you did," Cassandra said. "If you could call next time, I'll let you know when it's a good time to stop by."

Yet now that they'd started talking, Judith really wanted to say so much more.

"I did text you this morning, darling. When I didn't hear anything, I thought it wouldn't hurt—" she blurted as she went in for a goodbye hug but stopped halfway. She needed to say something real, something her daughter wanted to hear. Cassandra was already stepping back, reaching to close the azure door. "Your grandmother died like that too. It was actually very hard for me to see it again. To sit there and just watch . . ." She turned on her heel and stumbled off the last step of the porch. Embarrassed, she looked back.

Cassandra's expression was quizzical. "Mum?"

Judith adjusted her handbag on her arm so she could rummage inside for her car keys. "Gladys was nice at the end, I thought," she said. "Mother was . . . not so nice."

"Mum, I don't think we should speak ill of the dead." Cassandra's cheeks were pink, her expression still confused.

"Of course," Judith agreed immediately. She knew she hadn't made anything like a point and gave herself one more chance. "Do you know the last thing your grandmother said to me?"

Cassandra shook her head.

"'The doctor's coming in, Judith—for God's sake, put some lipstick on,'" Judith said, feeling more foolish than ever. "She never—maybe she loved me, but she never liked me, my mother. You should know, Cassandra, that I love you, and I really like you too. Anyway. Sorry, I'm a silly sod."

She found her car keys, marched through the gate, and got in her car. She waved through the window and didn't risk looking to see if Cassandra was still watching. She wasn't silly enough to think that Cassandra was going to accept her apology and want a relationship with her. She had said mean things about Marigold, which Cassandra wouldn't like either.

Judith buckled her seat belt. "Well, even if I was a terrible mother, at least I did something real with my life, not like Marigold," she defended herself in the silence of the hot, stuffy car. She could safely say that she'd never put Cassandra under any kind of pressure to be a perfect housewife. She pressed the ignition, carefully pulling away from the curb. She had been more interested in how Cassandra's university studies were going and whether she was reading newspapers and wonderful books and still practicing the piano—she had always played so beautifully. She had always warned Cassandra that making a positive contribution to society was far superior than doing all those silly home decorating courses.

And she had always encouraged her to come and volunteer in Kenya so they could work side by side and—

Judith gasped when the realization hit her.

"Oh," she said. "Oh. No."

TWENTY-EIGHT

JUDITH WAS DETERMINED TO STAY BUSY UNTIL CASSANdra needed her again, and her outdoor renovations certainly occupied her time. But it was the first day of April, and she was having most conversations with Cassandra by text and still hadn't been invited over the threshold of the blue door since her drop-in visit.

It gave her a hollow feeling every time she remembered that the overriding reason to stay in Adelaide had been resolved. Cassandra was coping with her daughter's health issues, and Emily was thriving. Judith had accepted that t*hat Andrew* actually cherished and respected her daughter. Their relationship wasn't what Judith had wanted, yet Cassandra was genuinely happy.

So, what purpose did Judith serve? The mission was over. Usually, this was when she headed home. Home. Did she want that to be Adelaide? She had never been a patient woman, and the "should I stay or should I go" dilemma was driving her quite mad.

She finished framing a photo of a beaming Emily wearing a silly pink bandana on her head that Cassandra had sent her via text. She wondered if it really would have made Cassandra happy to have a mother clanging around the house all day—baking, doing laundry, and feeling hideously unfulfilled. She put the new photo frame on the silent Queen Anne shelf, arranging it in front of the others.

Did all working mothers get the same guilt trip from their grown children? She would ask at the next ladies' lunch. Bev had worked fulltime while raising her two boys. Maybe Marg had, too?

It was after five o'clock. That meant the workmen building her garage had gone home, so she headed out to weed her front yard—it was blessedly cooler now with the arrival of autumn. She'd just settled on her foam kneeling pad, gardening fork in hand, when she saw Billy rifling through the contents of the Thompsons' mailbox. She called out a greeting, and he stuffed a letter into his pocket before coming over to sit on her porch step.

"Real mail's a bit of a treat nowadays, isn't it?" she said as she dug out a stray dandelion.

"The school found out Martha doesn't have email." He leaned his chin into a palm, his tired expression making him look older than he was. "I'm failing a couple of subjects, and they want to let her know. Like she's gonna be able to do anything." He rolled his eyes.

Judith sat back on her heels. "Which subjects?"

"English and history," he said. "Which is stupid, because I speak English good enough, and no one needs history to get a job."

She went back to stabbing at weeds, trying to dig them out of the hard, baked soil. "Everyone needs to have an understanding of history, Billy. It's only by knowing where we've come from that we can know where we're going. It's how we avoid our past mistakes."

"Don't do that, Mrs. Drainger."

Judith looked up, startled by the vehemence in his tone.

"Don't talk to me like I'm a bloody idiot," Billy said. "I know why I need to study history. I was being sarcastic. I hate dates, okay? I don't want to remember a pile of shit that a pile of shitty white guys did and act like it's important to me. I'm not a hypocrite."

Judith considered his argument. "Fair enough," she said finally.

A chatty neighbor from around the corner and her golden retriever stopped at the fence and commented on Judith's blooming frangipani tree. She couldn't remember the neighbor's name, but she accepted the compliment with thanks, wishing her and the dog a good evening. During this interaction, Billy had picked up a spare hand trowel and was now digging at the weeds next to the front steps. His face grew alien as the shadows stretched, making his cheekbones more prominent. In the gloaming, he looked like he had the first time Judith had seen him standing in her house, the night he'd robbed her. He was the same wild, desperate boy, struggling not to care when he disappointed a person he might love.

"You know, Billy, I was an English teacher," she said. "I can even show you my qualifications." The joke fell flat.

He stabbed viciously at the ground.

"How about I tutor you?" she suggested. "Just until you get your grades back on track, of course. I could always help you with history while we're at it."

"It's Australian history," he said. "You're British."

She tapped her chin with a gloved finger. "Didn't the British have something to do with the European invasion of Australia? Maybe we could start there?"

Billy frowned, and Judith knew she hadn't won him over. He threw the gardening trowel down and got up. "Yeah, actually the British sent a bunch of shitty white guys over here to do shitty things to the peaceful Aborigines. It was a bloodbath. Complete and total genocide. You should be really proud of your people. See you, Mrs. Drainger." He left, slamming the gate behind himself so hard it bounced open again.

Judith took her own irritation out on the rude clover weeds growing all over the daisy seedlings who were just trying to live in peace.

It was only when the porch sensor snapped the light on that she realized night had properly fallen. She went inside to make herself a bit of dinner with gluten-free noodles and stir-fried chicken and veg. Though not as good as Cassandra, she was getting better at handling a wok. Sitting on the back step, she was enjoying the cool of the evening and the *shush-shush-shush* of her fancy new sprinkler when she heard Martha shouting and the Thompsons' back door slam. A moment later, Billy launched himself over their dividing fence and jogged across her yard. He threw himself down on the concrete step next to her.

"So?"

"So." He huffed a sigh. "About those English lessons?"

"Billy!" Martha's head popped over the fence. "Don't run away from me when we're talking about your grades."

"Mum, I didn't run away from you!" He looked affronted. "I am speaking to Mrs. Drainger about tutoring me, like I told you I would."

Martha frowned, unconvinced. Judith didn't want Billy to think he held the balance of power, but this time she decided to help the kid. "I did offer to tutor Billy, if that's all right with you, Martha?"

"Well, what's he going to do for you, then?" Martha asked. "You're already giving him driving lessons. I don't want Billy taking advantage of your generosity, Judith."

Judith and Billy exchanged a look.

"I could give you Australian history lessons," he offered. "You sounded like you needed a few." He grinned. "Or I could get rid of your nettle bushes for you."

"Both, please."

Billy held out his hand, and they shook.

"All right, Billy," Martha said. "Let's leave Mrs. Danger to finish her dinner in peace. I made you a lemon delicious for dessert." She disappeared from the fence.

Billy didn't move except to stretch his long legs and kick the edge of the lawn. "Doesn't it bother you that everyone gets your name wrong all the time?" he asked.

Judith forked up a piece of carrot. "I'd prefer they got other things about me right first."

"I get that," he said, then gave her a squinty look, one eye closed. "You know what? You're all right, Mrs. Drainger."

She avoided accepting the compliment by checking her phone, but there were no messages to read.

"Cassandra still not talking to you?"

He must have known it was none of his business. Judith was too tired to lie, so she nodded. "She doesn't need me anymore, and neither does Emily. They're doing great together without my interfering." She forced a smile for his sake. "I really should get a hobby instead of stalking my daughter. I did always promise myself I'd go traveling when I got to Australia, and it's not like I have to be here if I'm not wanted." The silence stretched between them, filled with the *shush-shush-shush* of water and the whirr of cicadas.

"Your lawn is looking good now," Billy said, a little crack in his voice. "I might have to mow it more than once a week."

Judith opened her mouth, but Billy wasn't finished. "You better let me know when we can have our first tutoring session. Martha's really on my case to pass my classes this year. She's even talking about giving me her old Nissan if I do really well. Do you know how cool that would be, having my own ride? I could even get a weekend job to help my family out with bills and stuff. Maybe I could even save a bit for uni. I've really fucked school up, and I can tell you that no one at Adelaide High thinks I'm a bloody diamond in the rough. I've been doing it on my own for so long now—"

"Fine."

Billy raised his eyebrows. "Fine. You'll stay?"

"I meant while you finish the school year, just to help you get through." Judith scraped up the last of her noodles with her fork, holding them in front of her lips. "Billy, it's not that big of a deal. You're a smart young man—you'll catch up in no time." His expression was hard to read, but she knew that he was rethinking her kindness. "I'm not helping you because I have to; I'm helping because I want to. I miss teaching a lot, as it happens. You'll almost be doing me a favor."

Billy was grinning again. "In that case, maybe you could—"

"Whatever it is, not a chance, kid," she quickly added.

They both chuckled and went back to watching the sprinkler. The water caught the porch light, glittering like diamonds as it arced over the dark lawn.

A rustle of noise made Judith look over at the fence. Martha had stuck her head up again, watching Judith with her foster son. She gave a tentative thumbs-up. Judith returned the gesture. Martha screwed up her face and mimed wiping sweat from her brow, then dropped away again.

What had Judith just agreed to? She had accepted her share of Billy's care from Martha and also committed herself to staying next door. They were linked now, the three of them—Martha had adopted them both. She grimaced. Sod it, that woman really did have a heart of gold.

Like a spring releasing, Billy jumped up. Brushing off his jeans, he headed for the fence.

"Four o'clock tomorrow, Billy, straight after school," Judith called out. "Bring your textbooks with you."

He pulled himself straight up to the top of the fence, triceps bulging on his skinny arms. "Yeah, yeah," he grunted and swung his legs to the side, dropping out of sight.

Judith frowned at the green paling fence. Then she heard a shout, "Good night, Mrs. Drainger!" followed by the crash of the Thompsons' back door.

Her frown smoothed away. "I know what I'm doing," she whispered.

TWENTY-NINE

IT WAS THURSDAY MORNING, AND JUDITH HAD TO get ready for her date. No, not a *date*, an appointment. She brushed her short hair into place and searched for her one lipstick. She was wearing her nice guipure blouse with the blue linen slacks. The waistband was a little tight now, and she told herself not to mind that at all. It was fine. Harry was coming, and she wanted to make an effort.

When she'd called the office to speak to him, she'd been told by the receptionist that Harry was a salesman and it wasn't usual for them to make time to see construction jobs. So she had booked an appointment for a new project and asked specifically for him. Maybe she did really need a backyard gazebo? It might tizzy up the place quite nicely.

Harry was on time, to the minute, for their appointment—a fact that Judith appreciated, knowing how difficult it was for Australians to be on time for anything. He was carrying a pile of catalogs and color samples and wearing a blue-checked shirt that sat well on his rotund figure. As she stood aside to let him enter the house, she realized that she was slightly taller than him. The idea disappointed her—height meant strength and masculinity. Then she felt an odd sense of relief when she considered that Harry could never make her feel small.

She had already laid out the tea set on the dining table and went to put the kettle on. It only took a minute, as she'd kept it hot. Though when she returned to the table, she soon realized that the noise of the power drills and jackhammers outside was going to make it very difficult to have a conversation.

"You're brave, putting up with all this construction noise," Harry said with a wince and a grin. "Doesn't it drive you bonkers day after day?"

She shrugged. "I spent most of my working life surrounded by chaos and noise," she said. "At least there aren't gunshots."

His eyes widened, impressed. "What did you do for a crust, if you don't mind my asking, Judith?"

She told him, braced for the deluge of praise and questions everyone asked. Harry just nodded and let her talk, his eyes drifting to the pictures on the Queen Anne shelf. She quickly got through her little speech about how she had only stopped working to move closer to her daughter. Yet after the description of her life's work, she worried that it sounded so selfish to say that she was only concerning herself with one little family in the world now—one daughter, one granddaughter. It still made her cringe when Andrew called her Mum, so she didn't include him. He had his own mother, after all.

"I did a stint in South Africa," Harry said, "about a hundred years ago now. I went over with World Vision and spent three months in a little village a few hours out of Soweto. Helped dig a well and worked in the school for a bit teaching English. I don't think I've ever felt so useful in my life."

"Would you go back?" Judith asked and wanted to kick herself for her nosiness.

He thought about it, a frown wrinkling his wide forehead. "I can't honestly say I would," he answered. "It's tough to be on the ground in a rough place like that. And with my bad back and no flushing toilets, I'm afraid to say I'm too precious now. Still try to do my bit by working with the local Rotary, raising money and helping host events, but it's all I make time for."

She rushed to reassure him. "Rotary does amazing work."

"That's why I help them."

Harry didn't seem to need her approval, which stopped Judith before she assured him that every little bit counts and it's important to stay aware of issues. She bit her lip and wondered what she thought about his lack of guilt. He seemed happy not to be a saint.

"Look, Judith, I don't want to be too forward, but how do you feel about moving this meeting of ours to Beans and Brew at the end of your road?" Harry's neck was bright red, though his smile was still wide and easy. "We can get away from the noise, and I could . . . buy you lunch?"

Judith blinked. "Like a date," she blurted.

He laughed. "Like a meeting with lunch," he replied, and before Judith could die of embarrassment, he added, "so you could see if you might like it if . . . I could, you know, take you out to dinner sometime."

She felt her blood run hot, then cold, then hot again. Her palms were sweating, yet she tried to match his airy tone. "Of course," she said. "That would be lovely." She checked his left hand. No ring, but. "You aren't married, are you, Harry?"

He smiled ruefully. "Divorced for eight years now," he said. "I've got three boys, all grown but still costing me money." He chuckled and shuffled his papers together, gathering up the catalogs.

Judith didn't know how to respond to someone else's divorce: *I'm sorry, Never mind,* or *Wonderful!?* She settled for, "Me too. Divorced, but no boys. I have a daughter." Harry chuckled. Of course he knew she had a daughter—she'd just been prattling about Cassandra for the last ten minutes. She flushed again. He didn't try to tease her, only extended his hand and invited her to head out the door. She had another flustered moment trying to find her keys and handbag, then eventually got them out of the house.

Harry greeted all the "boys" working on the new garage and fence. Like a gentleman, he held out his hand again, this time to help Judith step over the pools of setting concrete that would be her new fence posts.

They were easy to cross, but the gesture still made her trill, "Thank you, Harry!" She took a moment to pull a biodegradable waste bag from her mailbox and pick up a dog poop from the verge. She only shrugged when Harry complimented her neighborliness.

"Where's that lovely new car of yours?" He looked up and down the street. "Are you enjoying it? I've got an earlier model Volvo, still the S60, but from five years ago, and I'm thinking of upgrading—"

Judith's gaze traveled the curb outside her house. She'd had to park a few houses away last night when she got back from Bev's book club. However, she was sure she'd seen the car that morning when she'd done her watering. They began walking to the café, and she checked the Thompsons' driveway, peering into their open garage on the way past. Her heart thudded, and the blood rushed in her ears. Harry was still talking as Judith searched, checking every parked red car they passed on the street.

The Volvo was gone. She felt a stone drop into the bottom of her stomach. Her car had been stolen in the middle of the day. Honestly, who would steal a car in broad daylight on a suburban street, really? That took some kind of cheek.

It'll be that boy, Marigold whispered. Because of course Marigold would be back when panic was shaking her. *That nasty boy Billy would steal your car, my girl. He isn't your friend. He thinks kindness is a disease.*

Judith knew she should do something and do it now if she wanted to get her car back in one piece. Stealing a car would mean jail time for Billy, so what the hell could he have been thinking?

"Judith, are you all right?" Harry's forehead was shiny, and the red flush on his neck had crept up to his chin. "I'm sorry if this was a bad idea. I didn't mean to overstep."

They hadn't made it to the end of the street when she stopped walking, and so did he.

"Harry," she said, "it's not you, it's just that I—" She wouldn't blame Billy before she knew it was him. "Remembered that I—" Just then her phone beeped, and she automatically fumbled with her handbag as she tried to think of something to say that wouldn't hurt Harry's feelings or show how much she was panicking. She checked her phone to see a message from Cassandra:

Mum, Emily just threw up her lunch.
Can you come over?

Triage loomed with its numbing clarity to still the panic and anxious chatter in her mind. The problems fell into place:

First, her car had been stolen, and she needed to inform the police right away to help them find it—even if it might have been Billy who had taken it.

Second, she was almost sure that Emily throwing up her lunch had a perfectly normal explanation—no reason to visit, as she'd been doing so well with her weight.

Third, Harry was nice, and it'd been forever since a man was sweet enough to ask her out for lunch—though this relationship would probably go nowhere, like every other relationship in her life.

Suddenly, Judith decided all these questions had to be felt. With no ceremony, she yanked all her emotions out of their boxes. Today, right now, in this moment, she chose not to be numb. Yes, the anxiety made adrenaline course through her system and caused her heart to race and skip. Yet it wasn't the only thing. Her pulse was also racing with excitement at Harry's flirting, and her heart clenched with delight at Cassandra's request for help. Even the comfort of knowing she had friends to help her with the car situation eased her soul-deep vulnerabilities. She wasn't alone, and she didn't need to pretend to be.

With a rattling heart and a busy mind, she examined her list and knew exactly what she had to do.

Judith opened the car door and thanked Harry once again for the lift. "I am really sorry to cancel our appointment. Believe it or not, I did have a deadline for getting all these house renovations done," she said, failing to control the girlish pitch of her voice. "I'd love to reschedule with you."

"The appointment or the lunch?" he asked, softening the question with a chuckle. She saw the blush creeping up out of his collar again.

"Both," she said in her normal voice. "I'd really like to see you again, and you don't even have to bring your lovely color charts with you." They laughed together, and it felt very natural. She waved as he drove off, then quickly dialed Billy's number. It went to voicemail. She sent him a short text asking him to call her and then knocked on Cassandra's bright blue door. Hearing footsteps coming, she braced herself for whatever Cassandra's mood might be.

"Oh, Mum, I didn't realize you'd be here so quick." Cassandra was flushed, her eyes swollen and red like she'd been crying. "Emily was just about to go into the bath again."

"It sounded urgent on your—" Judith began, then realized that Cassandra might think she was accusing her of being dramatic. She changed tack. "I wanted to come and see Emily for myself. How are you both?"

Cassandra shrugged and turned from the door without inviting Judith inside. Either she was being deliberately rude or she was completely shattered by fatigue. Judith followed her daughter and noticed she was looking a little fuller in the behind. There was a roll of flesh just over the waistband of her jeans. Clearly Cassandra wasn't looking after herself, and that was a worry.

A little hand waved into Judith's line of vision. She looked up from Cassandra's jeans and saw that Emily was staring at her.

"Hello, Emily," she said and wiggled her fingers. Emily's face broke into a wide grin, all pink gums and sticky cheeks. Judith's heart lifted in her chest. She was surprised to see Emily reach out, her arms waving. "I think she wants me." She waited for Cassandra to assess the baby before she could really believe it.

"Take her, please." Cassandra sounded relieved as she swung a giggling Emily through the air to Judith's waiting hands.

"Do you want me, darling?" she asked Emily, just to double-check she was doing the right thing. "Do you want your silly old Grandma Judy?" She looked up for confirmation that it was all right to claim the title of grandma and saw that Cassandra was staring. "What? I think 'Judy' will be easier for her to say later on," she said, distracted by Emily's sticky hand patting her cheek. "Bathroom is upstairs, isn't it?" She put Emily on her hip and headed to the stairs.

"Mum!" Cassandra had found her voice again. "Sorry, you've never bathed her before, and I haven't shown you where everything is."

"You still wash babies with soap and water, I take it?" Judith called back, letting a little humor touch her voice. "We're going upstairs, and you're going to get off your feet, Cassandra. Make a cup of tea. We'll be fine."

She found everything she needed in Emily's ridiculously organized and over-equipped bathroom. "I've bathed babies in an old cow trough before," she told Emily, who giggled and shoved her toes in her mouth. "It's really not as complicated as your poor exhausted mummy might think." She tried to remember the best way to strip a wriggling baby. Soon Emily was happily in the water, sucking on a facecloth as Judith washed her with a bit of organic soap-free gel that smelled delicious.

"You have nice, clear urine," Judith told her granddaughter when she peed in the bath. "That means you're well hydrated. This chubby tummy means you're still thriving." She continued her examination. "Clear whites of the eyes, so no jaundice. Good color in your cheeks. That cradle cap on your hair is a little smelly, so I wonder if Mummy knows that coconut oil will work wonders to clean that off." Emily squeaked back at her. "No, you're right, it would be better if you tell her," she said. "I'm just lucky that I got to be here today."

It took longer than she thought to pick out clothing from Emily's extensive wardrobe, but in the end, she dressed the baby in a romper decorated with flowers. She called Billy one more time and again got sent to voicemail. When she brought Emily downstairs, she was sure that the baby needed to eat but was unsure how to phrase it to a sensitive Cassandra. She didn't see her daughter in the immaculate kitchen area, so she headed for the back door, thinking she might be in the garden getting some April sunshine.

"Sorry, I know she threw up before, but I really think that Emily might want to nibble on—" Judith stopped when she spotted Cassandra sound asleep on the couch. Her feet were still touching the ground, as if she had just fallen to the side out of sheer exhaustion. Which was very likely the case. Not only was Cassandra not getting enough sleep, she was a fanatical organizer. The house itself was a bastion of tidiness and spotlessly clean. It wasn't normal or, in Judith's opinion, healthy for a baby to be in such a sterile environment. Nor was it healthy for one woman to try and do it all by herself.

"Mummy's asleep," she whispered. "Dare I feed you without her knowing?" Emily seemed pleased by the idea and broke out into chortles.

In the fridge, among the half-empty wine bottles and takeaway containers, Judith found more than a dozen uniform Tupperware boxes, neatly stacked, with penciled labels listing their contents. She picked up one labeled "Pear And Spinach". With the baby perched on her hip, it wasn't easy to pull off the lid. She showed Emily the pale green goop. "Yummy?" she asked. Emily raised a little red eyebrow at her, the answer obvious. "Then how about some mashed potatoes, peas, and grilled sausages? That'll stick to your ribs," she said and began searching the pantry.

By the time Judith got Emily into the high chair, she was already feeling the strain of carrying the wriggling baby. Feeding Emily was another matter entirely. She kept putting her hands on the spoon, getting the food everywhere but her mouth.

"Emily, if you don't eat, you'll be hungry," Judith explained. She went in again with the spoon, trying to dodge those little fingers, but Emily was too quick and tipped the food all over her clean onesie. Judith took a break to send Billy another urgently worded text message. Turning her attention back to the baby, she picked up the spoon. "Right, let's try this again, young lady."

Emily squealed happily, and another plastic spoon appeared over Judith's shoulder. Emily took it and shoved it straight in between her chomping gums. "Don't worry, her mummy knows what a rascal she is," Cassandra said as she dropped onto the dining seat next to Judith. "What have you put in her food?"

Judith felt guilty. "Sorry, it's just a little bit of rice cereal," she rushed to explain. "I found it in your pantry."

"Mum, it's fine, really." Cassandra might've been annoyed or content —it was hard to tell behind her jaw-clicking yawn. "You shouldn't have let me go to sleep."

"You needed it, my girl," Judith said, risking some sensible advice.

"But if I don't go to sleep, then I never realize how tired I am," Cassandra said, slumping on the tabletop with her head in her hand. "It's better just to keep going."

Judith felt a hundred more pieces of advice poised to spill from her lips. Cassandra was talking nonsense and should ask for help, even if it wasn't from Judith. Still, she'd learned better now. "You know best," she said instead. "I'm exhausted after just a bath and bit of dinner. I don't know how you keep it up all day and night."

"Because I love her," Cassandra said. "And because I enjoy it, even though I'm shattered most of the time. Being a mother is the greatest thing I've ever done."

Judith felt her spine stiffen. Yet as she watched Cassandra gaze at Emily, she realized that this had nothing to do with her. Cassandra wasn't judging her own mother—she was just rejoicing that she was one. "It suits you too," she said quietly.

"Thanks," Cassandra said, just as quietly. The baby offered a loud burp, and both women laughed.

"I'd better go." Judith handed over the bowl of food and stood up. She wanted Cassandra to ask her to stay, though she presumed she'd probably have to wait longer for an invitation like that.

"Thanks for coming, Mum. I just wanted you to have a look at her, not let me have a nap." Judith thought she sounded more embarrassed than upset. She decided that this was progress. "Andrew will be home soon, and I promised I'd make something more than pasta with sauce tonight," Cassandra added.

"He'll be lucky to get a hot meal at all with how busy you are," Judith said, defending her daughter from the dentist and his expectations.

"I enjoy cooking," Cassandra said, her tone sharp again. "Andrew loves my food."

Judith felt her protective bluster leak away. Cassandra was so happy to be everything that she never was. A sweet and tidy homemaker with a hot dinner on the table for her hardworking man. It made her skin crawl. Clearly she'd left her alone with Marigold too many times. "Well,

I'll just get out of your way," she said and hurried to the door before she remembered she'd have to walk home or get an Uber.

"What're you doing?" Cassandra asked when she saw Judith fiddle with her phone. "You didn't come in the car?"

Judith was annoyed to see there wasn't an Uber in her area. "No, I think it got stolen," she said as she tried to refresh the app.

Cassandra jiggled Emily on her hip. "Sorry, did you just say you *think* it got stolen? For goodness' sake, why are you here when you should be at the police station? Oh, your lovely car! Mum, what a shame!"

Judith really wanted to tell her to stop being so dramatic—it wasn't Cassandra's car. Instead, she took a deep breath and explained what she thought might have happened and that Billy simply couldn't have another criminal charge or he would be going to juvenile detention for sure.

"Mum, that's ridiculous!" Cassandra was incensed on Judith's behalf. "If that kid has stolen your car, he deserves to be in trouble."

"I'm sure Billy didn't meant to steal it," she said. "You don't know him like I do, Cassandra, and honestly, he's a really careful driver. But if neither he nor the car is back by the time I come home, then—" She took a deep breath. "I'll talk to Martha first."

"I can't believe you got your car stolen and you rushed over here to help me with Emily," Cassandra said, sounding mystified. Which was nicer than hysterical, Judith thought.

"Actually, I was about to go on a date, sort of, when you messaged me."

Cassandra bugged her eyes, looking like Emily. "A date!"

"Sort of." Judith squirmed in discomfort having mentioned something so potentially upsetting to Cassandra. "It was actually a prelude to a date. We were going to talk about a new gazebo and then find out a bit more about each other."

"Sounds romantic." There was an amused wobble in Cassandra's voice now.

"Oh, I don't know about all that," Judith said. She coughed into her fist. "Actually, while we're chatting, I've been meaning to ask if you'd like Mother's Queen Anne shelf?"

Judith watched Cassandra's pale green eyes scan her open-plan room with all its modern beige furniture. Her forehead crinkled, then released. "Sorry, Mum, it's a beautiful piece, and I know it comes with so much history, but it just won't work here."

Judith agreed. "It doesn't work for me either," she said. "I'll donate it to charity, I think."

Checking to see if her Uber trip had finally been picked up, she saw her phone was ringing. Fumbling with the electronic buttons, she answered more sharply than she meant to. "Billy, where are you?"

"Where're you, Mrs. Drainger?" She could hear traffic behind his voice. "I'm waiting at your house. We had an English lesson today, remember?"

"Oh!" Judith swallowed. "Then where is my car?"

"How would I know?" He sounded irritated. "Look, if you're trying to get out of giving me another highway lesson because I'm no good at changing lanes yet—"

"My car disappeared sometime this afternoon," she said. "I think it might've been stolen."

"Did that boy take it?" Cassandra interrupted her. "Tell him to bring it home right now."

Judith waved her daughter to silence. "Billy, you didn't return my calls, and I didn't know if you had it. I thought, maybe—so I didn't call the police yet."

"You thought what?"

She imagined Billy's expression as he digested her suggestion, then she said, "I wanted to talk to you before I spoke to anyone else."

"What in the hell?" Billy was as incredulous as he had every right to be.

Judith thought she might as well keep being honest. "I was thinking if you'd borrowed it—it only would've been to help someone out. I wanted to give you a chance to talk to me first."

"Ride or die, eh, Mrs. Drainger? I like your loyalty," he said. "But you realize you've probably let the thieves get her all the way to bloody Sydney by now. Please, call the cops—I love that car!"

Huffing a sigh of relief, Judith hung up the phone. Only Cassandra's expression gave her pause. "What?"

"It's just—you're so calm," Cassandra said. "I mean, it's kind of amazing."

She shrugged off the compliment. "No use crying over spilled milk."

"Well, I guess. Still . . . " Cassandra swung Emily onto the other hip. "Do you need a lift? I can—"

"No, really, it's fine. You get a start on dinner," Judith said and suddenly felt very happy. "I'm going to walk home and enjoy this beautiful autumn sunshine." She hurried out the front door and made it to the gate, remembering to turn and wave back at her daughter and granddaughter. "I'll see you again soon, my darlings," she called.

Cassandra waved Emily's hand for her. "See you later, Grandma Judy."

Judith furiously blinked the silly tears away as she strode off down the street. Billy would be waiting for her when she got home, and they were going to be busy. Best to get on with it before she went under it.

ACKNOWLEDGMENTS

First and foremost, I have to thank Shanna McNair and Scott Wolven for seeing so much in the first draft of this manuscript. If it wasn't for your clear-eyed critiques, your wonderful writing conference, The Writer's Hotel, and your affectionate support, this book might not have progressed at all. A thousand thanks for selecting this story to be published by High Frequency Press.

My thanks to early readers Monica Hall and Leila Hall for your outrageous encouragement as I was trying to make sense of the story. You helped me see what was important and pushed me to continue.

I would love to thank my first editor Ernesto Mestre at The Artful Editor for your insight and ability to discern what I meant despite the hash I made of those early drafts. You helped me get out of my own way and bring more meaning to this story. Thank you.

I'd love to thank everyone at The Artful Editor. The wonderful, Naomi Eagleson, who has always had my back from the very first days of my writing journey when I was scribbling away all on my own. She always encouraged me and offered up the perfect editors who all helped me become a better writer. My sincere thanks to Denise Logsdon, rockstar copy editor, whose tireless dedication to teaching me the grammar of my mother language is much appreciated. You are the Queen of Commas.

To my family and friends who've had to hear about these characters for so many years now. Yes, this book is finally finished! Thanks for listening. It meant so much.

ABOUT THE AUTHOR

Alexandra Addams is an Australian novelist and screenwriter living in Switzerland. She has one less than half a dozen children who provide much of the trauma and wild inspiration required to write novels. *The Self-Made Saint* is her first published work of fiction.

Addams loves talking to readers and writers. Please contact her at alexandraaddams.com to sign up for her newsletter or follow her on Instagram @AAddamsWrites.

www.ingramcontent.com/pod-product-compliance
Ingram Content Group UK Ltd.
Pitfield, Milton Keynes, MK11 3LW, UK
UKHW021948090425
457258UK00013B/54